Her Shallow Grave

Dan Padavona

Copyright Information

Published by Dan Padavona

Visit our website at www.danpadavona.com

.

Her Shallow Grave

CHAPTER ONE

Letters in the Attic

She found the love letters stuffed inside a cardboard box in the attic.

Like finding a scorpion under the pillow.

He hadn't hidden the box very well. It was nestled between the vinyl records and antiquated VHS movie collection, a dagger's throw from her wedding dress.

She hadn't recognized the box, its grime-free top marking it as recently placed amid so much dust, so she took off the top and removed a newspaper. And there lay the notes underneath.

I won't cry.

Yet she did. Angrily swiping the tears onto her shirt sleeve, she stuffed the newspaper back into the box and shut the lid. The wedding dress hung and swayed, looking old and tattered. Old and tattered like Marissa. Somewhere a horn honked and pulled her out of her haze.

She recalled hearing Tristan stomp around in the attic three nights ago. She'd wondered why he was up there after she'd gone to sleep when he'd last been on the couch, one eye on the news and the other impatiently watching the staircase.

Waiting for her to fall asleep so he could creep up the stairs and hide the letters? Did he think she was stupid, that he could conceal them one floor above their bed?

Before Tristan, when she was young, she'd viewed romance as a temporary oeuvre, a piece of art to quickly consume before the colors faded.

If only she'd remained true to her original intuition.

Tristan was the most sensual man she'd ever known, chiseled physique matched by a youthful face that never seemed to age. Upon first meeting him at Brown, she thought he looked like a Hollywood actor, then decided his dark eyes and erotically sullen disposition reminded her more of a rock star. He had a magnetism about him, this one. Something hot and fiery under the surface that attracted her in ways no man had before. Their bodies felt made for each other, each muscle and angle destined to fuse and grab and lust. Simply holding his hand set her heart hammering and her skin prickling.

After graduating with honors from Brown, Tristan worked as a floor trader on Wall Street. A windfall of profits allowed him to start a small brokerage firm on Cape Cod, which became an instant success, though the business required him to travel. While many of Tristan's clients were New England-based, others lived as far away as Florida.

A ring on her finger. A comfortable life that afforded her all of the good things. A beautiful home near the ocean, just ninety minutes from Boston if the tunnel wasn't jammed. Sex so intense she tingled for days, longing for him.

Maybe that's why she tolerated his growing aloofness.

Below the beautiful features was a dangerous severity she couldn't place. With the snap of a finger, he could switch from seductive to detached, as though an electric fence shot up between them.

Often after arguing he would sit outside in the cold,

fixated by the flames snapping in the fire pit, unwilling to respond to her. Strangely, she knew he wasn't freezing her out—he simply couldn't hear her. When angry, his face was a storm of hidden secrets. Staring into his eyes was like watching a hurricane churning up the eastern seaboard, never certain if the storm would rain itself out or smash the coast to splinters.

They'd married on an overcast, frigid November day, a week after the last of the Halloween pumpkins lay moldering and the wildflowers leaned over to die, smothered under the dead vestiges of summer. Marissa never once considered leaving Tristan, figuring she could save him from himself.

Yet she couldn't change him. Instead, he became increasingly distant, prone to drive off to who knows where in the middle of the night to clear his head. Often he was gone for hours, Marissa climbing the walls worrying he'd gotten into an accident or driven into a ravine. Tristan's excursions only became more frequent. Under the guise of visiting clients, he was gone for several days at a time without so much as a phone call to assure her he was fine.

She tried to justify his behavior. She knew how bad his upbringing had been—the mother who'd walked out on him when he was a toddler, the frigid, alcoholic father who she suspected beat his son. Visiting Keith on the holidays was frightening and painful. Tristan's father seemed perpetually on the cusp of violent outbursts. One Christmas, Keith and Tristan argued with such ferocity that the father shattered a chair against the wall, blowing a twelve-inch hole through the plaster.

Marissa loved Tristan despite the mood swings and disappearances and always gave him the benefit of the doubt.

Now this.

Marissa caught her reflection in the window and suddenly understood why Tristan would cheat. Forty-five and not looking a day under sixty. Face gaunt, hair brittle and rapidly graying, eyes lost down twin craters digging into a fleshless skull. She bit her tongue to stifle a scream and cried into dry, chapped hands. When had this happened? It seemed she'd aged fifteen years in the last six months.

Stumbling as she tried to rise, she grabbed hold of an overhead joist and narrowly missed impaling her palm on a rusty nail. Walls moved. The floor tipped away from her like a fun house trick.

As her heart raced, she realized the dizzy spells and headaches were increasing. She tried to remember her last doctor's appointment and couldn't. Last year she'd been fit with the heart and chiseled legs of a runner.

Her phone was in the bedroom. Otherwise, she would have already dialed 911. After a moment, the spell passed and her heart slowed. Marissa tiptoed away from the wall, half-expecting the floor to shift on her again. It didn't. Still jittery, she clutched the rail and descended the stairs one at a time.

It's nothing. It's the flu.

Or Lyme disease. She enjoyed trail running and fresh forest air, liked how the soft-packed floor lessened the pounding her knees took on concrete. A tick might have bitten her. Yet she couldn't recall her last run. It seemed the last several months were hidden behind a veil of fog, the salty, impenetrable kind that rolls across Cape Cod when the marine layer creeps ashore.

Her legs stopped shaking between the hallway and bedroom nightstand. Her hands remained jittery as she fumbled with the phone. Sitting on the edge of the bed, she scrolled through contacts, terrified by the realization she couldn't recall her doctor's name. She could see his face—Indian, glasses perched on the end of his nose.

Patel. That was it.

Another wave of panic fell over her when she

couldn't find his name under *P* for *Patel* or *D* for *doctor*. She wondered if Tristan had deleted the doctor's number, though it seemed insane to think he would do such a thing. It was only when she whipped back through the list that she recognized the physician's practice.

Marissa was about to dial when a car door slammed outside.

Tristan.

She slipped the phone under the pillow, didn't want him to know. Ridiculous, as he was the guilty party, the one with the dark secret.

He wouldn't like her calling the doctor, another thought which made little sense to her. More evidence her mind was as diseased as her body.

A brain tumor.

That had to be the answer. Based on her rapid degradation, it was probably too late to cure.

The front door opened and closed before she could finish the thought, then he rummaged through the closet. Coat hangers clanged together.

Footsteps climbed the stairs. Her heart slammed in her chest.

"Marissa?"

She opened her mouth and found her throat too parched to speak. She sat frozen, a prisoner in her own home. If only he'd go away. She couldn't confront him now. Not with so many worries clouding her thoughts. Time was needed to think things through, determine the best way to encounter him.

He paused halfway up the stairs. The house was silent except for the tick-tock of the old wall clock in the hallway.

"Hon? You up there?"

Marissa's fingers clutched the bedspread. She eyed the closet, the window, the corner armoire, searching for somewhere to hide.

The stairs creaked. He was closer now. A little farther and he'd be at the top of the stairs and see her frozen on the bed like an animal in a hunter's trap.

"Marissa?"

A momentary pause, then he stomped back down the stairs and crossed the lower floor toward the kitchen.

A cupboard door shut, then the clink of wrench against pipe and the sound of water running. Another door opened. He was doing something under the sink. Probably cursing at the slow, persistent leak from the under-the-sink water filter. Marissa imagined him dabbing water with a hand towel and staring disapprovingly at the damp, warped wood under the catch pipe.

Now was the time to hide. She crept off the bed, hitching her breath when the floor squeaked under her weight.

Silence followed from below. He'd heard her.

The empty hallway ended with risers to the attic. If she moved fast—

Too late.

Footsteps thudded from the kitchen to the staircase.

"Marissa? That you?"

Quickly, she tousled her hair and lay back on the bed, careful the springs didn't groan. If he came upstairs, she'd feign waking up and complain of a headache. The latter wouldn't be a lie. Her temples throbbed and pulsed as though something black and spindly nested inside her skull.

A cool breeze blew up the staircase as he opened the front door. Then it shut and the whole house was dead quiet again.

On trembling legs, she padded to the bathroom and ran a brush through her hair. Clumps fell out and dirtied the sink. She caught a glimpse of the skull face in the mirror and nearly screamed.

Yes, she was dying. Most likely cancer as she'd theorized. Or some other insidious, incurable disease eating away at her.

I hope he chokes on tears at my funeral.

She reached into the medicine cabinet for her blush and stopped. No amount of makeup could feign the youthful features she'd so recently possessed. She gave up and left the brush, choked by a steel wool tangle of gray and black hair, in the cabinet.

After dialing the doctor's office she was placed on hold. An old Psychedelic Furs song she'd loved as a teenager played in the background, another reminder of how quickly life had passed her by. Ten minutes later and still on hold, she ended the call and decided to drive to the doctor's office. The walk-in clinic was her best chance to be seen. She'd have to put her faith in a physician's assistant rather than her own doctor, but she needed answers.

The October sun was at its afternoon apex when she stumbled out to the car. A chilly wind bit the back of her neck, a reminder of how cold the Cape would be once winter arrived. As she grappled with the keys a pair of dead leaves crab-walked down the sidewalk. She clutched her sweatshirt together, yet the cold found a way in and bit at her chest.

Center Street crawled with traffic, the after-lunch commuting crowd rushing back to work. The sun glared across the windshield, making it hard to see, and she had to pump the brakes to avoid hitting a bicyclist who appeared out of nowhere. A horn honked behind her. She checked the mirror, correctly assuming the horn was meant for another driver. A sports car shot around on her left, then the way forward turned blurry. She blinked and the haze grew worse. That was when her arms filled with pins and needles, and the sun seemed to hurtle into the windshield.

The last thing Marissa remembered was glass

smashing and people screaming. The world went black.

CHAPTER TWO

The Crash

"Mrs. Carrington?"

The voice sounded far away and muffled, as though it came from the other side of a padded wall. Black and interspersed blasts of colorful light clouded her vision. She blinked twice, and the reds and blues swept across her eyes, forming and reforming like water colors lit from below.

"Can you hear me?"

A dark shape hunched over her, too blurry to make out. More shapes appeared to sweep in on her.

"Mrs. Carrington?"

"Yes," she said. "Where am I?"

Her throat was dry, head throbbed, arms stinging as though covered by Texas fire ants. Odd, she thought, that sweet, spring-like scents filled her nostrils amid so much confusion.

She started to sit up, and a hand gently pressed back against her chest.

She could see his face now and make out the police badge affixed to his cap. He was young, with probably no more than a few years on the force. His name tag read *Stevens*. His eyes surveyed Marissa and the confused scene with the intensity of a rookie in over his head. An ambulance blared its siren once to scatter a growing number of onlookers and pulled to the curb.

"It's best you don't move until the paramedics check you over."

"Paramedics?"

Sensing her anxiety, he said, "Just a precaution. You have minor abrasions and a bruise down the side of your face, probably where the airbag hit you—"

"Oh my God. Are you saying I was in a car accident?"

He looked more concerned now. His brow furrowed as he studied her eyes.

"You don't remember driving across the median? You drove through a plate glass window, ma'am."

Marissa's stomach lurched. At this time of day, shoppers crowded Center Street's sidewalks. Families with children.

"Mrs. Carrington, do you remember feeling sick?"

I've been sick for as long as I can remember, she wanted to say. That didn't seem right, either. She'd run the Boston Marathon last year—or was it two years ago? Everything seemed so muddled together—in less than three-and-a-half hours, a faster pace than she'd run in her twenties.

"I haven't been feeling well," she said.

"Sit still. Everything is fine and nobody was hurt. Your husband is on the way."

"My husband…"

"Tristan Carrington is your husband, correct?"

She shook her head even as she mouthed, "yes," drawing a perplexed look from Officer Stevens.

Two paramedics knelt beside her. An assistant who looked no older than seventeen checked her blood pressure while an older-looking, overweight paramedic shined a light in her eyes and asked her a battery of questions. Yes, her heart felt fine—no chest pains or fluttering. No, she'd never fainted before, and no she didn't use recreational drugs. The assistant raised his eyebrows and shared a look with the fat technician. She was about to ask what the meaning of their question was when the boyish police officer turned to calm a belligerent man who Marissa recognized as Hal Burkovich, proprietor of Burkovich Flowers. The front of Marissa's RAV4 steamed inside the florist's shop. Chaos in the form of multicolored flowers lay scattered across the sidewalk, attracting more bystanders who snapped photos with their phones. A shard of glass hung from the storefront's top like a guillotine.

Despite her protests, they loaded her onto a gurney under the watchful glares of people she recognized. There was Yvonne Kimble peering over the crowd with a mix of fright and alarming curiosity on her face. The gossiper regarded her as though Marissa were a derelict led out of a meth lab in handcuffs. News of the car crash would be known throughout town before dinner time.

She felt thankful when the gurney slid fully into the ambulance, out of Yvonne's view. The paramedics sat down beside her as a shadow passed across the interior.

"This is the husband," she heard Officer Stevens say as Tristan climbed into the back of the ambulance. The vehicle shook with his weight.

Tristan's was the last face Marissa wanted to see, but he was here now, bending to kiss her forehead and hold her hand.

"You okay, hon? You gave me a helluva scare."

She saw no sign of cold distance in his eyes, which held the warmth of afternoon trysts at Brown. The love letters were still on her mind, yet all she saw was the man she'd been infatuated with for over two decades. Perhaps the letters were some kind of mistake, some misinterpretation on her part.

"Talk to me," he said. "I'm here now."

The ambulance started to move, backing away

from the curb with another blast of siren. Then they were in forward motion with the macadam rumbling underneath.

"I don't know what's happening to me," she said, choking on each word.

"Nothing is happening to you. You got into an accident, nothing insurance won't pay for. And we have three vehicles—"

"It's not the money I'm worried about. I'm sick, Tristan. Something is seriously wrong and I don't know what it is."

The overweight paramedic checked her pulse and said, "Breathe normally, Mrs. Carrington. We'll be at County General in ten minutes. You're doing fine."

"Do I look fine?" she asked. "I put my car through a plate glass window and don't remember a damn thing."

Tristan brushed the hair from her eyes and cleared a tear with his thumb.

"You look beautiful," he said. "Like the day I met you."

"You know that's not true," she said. "You don't think I see the face in the mirror? I'm dying."

"We're going to need to calm her down," the paramedic said as he reached behind him for a medical supply kit.

"Don't you dare," she said.

The way she spat the words caused the paramedic to glare at his assistant.

"I think it would be for the best if—"

"No medicine," Tristan said. "Leave her be."

The paramedics wheeled Marissa into County General. It was busier than normal. Another stretcher raced past her, driven by three orderlies in green scrubs and masks. She couldn't see who was on the other gurney, only a woman's arm riddled with veins, liver spots, and wrinkles, hanging like a dead snake.

Marissa lay in a small room behind a drawn curtain. Tristan sat by her side and stroked her hand. Every time his phone buzzed, she wondered if the other woman was messaging Tristan, asking him when he could slip away.

Soon, when I stop breathing.

Stop it.

She waited nearly an hour before a doctor saw her. Another half-hour passed before the next doctor arrived. Then more waiting and more doctors. No one seemed to have an answer.

After enduring four hours of seclusion and an MRI which revealed no tumor, aneurysm, no critical malady, she was finally allowed to leave when the blood tests came back. That they declared her healthy made Marissa worry about things like malpractice and incompetence. She knew how sick she felt, how cloudy her thoughts were. The doctors were missing something important.

It was the last doctor she saw, a middle-aged tall man with kind eyes and a strong chin, who concerned her with his line of questioning.

"And you're telling me the absolute truth," he said. "You don't take recreational drugs."

"I smoked a little weed in college if that's what you are implying."

He sighed. The doubt was plain on his face. He started to protest and stopped.

"My wife doesn't put that garbage in her body," Tristan said, rising to challenge him.

Tristan met him eye-to-eye. The doctor's forced smile slipped off his face like dripping oil.

"Her blood tests are consistent with—"

"You obviously made a mistake."

Undeterred, the doctor handed Marissa a pamphlet as she reached for her clothes.

"What is this?" she asked.

The pamphlet offered free and anonymous counseling for drug users. The 1-800 helpline was repeated on all three pages.

Marissa threw the pamphlet down on the cot.

"I don't have to listen to this anymore."

"As you say, Mrs. Carrington," the doctor said. He shifted uneasily away from Tristan. "Your hair loss could be caused by many things: certain infections, complications with medications, even environmental exposure to chemicals. In the vast majority of cases, the hair loss is reversible once we determine what the root cause is. I'd like to run a few more tests—"

"I think you've poked and prodded my wife enough," said Tristan.

The pamphlet drifted to the floor as Tristan grabbed his wife and pushed past the doctor.

"Maybe we should let him run a few more tests," she whispered while he pulled her through the curtain.

"These doctors are worthless. I'll take you to Boston tomorrow."

He never did.

The sun was down and the cold breath of autumn hung in the air by the time they made it home. He helped her through the doorway and paused until she showed she was capable of hanging her coat without tottering over. The chrome hangers clinked together like wind chimes long after she closed the closet door.

"Really, I can make it by myself," she said as he walked her from the foyer to the living room couch.

"You sure you're okay to walk?"

She sank heavily into the cushions and pulled a blanket over her shoulders. She couldn't get warm.

"I'm fine."

Hands on hips, he groaned and rolled his eyes.

"Still have a ton of work to get through. It's going to be a late night."

"Tristan, you don't have to watch over me. Go finish whatever you need to work on."

"No, really. I can't—"

"It's okay. I'm just going to watch TV for a bit."

"You're sure?"

"Go."

"All right then. Sit still. Call me if you need anything."

She heard him sit down in his office, then the wheels of the rolling chair moving across the floor. Turning on the television, Marissa thumbed the remote with disinterest. Between her swimming head and racing mind, she couldn't concentrate. She didn't hear him typing anymore.

The upstairs was silent. She worried about love letters and secret conversations.

On unsteady legs, she shuffled her way to the staircase and listened.

Quiet.

She climbed the stairs, a 45-year-old who'd biked the Massachusetts coast and ran marathons, tottering with the cautious gait of a grandmother, joints inflamed and popping. If Tristan heard her coming he made no attempt to hide his activities. No, the love letters were making her crazy with jealousy. For all she knew the notes were written during high school or college, predating their relationship.

A rectangular shaft of light leaked out of the study. From the top of the staircase, she couldn't see Tristan yet, didn't hear him. Marissa edged closer. She looked over her shoulder. The bathroom door was open, the light out. One lamp shone in the bedroom, the empty bed visible from the hallway. No Tristan. He had to be in his study. Hiding something.

One trembling hand reached for the jamb.

She pulled herself over the threshold and gasped. Whoever the woman on his laptop screen was, she was beautiful.

He must have heard her. Tristan grabbed the screen as if meaning to slam it shut, then stopped.

"You shouldn't sneak up on me like that," he said, wheeling his chair around.

Heat flared in his eyes, so briefly she almost missed it. Then worry.

"Don't tell me you thought it was smart to climb the stairs alone. For goodness sake, Marissa, you just came home from the hospital."

Her mouth hung open. It was perplexing that he made no attempt to hide his activities, didn't swivel the chair to shield the screen from her. The woman was even prettier than Marissa had first noticed. High cheekbones, dark curls tumbling past her shoulders. Marissa saw another picture on the screen, a second woman. Younger. Possibly a teenager. Though the second photograph was much smaller, Marissa noticed how similar the two women looked. Mother and daughter, perhaps.

His eyes followed hers to the screen, and then he grinned and leaned back in his chair, self-assured and not the least bit concerned.

"Facial recognition software," he said. "Neat, isn't it? You put in someone's photograph, and the software scans social media and search engines for the best match."

Marissa stepped closer, one hand on the wall. Had she not been so sick and blurry-eyed she could have seen the screen clearly. All she discerned were the faces and an address in the corner, the text too small to read.

"Why are you looking at her picture? Is that her address?"

He slammed the laptop shut.

The fury she'd seen in his eyes flashed again. There and gone. As if it had never been there.

"Please, sit down."

He rose to help her into a chair. She pushed his hand away.

"I'm fine standing."

"Marissa—"

"I've been sitting all day."

He looked down at his hands, folded in his lap.

"Clearly I owe you an explanation. I can see why this would trouble you."

"She's quite beautiful, Tristan," she said, her lower lip quivering. She bit down on it, refusing to cry in front of him.

"Is she?" He opened the laptop, studied the photograph with the detached interest of a jeweler scrutinizing fool's gold. He closed it up. "I suppose she is. I'm just happy I found her."

Marissa's heart stopped. She willed her legs not to crumple.

"If I get her account, we're set for the year, hon," he continued, making it all seem so obvious. Seeing she didn't understand—and how could she?—he sighed. "Liam Brady turned me onto her during my trip to New York. Said she was frustrated with her broker's performance during the last market downturn. I told him how stretched we were, that I couldn't take on any new business. Liam insisted I look over her portfolio. Marissa, it's three times larger than the Byrne account, and you know how much his business meant to us last year."

"But why are you looking at her picture?"

He leaned back and laughed.

"I was so nervous I'd blow the deal that I somehow misplaced her contact information. All I had was a scanned photo and her Goldman Sachs holdings. I wasn't about to call Liam and admit I'd forgotten her goddamn name. He'd never again recommend a client of that size to me. So I popped her photo into the computer and voila: the magic of modern technology. I have her name, address, and phone number again."

"Then who is the other girl on the computer?"

"Oh, the smaller photograph? The software spits back the best matches. Fortunately, there were only two, and the other woman wasn't the correct match. Smile, Marissa. Carrington Associates will be a publicly traded company inside of five years at the rate we are moving."

What little distrust remained vanished when he took her hands. She was a fool. An overreacting, jealous fool confused by illness.

She fell into his lap, her face nuzzled against his chest as he stroked her hair. An account this large would mean less travel, less time spent away from home.

"Why didn't you tell me sooner?"

"Because I wanted it to be a surprise."

"This is wonderful, Tristan. I'm so proud of all you've accomplished."

"All *we* have accomplished, hon. I couldn't have done any of this without you."

Hearing him say it was sweet, though she knew it was untrue. If anything she bogged him down, tethered him, sick as she was. Though he traveled as much as ever to keep pace with an ever-expanding client base, he shortened the lengths of his trips so he could come home to her.

Truthfully, Tristan could have attained anything he wanted in life. When they'd first met at Brown, he was a chemistry student, top of his class. Late in his sophomore year, he switched majors after a disagreement with one of his laboratory professors. The change was shocking since Tristan was fast-tracking toward a career as a materials scientist, and there was little doubt he'd be one of the nation's foremost inside of ten years. The switch to economics had been silky smooth. By the following semester, no one doubted Tristan would be just as successful in high finance.

"We should celebrate," she said. "Tell me what you want me to cook for dinner. Lobster? A nice filet mignon?"

"Stop. You had a long day. I'll not have you cooking. How about I take you to Marina's?"

"Oh, Tristan. I don't want anyone seeing me like this."

"Seeing you like what?"

"Sick."

"You look beautiful."

She kissed his cheek. He hadn't shaved the last few days. She liked a little stubble on his face, thought it made him look straight off the set of a Hollywood action movie.

"That's sweet of you to say, but I can't stomach having people staring and pointing at me. News of the accident must be all over town by now. No, I don't think Marina's is a good idea."

"No one will bother you. It's all in your head."

"Is it?"

"Fine. I'll get takeout. Won't take me more than half an hour," he said.

She agreed and kissed his forehead. They walked down the stairs hand-in-hand as they had as newlyweds. He slipped into his jacket and kissed her full on the lips, still astonishing after two decades, enough to make her heart flutter.

"Take a nap. I'll be right back."

The door shut behind him. She listened to him clog down the porch steps, then the dampened thud of the car door shutting. The engine revved and faded down the street.

She was alone again. The cold emptiness of the big house poured down from the ceilings.

Sitting on the sofa, she opened a Dean Koontz novel and turned down the television. Three chapters later, she glanced up at the wall clock. Thirty minutes gone. Tristan was due back unless traffic slowed him.

After an hour passed with no sign of Tristan, Marissa's thoughts returned to love letters and clandestine rendezvous. Another fifteen minutes ticked by.

It was after nine. She paced the downstairs, then returned to the couch with a glass of chardonnay. Peeking through the curtains, she saw the soft glow of lights shining out of windows up and down the cul-de-sac. Mrs. Valle was out walking her Pomeranian. Otherwise, the upscale development appeared deserted.

Her eyes drifted to the stairs.

Marissa swallowed the last of her wine and set the glass on the end table. One last glance at the driveway confirmed Tristan still wasn't home. He wouldn't be so callous as to cheat on her after bringing her home from the hospital.

No, she wouldn't allow herself to believe he'd been unfaithful. The letters had to be old.

Before she could talk herself out of it, she climbed the stairs with a dizzy head. She hadn't eaten since breakfast. Besides the wine, she'd drunk only a tall glass of water after returning home. Tristan insisted she stay hydrated.

Stopping outside his study, she heard a car door slam. If it was Tristan, she should have heard his car approach. The engine of his restored, vintage Camaro was unmistakable.

What if he really was having an affair and caught her sifting through his letters? She froze on the riser, one hand clutching the banister. An owl hooted outside. She waited to hear Tristan pounding up the porch steps.

Nothing. Not a sound.

Maybe it was smarter to wait until tomorrow while

Tristan was at work to read the letters. She needed to know, needed to understand.

Marissa peeked into the study. The laptop was open. An orange, bird-like creature ascending out of flames was on the screen. The mythological scene tickled her memory.

Her vision went blurry again as she plodded up to the attic. The doorknob was frigid in her hand. Nothing prepared her for the chill that swept down the risers when she pulled open the walk-in attic door.

Cupping her elbows with her hands, she lowered her head and struggled up the stairs. Pulling a string turned on one overhead light. The corners were dark. Everything smelled of dust and wood.

She pushed aside a box and climbed over another. The wedding gown danced and swayed like a ghost as the coming winter pushed through the soffit vents.

Marissa stopped short of her wedding gown.

So much darkness.

She expected a hand to shoot out from the gloom and grab her. The cold was into her bones now.

When she tried to push past the gown the fabric wrapped around her face like a spider web.

Crying out, she threw it aside and saw the box.

Dropping to her knees, she tore off the top as footsteps scuffed outside. From the driveway? The wind gusted and screamed over the roof.

Marissa ripped away the newspaper as the sounds drew closer to the house.

She saw the notes. Terror crawled on spider's legs down her back.

"No," she said, sobbing.

She ripped open the first note and threw it away with a shriek, thinking something had to be wrong. The next note nearly made her faint.

She'd torn every last note from the box before

falling to the cold, dirty floor with tears streaming down her face.

It can't be.

What's happening to me?

The letters weren't written by a lover.

The notes were from Marissa.

CHAPTER THREE

Takeout

Marissa lay huddled under the bed covers with knees drawn to chest.

While the October cold bled into the house, the last bit of evidence that she'd lost her mind collected dust eight feet above her head. Seeing the long-lost notes brought forth a flood of memories. She'd written those notes at Brown, placing one under Tristan's pillow, hiding another two in his coat pocket and over his Camaro's visor, slipping a letter into his chemistry notebook before he left for class. Perhaps it was juvenile—before then she hadn't written a love note since the eighth grade— but she loved to please and surprise him, hungered for the passionate side of Tristan to emerge and take her to bed with him. She recalled writing one letter on a warm September afternoon after their first date. Still another she'd penned in the university quad, seated in the grass wearing cutoff jean shorts and a crop top, reveling in the comfortable shade of an old oak tree the morning after they'd first had sex. He'd always said they were destined to be together, acted as though they were long lost lovers finally reunited.

The idea of Tristan saving the notes all these years only made the pain worse. How could she have looked at her own handwriting and mistaken the notes as another woman's? Soon she'd see ghosts or hear witches cackling in the attic.

Perhaps the sickness weighed on Tristan as much as it did Marissa. Lately, she sometimes awoke to him tossing and turning in his sleep, muttering angrily. The doctor had prescribed him something, perhaps sleeping pills, and he wasn't taking them. He kept the pills stuffed in his glove box, obviously humiliated. Strong men didn't want to rely on anything, especially medication.

A bang from downstairs brought her up and out of the covers.

"Tristan?"

"It's me."

He said something else. She could have sworn he called her *Jess,* but her head was cloudy. And didn't *Mariss*, as he sometimes called her, sound like *Jess?*

She exhaled and checked the clock. He'd been gone nearly two hours.

She heard him cross the floor into the kitchen. Water ran in the sink, then he walked back to the stairway.

"I started to worry something had happened to you."

She couldn't see him yet. The stairway was all shadows and darkness. She heard him climbing the steps, coming closer.

The dark congregated outside the doorway, barely held at bay by the bedside lamp. His shoes were heavy on the stairs. The planks squealed near the top.

She could see him now, a beast's shadow cast against the black.

He flicked on the hallway light. She squinted her eyes from the glare.

In the light, he no longer looked monstrous.

"What on earth took you so long?"

He shook his head in disgust.

"Route 6 was a mess. Tanker truck overturned

near Barnstable and backed traffic up for a mile or so. I should have checked the road reports before I left. I must have been stuck for an hour-and-a-half."

He shook two grease-stained paper bags and said, "This stuff will probably kill the both of us."

His laugh disarmed her.

The bed springs protested when he sat beside her, the mattress tipping toward him.

"Thank God you weren't caught in the accident," she said, feeling guilty for thinking he'd cheated on her tonight. "Sometimes I worry that you're hurt or lost when you're on the road for so long."

The bag he handed her smelled of shrimp egg rolls, fries, and teriyaki chicken.

"Well, don't."

"Why didn't you call me, at least? You have your phone."

He pulled a cloth place mat from his coat pocket and laid it in front of her as she propped herself up on her pillows to comfort an aching back.

"I tried," he said "Damn network was down again, and you know how lousy coverage is on that road. Maybe it was better that you rest."

"You know I can't rest when you're out on the road so much. I worry about you."

Fishing his hand into one of the bags, he removed two french fries. He put one in his mouth and slipped the other into hers. It tasted salty and wet and altogether wonderful.

"Good, isn't it? But first," he said, handing her a big glass of water. "Drink up. No more food until you're hydrated."

"Tristan."

"Do it."

She gulped half the glass before coming up for air. The water flooded down her parched throat.

"Finish all of it."

"Yes, boss."

When she was done he placed the glass on the bed stand and opened the takeout bags.

The comfort food filled Marissa too quickly and left a dead weight at the bottom of her stomach. Half the bag remained when she pushed it away.

"I can't handle the smell any longer," she said. "Take it away, would you?"

"What's the problem?"

His hands were soft and warm as he brushed the hair from her eyes. She desired him, would've wished for him to sweep the food off the bed and climb atop her had the fatigue coursing through her body not ensured she'd fall asleep under him. Then what would he think of her?

"I want you to rest," he said, easing Marissa to her back and pulling the covers up to meet her chin. "Sleep in tomorrow."

"I don't want to sleep. That's all I ever do anymore is sleep."

Her voice sounded distant and lost. A small part of her hoped all she needed to wake strong and vibrant again was sleep. Another part wished she wouldn't wake at all.

"Where are you going?" she asked, her voice barely a whisper now.

Marissa was aware of his footfalls leaving the room. The table lamp painted deep orange across her closed eyelids. Something scuffed in the room, and she forced herself up from impending slumber. He placed a box fan at the foot of the bed and turned it on, aiming it away from her.

"The noise always helps you sleep," he said.

She'd become accustomed to white noise at Brown, using a big box fan to drown out her dormitory neighbors talking in the halls at night.

"Thank you," she whispered.

Her eyes were cemented shut when he kissed her forehead and turned off the lamp. The room was dark and the fan a gentle lullaby.

Then he was gone from the room.

She thought she heard the front door ease open and close before she fell asleep.

CHAPTER FOUR

The Golden Caribou

The Golden Caribou was overflowing with locals when Michael Tompkins took the first open barstool. A country band he didn't recognize played on a small stage set at the back of the bar, where several people danced and raised beer bottles to a Garth Brooks cover. It was fish fry night, and the bar smelled of charred bass and grease. The cook, Dickie Nicks, had burned the fish again. When the rowdies celebrated a poor rendition of a Jimmy Buffett classic, Michael decided to find a quieter bar.

He swiveled on his stool and saw Tristan Carrington standing in the doorway, surveying the crowd. Michael didn't like Tristan much, and it wasn't because he felt a pang of jealousy over Marissa. His own wife, Beth-Anne, died of a stroke in her thirties—almost ten years ago, Michael realized, watching couples dance as though life was endless. Now it was just Michael and his thirteen-year-old daughter, Jennifer. Though Michael still loved his wife, Marissa was one of those rare women who drew men like a magnet—or at least, she had before she turned so sickly; in truth, Michael felt even more attracted by her vulnerability—and it seemed to Michael that Tristan was too tied up in his business activities to look after his wife.

"Howdy, Michael. What can I get you?"

Michael looked up, surprised. Renee Gardner had a harried look on her face as she filled foaming mugs and passed them down the bar. Her father, Bill, owner of The Golden Caribou, ran the business like Ebenezer Scrooge. Damned if Renee needed two or three people helping her behind the bar. The books needed to stay in the black.

"Sam Adams," he said.

"You got it."

Michael fixed things. It's what he'd always done best. As a child, he fixed his friends' bicycles, oiled the chains, changed the brakes, and kept the gears shifting like oil on a hot pan. Later, with his father's guidance, he expanded his skills to servicing and repairing lawn mowers, trimmers, any motorized yard equipment that began to belch smoke or refused to start. By his eighteenth birthday, Michael earned enough money from neighborhood plumbing repairs and painting jobs to buy himself a car, a rusty Chevrolet Celebrity with over 150,000 hard miles on it. That led him down the road to automobile repair, and somehow he kept that Celebrity purring through trade school before the car finally gave up the ghost.

But he couldn't fix Marissa anymore than he could've fixed Beth-Anne, and didn't even know where to begin troubleshooting. It didn't make sense: a woman in outstanding physical condition and barely into her middle years suddenly falling ill and looking twenty years older. All the worrisome specters visited him when his mind wandered—cancer, Lou Gehrig's disease, an early onset of Alzheimer's. Her doctors should have identified those diseases, yet they had no answers. Alcoholism? Drug addiction? The latter worried Michael the most, though he couldn't say why. No, Marissa would never poison her body with drugs. She took pride in her conditioning, and until six months ago it showed. Michael had never met a woman her age with such strength, vibrancy, and natural beauty.

She was slowly wasting away, perhaps dying, and the bastard in The Golden Caribou doorway didn't give a shit.

"Here you go." Renee put the beer down and cocked an eyebrow. "What's up with you tonight?"

"Huh?"

"You seem distracted. Everything okay?"

"Just a long day on top of a long week. If I get one more plumbing job that requires me to rip out the floor and re-pipe, I'm going to turn into Jack Torrance."

"All work and no play…"

"Yes, makes Michael a dull boy."

He glanced back to the doorway. Tristan was gone.

Good. He didn't want to talk to that piece of shit, anyhow. Michael slapped a generous tip for Renee on the bar and took the bottle with him. Ducking behind the crowd, he weaved his way toward the exit. The band was all bass and drums. His ears started to ring.

It was after ten. A homeless man in torn jeans and a flannel jacket curled on a bench, trembling each time the wind ratcheted up. That was the problem with the weather on the Cape, Michael thought. The wind always blew. In the summertime, when the air was hot and the humidity swamp-like, the wind was a Godsend. But as winter approached, each gust from Mother Nature doused you with ice water. By December, the locals would wish the wind never blew again. Michael dug a five out of his pants pocket and handed it to the man. As Michael braced against the cold and started down the street, the man recited gospel.

Nobody else was out tonight. The shops were closed. Michael passed the Pink Dolphin, a touristy shop with Patriots and Red Sox beach towels hanging in the window. The shop was closed until tourism picked up in May. The seafood buffet across the street was shut down for the season.

The bar sounds faded behind him and were lost to

the wind whistling in his ears. His truck was a block away in an unlit parking lot. Living on the Cape tended to isolate residents from the dangers of the big cities. Still, it chilled him to squeeze between vehicles in the dark. You never knew if someone was hiding back there, waiting to stick a jackknife into your belly and run off with your wallet.

Michael turned the corner and nearly walked into Tristan.

"Hello, Michael." Though Michael was a big man, he looked up into Tristan's eyes. Michael took an involuntary step backward. "Out kind of late, aren't you?"

Michael lifted the bottle of Sam Adams.

"Just grabbing a drink before I call it a day."

"I saw you in The Golden Caribou. A sane man would have finished his drink inside, and yet here you are in the cold."

Laughing nervously, Michael tried to edge his away around Tristan but found himself blocked in.

"Yeah, it sure got cold early this year. I should really get back to my daughter."

"Yes…Jennifer," Tristan said.

Michael saw hate deep down in Tristan's eyes. For what, he couldn't imagine.

"I need to go. I'll see you around the neighborhood, yeah?"

Michael tried to walk around Tristan. Tristan stepped over to block him. They thumped chests, and Michael nearly fell backward.

"I see the way you look at her."

"I have no idea what you're talking—"

"Don't fuck with me. You think I don't know what the two of you are up to? What's the end game if you turn her against me? Jess has a tendency to wander, as I recall."

"Jess?"

Looking confused, Tristan stepped back and rubbed his head. His eyes were unfocused. He had to be drunk, though Michael didn't smell alcohol.

"Jess...what did I..."

"Whatever it is you think I did, you're mistaken."

Tristan touched his jacket. Michael heard pills rattle around.

"Are you all right, Tristan?"

"No," Tristan said, looking as if Michael splashed him awake with ice water. He shook the cobwebs from his head and checked his watch. "I'm sorry. It's been a long day, and I need to get back on the road."

"On the road tonight? Maybe you should rest awhile before you drive. Let me call you a cab."

"I said I'm fine."

Tristan walked away. He shot glances over his shoulders as if shadows followed him.

Michael took one last swig from the bottle and tossed the remains into a trash can. Jess?

Fading back into the shadows of a shop's entryway, Michael watched him go. Tristan stopped at the corner and called someone on his cell phone. Tristan was too far away for Michael to hear, but he kept turning in circles and looking behind him, nervous someone might overhear his conversation. The call ended. Tristan stuffed the phone into his pocket and disappeared around the corner, heading back toward the closed shops and restaurants.

Yet Michael couldn't shake the feeling that Tristan had tricked him and was waiting in the shadows.

Leaning against a cold brick wall, Michael breathed and waited, breathed and waited. When he was sure Tristan was gone, Michael hurried out of the entryway and crossed the lot to his truck.

CHAPTER FIVE

The Bathtub

It was five minutes past eight when Marissa's eyes opened. She glanced over at the clock and groaned. The heaviness in her head made her feel as though she'd gone on a midnight bender.

She couldn't recall the last time she'd slept so soundly. Her bladder was full to the point of hurting, thanks to the glass of water Tristan made her drink before bedtime. She yanked open the blinds. Sunshine seared the windowpane and flooded the room.

Something was different.

She felt alert, awake. Swinging her legs off the bed didn't provoke the battery of joint aches she'd come to expect.

As she carried the glass to the bathroom, her hand didn't tremble and her legs felt steady. Her heart beat with new urgency, felt like it wanted to leap out and run. It was as if a long lost power switch had been thrown. The strong, vibrant Marissa was down in the depths and swimming to the surface.

She shuffled from the bedroom to the bathroom and relieved herself. Checking the mirror, she saw too much gray crawling out among the black strands like weeds. Her skin was dry and pale, but the circles under her eyes had lightened.

Yes, this was different.

"Tristan? Are you downstairs?"

Her voice rang off the walls unanswered.

Tristan was probably at work by now, though it was odd she hadn't heard him leave.

She brushed her teeth and washed her face. Feeling inspired, she reached up and removed a rose flower hydration cream, her favorite, off the top shelf. As she rubbed a little into her parched skin she realized she hadn't applied the cream since before she fell ill. She longed for healthy skin, wanted to look attractive for Tristan again. Setting the cream aside, she determined to use a full application after showering.

With a strong grip on the banister, she padded down to the kitchen where she filled the kettle and set it to boil. An idyllic autumn scene unfolded out the window —orange, red, and yellow leaves set ablaze by the sun, the morning frost melting into the grass and glimmering. Maybe she would take a walk through the neighborhood. The old Marissa would have already been out on the trail, running and working up a sweat.

Small steps first.

As she ate a poached egg with a slice of wheat toast, she checked the weather forecast on her phone. Breakfast settled peacefully. Her fingertips tingled. Each bite of food was kindling on a smoldering fire.

After her tea was ready, she sipped from the cup and read the note Tristan left her on the kitchen table:

In the office all day. Be back before dinner
I love you
Tristan

Something about the tea tasted acrid. She loved pure green tea, unsullied by sugars and flavorings. Marissa could recognize the taste of organic green tea, and this wasn't it. Perhaps being sick for so long had altered her sense of taste. She sniffed at the tea. It smelled fine.

Plugging her nose, she swallowed the last of the tea and cleaned the dishes. Afterward, she brought a small load of laundry down to the basement, then climbed the stairs with a hint of a hop in her step. Marissa couldn't remember the last time she'd felt so clear-headed.

Damn her doctors. If they couldn't help her, she'd nurse herself back to health. If you wanted anything done right, you had to do it yourself.

The phone rang as she finished putting away the dishes.

"Marissa?" It was Michael Tompkins, her home repairman and neighbor from the far end of the cul-de-sac.

"Hey, Michael. How's Jennifer?"

"Doing well. Beginning to discover boys, I fear. I suppose she's reached that age. Anyhow, I apologize if you think I'm prying, but I heard about the accident yesterday. You weren't hurt, were you?"

Marissa sank into the chair. Small town rumors spread quickly.

"Just my pride. I'm rather embarrassed over the ordeal."

"I heard it was a black out."

"Yes, I suppose it was."

"What did the doctors find?"

"Nothing, which scared me a little. Then I got to thinking about it and realized it was good news. At least they ruled out anything serious."

"Thank God for that. But, Marissa..." She could hear him wrestling for the right words. "Listen, I don't want this to come across as forward, and you've always been so good to my daughter, but if you ever need someone to check on you or drive you into town, you only need to pick up the phone."

"That's very sweet of you, Michael. I really shouldn't impose—"

"You wouldn't be imposing. I'm serious about this, Marissa. There are plenty of neighbors who care about you and want to help. You shouldn't have to shoulder this alone."

"I'm not alone. Tristan takes care of me."

He went quiet for a second, then, "Of course, he does. But I bet he wouldn't mind if some of us looked in on you while he was away. Maybe he wouldn't have to know. Just a quick phone call or a knock on the door."

Tristan wouldn't like it. The offer would make him look weak and be taken as a personal affront.

"For what it's worth, I think you're doing plenty already."

"How's that?"

"You're checking in on me now, and that's an awfully kind thing to do. But I don't want to burden you. You have your daughter to look after, and with all those boys who will be knocking on your door soon…"

"Ha ha. You got me there. Anyway, it wouldn't be a burden. I'm back-and-forth on this street several times per day. It wouldn't be anything to knock on the door and see how you're feeling."

"Well, since you brought it up," Marissa said, smiling. "I feel great this morning. Better than I have in weeks."

"That's wonderful news. Maybe you're finally kicking this." The phone beeped. "Uh-oh. That's the Kensington's calling me about their water heater again. I better take this call. Feel better, okay?"

Smiling to herself after the call ended, Marissa tousled her hair in the window's reflection, then tied it in a ponytail.

Better.

She stepped into the shower and left the bathroom door cracked open for ventilation.

The cascade of water was warm against her back. A fine mist grew and clung to the ceiling as she relaxed.

A moment later, her legs gave out and she slammed headfirst against the porcelain.

CHAPTER SIX

Cloak-and-Dagger

Twin streaks of sunlight beamed through the bedroom window, igniting dust motes which floated and glimmered. Muted voices and laughter followed from outside. Two neighbors were out for a walk, wholly unaware of what was happening inside her bedroom, and this excited Denise Moretti, deepening the cloak-and-dagger aspect of the rendezvous.

She was naked except for her bra, her abdominal muscles chiseled beneath sweaty flesh as she reached up and stroked the hard lines of his chest.

Denise didn't believe in one-night stands—or one-morning stands for that matter—but he was so strong, so breathtakingly beautiful, and she'd desired him from the moment he first strode into First Burlington Bank. A chance encounter. Their eyes met and, for a brief second, she'd sworn he recognized her. But that was impossible. She'd never seen him before and never would have forgotten a face like his.

Tristan.

He looked like a Tristan, she thought, giggling to herself. Broad shoulders, muscle sliding over muscle as if pythons curled under his skin. Stripped except for his jeans, he moaned and went about working her bra clasp free. It popped open. He tossed it to the hardwood floor.

She popped the button on his jeans and slipped her hand inside. Running her fingers from hip to groin, she smiled at the boyish laughter she invoked by inadvertently tickling him. Then she plunged her hand deeper and grasped. He moaned and rolled his eyes.

The rotating fan swept a chill across her skin and raised goosebumps. Denise yanked on the waistband with a frantic desperation, flipped him over to his back and ripped off the jeans. My God, he was stunning. In the dim light the tanned flesh seemed painted over his muscles, energetic and somehow ageless, no hint of middle-aged softness at the abdominals or anywhere else she could see.

And she could see all of him now.

Tristan turned her over and pinned her hands to the bed. She lay panting and greedy and utterly at his mercy.

She slid across the silken sheet.

Like a whisper at midnight.

Tristan slipped down to meet her body, helped her wiggle her way past the pillows, where she grasped hold of the slats.

She wanted him. He slid his fingers up and between her thighs and provoked a rapid hammering in her chest.

The smell of freshly laundered bedsheets was powerful around them. He slid into her, harder than she anticipated. A gasp, then she felt herself loosen.

She thrust up at him and felt the fan blow across her legs. Sitting up, he grasped the headboard.

Arms flexed and taut, he used the headboard more to exert his dominance than support himself. He was Icarus, son of Daedalus, rising high into the fiery sunshine burning through the window. And he was Adonis, the beautiful, the man she desired.

Already teetering on the edge of orgasm, Denise trembled and looked up into eyes where fire and darkness converged. She began to grind.

So enraptured was she with lust, she almost missed it when he whispered, *Oh God, Jamie*. Or maybe it had been *Amy*. Or *baby*. All sound was lost to the rhythm of the bedsprings.

"Please kiss me," she said.

Tristan's kiss was breathtaking, needy, colored by an undefinable danger, as though they lay upon a cliff edge, the sharp rocks below the ultimate punishment for the morning's debauchery.

His breath was hot on her neck. Animalistic. An untamed, primitive indulgence twisted his face.

"I'm ready," he said.

It didn't matter if she wasn't. He pushed faster and harder.

As she writhed he plunged his tongue into her ear.

Denise moaned. She wanted to slow down and make this moment last.

She couldn't.

The room seemed to turn a shade of red. Crying out, she let go as he exploded inside her.

His head was bent back, Tristan gulping air. Another flood of precious warmth.

Quivering, he collapsed onto her.

A friend once compared sex to a marathon, Denise recalled. Extreme effort forces the body to go queerly numb, blocking out exhaustion. It isn't until the runner stops that the legs turn into gelatin and refuse to respond. For Denise, that moment was now. Pins and needles tingled from her thighs to her toes. Her muscles wouldn't twitch. It was nearly enough to make her panic —she was paralyzed under Tristan, his weight smothering her on the mattress.

Eventually, the feeling came back to her legs, lessening the anxiety. She lay beneath him, the rise and fall of his chest the only sign he was alive. Strange he didn't move or say a word.

What did she know about him? Nothing really, other than he was magnificent. He was the owner of a small Cape Cod-based brokerage firm and twice visited her bank, the first time to meet with Regina Ulster, the bank president, regarding her financial holdings with his brokerage firm, the second time to get Denise's phone number. His guise had been a second conference with Ulster. A discrepancy existed with her paperwork.

Denise knew his real reason for visiting. He'd made his intentions obvious, always shifting his eyes in Denise's direction when Ulster wasn't looking. By the end of his second appointment, they'd planned their first date, a candlelight dinner at Little Napoli not far from the Burlington, Vermont university district. She found Tristan charming, charismatic, and deliciously mysterious. A gentleman, he opened doors for her and remained standing until she was comfortably seated at the table. He understood fine wine and ordered only the best, speaking fluent Italian with the waiter as she watched with rapt attention.

That had been three weeks ago. She had neither seen nor heard from Tristan until his text arrived late last night. He could be there by two in the morning, he'd written. And now here they lay, bodies melded together and dripping with perspiration as the bedroom window framed a perfect blue sky.

"Hey, don't you fall asleep on me," she said and gave his shoulder a nudge.

He groaned into her neck and made her skin tingle again.

"Don't forget I had a three-hour drive in the middle of the night. That took a lot out of me."

She massaged his back, all muscle under sleek flesh.

A car horn honked twice outside. It was almost nine o'clock, time for Eric Pendleton to wave goodbye to his wife, Christina, and drive to the office.

Denise fantasized what it would be like to kiss Tristan goodbye every morning and fall asleep next to him at night. Her marriage to Ben had been a failure, the knot tied fresh out of college. What had the rush been? It didn't take long before they both realized they weren't in love, and she'd seen the end foreshadowed from the beginning like a Greek tragedy. Now her ex was married again and happy and planning a family, and she was alone.

Alone in this perfect Colonial home Ben had left her in the divorce settlement, with its Norman Rockwell barn in the back. Alone with nothing to do except work and cook and sleep.

Maybe Tristan was married. It was possible. He didn't wear a ring, but that didn't matter. Guys removed their wedding rings all the time to pick up women. Perhaps the ring was buried deep in his jeans pocket or stashed in the car's glove compartment. She considered asking him and stopped. No sense ruining a tranquil moment and chasing him out of her bed.

She could have stayed like this all morning and afternoon if she chose—today was her off-day from the bank, and as long as he didn't have anyplace he needed to be…

He raised up in a push-up position and smiled pearly whites down at her.

"When can I see you again?"

"You aren't leaving already, are you?"

"I've gotta be in Boston by one, then back to the Cape this afternoon."

Sure, I bet that's when you told your wife you'd get home.

Denise swallowed her petulance. She wanted him to stay the entire day, longer if he was interested. Instead, she'd spend the day alone. The neighborhood block party and yard sales were only a few days away.

She was on the makeshift planning committee, really just a group of four women who were looking for anything to occupy their days while their husbands worked.

She rolled onto her side and pouted.

"I should jump in the shower before you convince me to have another go," he said.

"Would that be so bad?"

"Come on, you know I'd love to, but I have a full plate today."

"If you have Ulster's account, you must be doing pretty well for yourself. All that travel will only serve to wear you down."

"If I stop now, I fail."

"What does that even mean?"

"It means I planned for this day years ago, and I'm not about to slow down when I'm so close to getting what I want."

She threw her hair back and touched his chest.

"I want *you*."

Before the words left her mouth she knew they weren't true. She wanted companionship, not just sex, a person to come home to after a long day's work and share dreams and fears with. A man to grow old beside. That was the same logic that had roped her into her first marriage, the idea of love superseding love itself.

"And you'll have me again. Now answer my question: when can I see you again? I'll be up this way early next week."

"I'm off Tuesday. Does that fit into your busy schedule?"

"For you, I'll make it fit."

He kissed her on the forehead and crawled off the bed. Completely naked, he was elegant and purposeful as he turned the corner into the hallway. The bathroom door shut. Water showered into the tub.

Alone again.

She started to get up and stopped.

A buzzing came from his jacket, strewn across a corner chair. His phone.

She couldn't bring herself to read his messages or check his contacts.

Yet she needed to. It was a simple reconnaissance mission to ensure she wasn't strolling blindly into enemy territory. Better to find out now if he was married before she committed to him.

Denise edged back the covers and cocked her head around the bedroom door. The hallway was empty. She heard water cascading in the bathroom and the pop of the shampoo bottle opening.

He'd never know.

With a bed sheet clutched around her breasts, she stepped off the bed. The bare wood floor was cold to the touch. It whined when she stepped down. Tristan's clothes were jumbled in a pile with hers, his shoes beneath the antique chair where his jacket lay. From the center of the bedroom, she could see out the window. The Sandersons' Burmese cat was flicking its tail and watching something small scurry under the bushes. She knew the daylight was too bright for anyone to see into the bedroom, yet she adjusted the drooping sheet over her body when a car passed by.

The phone buzzed loudly. An angry sound. She jumped back.

Denise couldn't hear the water running over the rotating fan. It made her wonder if Tristan was standing right behind her in the doorway.

She spun around. The hallway was empty. She didn't know why she began shivering. It wasn't the cold of the upstairs. She turned around and approached the jacket again, throwing quick glances over her shoulder.

Reached out. Jabbed one hand into the pocket.

Not there.

She touched the hard plastic under the fabric, felt

its warmth burning from an interior pocket.

Something else jiggled. Candies or pills.

The lock on the bathroom door popped like a gunshot.

She covered her mouth to keep from crying out.

Denise tiptoed to the bed as he thundered down the hallway.

Tristan turned into the bedroom and caught her sliding onto the bed. She tried to look natural. Dark accusation flared in his eyes, hair dripping as though he'd rushed back to the room. He knew. Somehow, the bastard knew.

Then his features melted, and he stood grinning in the doorway with one of her embroidered cotton towels wrapped around his hips.

"You look like a kid with her hand caught in the cookie jar."

"Do I?" She felt something cold in the back of her throat. "Why do you say that?"

"No reason."

He smiled and watched her from the corner of his eye as he went about slipping into his clothes.

"That was a quick shower."

"Like I said, I have to be in Boston soon."

"Then back home to the Cape."

"That's right."

He tossed her clothes onto the bed. Denise sheepishly hurried into a nightshirt.

"Give me five minutes to cook breakfast," she said, elbows cupped by her hands as she slipped past him. She felt the humidity rolling off of him as he dripped in the doorway. Jesus, it was as if he'd known what she was up to. Who jumps out of the shower that quickly without drying?

Denise scrambled up some eggs and quickly plated them with a side of whole grain toast and half a grapefruit. As Tristan ate he studied her from across the dining room table. She began to feel uneasy. A dinner out on the town and a morning fling, and she still didn't know much about him.

He politely excused himself from the table and carried his dishes to the sink. The interrogating glares he kept slipping her made Denise squirm in her seat.

"Did you have enough to eat?"

"Cut the bullshit." Denise's mouth hung open. "What were you doing when I came into the bedroom?"

"Nothing…nothing. I was just—"

"You were going to search my jacket, weren't you?" He ripped the phone out of his pocket. "What gives you the right to see my clients' information? How would you like it if I went through your belongings when you stepped out of the room?"

"I didn't touch your phone. I heard it ring, but I swear I didn't go anywhere near it."

"I don't believe you."

In that moment, Denise felt the cold reality of knowing a stranger was in her house. It was like inviting a poodle inside and turning to see a rabid wolf in its place.

She'd moved too fast and shouldn't have allowed him into her bed yet. Tristan was hiding a secret. That much was obvious. Whether he had a wife or a girlfriend, she couldn't say for certain. What troubled her most was the sense of something dangerous crawling around inside of him.

"I think you should leave, Tristan."

The look he gave her was fury tinged by vulnerability. He hadn't expected her to throw him out.

"Fine."

As he walked through the doorway she stared down at her feet.

"I don't think you should call me again."

He swung around. She could feel the heat of his glare. His fingers trembled, clenching and opening.

"You're making a mistake. Remember what happened last time you did this to me."

She lifted her eyes to question him, but he was already thundering down the steps to his car.

Last time?

The car door slammed. She felt a measure of relief when he finally drove off.

CHAPTER SEVEN

The Basement

What happened…?

…cold…my head…

Everything wet.

Marissa awoke to the cold spray of water against her legs. Her skin was pruned and goose bumped, a topographic map of welts. Above her, the bathroom ceiling warped and spun, and her head felt locked in a vise.

Crying as she turned off the shower, she struggled to rise. Her feet slipped out from under her. With a scream she crashed down into the tub, her back clipping the faucet and tearing a small chunk of flesh away. Wracked by pain, she snaked her legs together and waited for her head to clear.

A clump of hair the size of a tennis ball blocked the drain, and the water was up past her breasts. Grimacing, she pulled the ball of hair from the drain and placed it in the corner of the tub. The water subsided, and she was left shivering and alone and frightened with the vent fan buzzing overhead.

Everything ached as she pulled herself out of the tub and onto the bathmat. There she lay in a ball with a towel as cover, listening to the quiet of the house.

No Tristan to help her. The phone downstairs on

the kitchen table. She might die up here before someone found her.

Reaching around to her back, she touched the wound, winced, and removed her hand. At least she wasn't bleeding.

The sun had departed the bathroom window and was on the west side of the house by the time she willed herself onto her knees. She knew it was late.

He'd be home from the office soon—she thought maybe she should stay put.

Marissa stopped in the doorway when the walls tilted in on her. Nausea clutched at her stomach before she could crawl back to the toilet, and she vomited breakfast onto the hardwood landing above the staircase. Wiping spittle away, she crawled around the mess and struggled into the bedroom where she slipped on a pair of sweatpants and socks. In the drawer, she grabbed the first t-shirt she saw and pulled it over her head with the pained efforts of an arthritic senior.

Next, she pulled herself up with the drawers to support her. The room spun again, but she held on until the spell passed.

It was almost four o'clock. Hunger pains wracked her, and her back screamed in protest. Her legs were steady now.

She moaned. No matter how awful she felt, she had to clean the sick off the floor before it ate into the woodwork. Tristan liked a spotless house and wouldn't approve of such an ugly blemish. It had cost them dearly to restore the hardwood.

The stairs appeared to slither and writhe as she climbed down. She clutched both hands to the rail, her only lifeline. From the kitchen utility closet, she removed a mop and bucket, then grabbed a handful of paper towels.

The climb up the stairs was longer and far more strenuous. She was heaving and out of breath by the time she reached the landing, though her eyes no longer played tricks on her. The puke dripped out of the paper towels in long, yellow strands as she plugged her nose and slung the slime into the waste basket. Mopping the mess away, she remembered only a year ago this month she was at the top of her Krav Maga class, too fast and strong for the soccer moms to spar with. The instructor paired her with men. She gave them all they could handle. It might have been decades ago, for now her knees crackled and popped, all her joints felt afflicted with arthritis, and her youthful appearance had been replaced by a witch's mask in the mirror.

I should call the doctor.

She put the thought out of her head. A team of doctors hadn't found a thing wrong with her, yet they made the ridiculous insinuation that she abused drugs. It probably was a tumor as she feared. The doctors had misread her MRI. She'd heard of tumors going undetected until it was too late.

The clock read nearly five by the time she dumped the remains down the toilet, washed her face, and worked her way to the kitchen. Tristan would be hungry when he got home. He often was after working all afternoon as he rarely had time to eat with so many clients to see. From the refrigerator, she grabbed a bluefish fillet. A breath of frost spilled out of the freezer as she grabbed a pack of frozen vegetables. She tossed the fish into a pan, picked up her phone, and dialed Tristan. The phone rang and rang. When his voice-mail message started, she ended the call and stuffed the phone into her pocket. It was after five and still no sign of Tristan.

Before the sickness, there had been spring days and rides along the coast. There had been the warm scent of spring rising off the salt marshes, Jimmy Buffett on the car stereo, and her childish, playful teasing over his long trips and what he did for fun while he was away. With a wink of an eye and a smile, she'd melt, and then his hand would be on her bare thigh, moving under the folds of her dress as she giggled.

Marissa reached under the sink for a bottle of dish detergent and sighed. The wood underneath was wet again. On her hands and knees, she saw water dripping off the filter. So that was it, then. It was definitely the filter leaking and not the pipes. She'd better call Michael, who'd installed the water filter and replaced a broken window another time.

The window memory made her uneasy. Tristan had become angry with her for questioning him over how late he'd come home and thrown a hammer through the bedroom window.

She remembered Michael watching her carefully while he fixed the window. He'd broached the subject, accepting Marissa's assertion that she'd stumbled and put the hammer through the window herself during a failed attempt to hang a picture frame. Dangerous with a hammer and ladder, she joked. For a while, Michael seemed to buy it as he laughed along. Yet she noticed flashes of concern in his eyes whenever Tristan's name was mentioned.

Before she could forget, she dialed Michael's number. He picked up on the second ring.

"Look, I'm finishing a bathroom remodel at the Sanderson's tomorrow," he said. "I could swing by your place when I'm done. Say between four and five?"

"Thank you, Michael. That sounds fine. Tristan should arrive home around that time."

It was uncomfortably silent before he spoke again.

"Everything else okay, Marissa? You sound different from this morning."

Marissa glanced at the stove. The burner flames flared under the pan. Clamping the phone between her ear and shoulder, she turned down the heat and dug under the fish with a spatula.

"No, it's just this leak. I'm worried I'll come into the

kitchen and find a swimming pool."

"Ha, that's not so likely. You know how to turn the water off if the leak gets bad?"

She did.

After the fish finished cooking, Marissa plated the meal and threw in a load of laundry. Cobwebs hung in the corner of the finished basement.

Once the washer started to fill with water and slosh the clothes around, she turned to head upstairs. Back by the sofa, which faced a wall-mounted 60-inch HD television, something looked out of place. She stood staring at the room, wondering what had changed. The recliner was where it was supposed to be. The ornate table they'd unearthed at a nearby antique shop appeared to be where she'd last seen it.

The sofa.

It was askew, if only slightly. The indentations from where the legs originally stood were barely visible on the carpet.

When she started to shove the couch back into place her heart froze. A folded note stuck out from underneath.

Dropping to her knees, she peered under the couch.

There lay the notes from his secret lover.

CHAPTER EIGHT

Bus Stop

The bus door hissed open. It was now or never.

Tristan watched the young brunette sling a backpack over her shoulder. She was running from something. He could see it in the way she avoided eye contact with the other four passengers preparing to board, in her clothes—dusty and beaten—and from her drawn-down face to her ragged high tops. She'd been on the road for days, weeks. Hiding.

She gave the impression of not belonging. If she was in a room with a dozen friends, she would be the odd one out, nervously shifting her feet in a corner while conversations carried on around her.

Sitting on a weathered, wooden bench, Tristan guessed she was sixteen or seventeen. She should have been in school at this time of day, another reason to believe she was on the run.

The last of the passengers climbed the steps into the bus. At any second, the driver would close the doors and she'd be gone forever.

The ticket in Tristan's hand would take him from Worcester to Saratoga Springs. He had no reason to go to Saratoga Springs except she was headed there.

Pulling up his coat sleeve, he read his watch. Almost two o'clock. Tristan wasn't supposed to be at the bus stop. He'd come to Worcester to visit his father, who he hadn't seen since early spring.

Plans changed when he saw the girl hurrying toward the bus station with her coat clutched around her. She looked so much like Renee, the pretty girl who grew up next door. Sure, this girl dyed her hair black and punctured her face with piercings, but the resemblance to his old classmate was uncanny.

Renee spoke to him sometimes, but never in school around her friends. Too popular for him. She didn't know how strong he was, couldn't appreciate his level of intelligence or what he would accomplish in life.

Renee's idea of religious worship was her parents dragging her to church on Sunday mornings. She wasn't well-read like Tristan. Simple girls couldn't understand his beliefs about reincarnation or accept that he'd witnessed his grandmother's soul rise in the form of the Phoenix.

"Renee?"

She didn't respond.

"Is that you, Renee?"

This time she turned her head.

"Renee Nichols?"

Shaking her head, she slipped behind a young man in army fatigues. The man shot Tristan a challenging glare.

The doctors thought Tristan delusional for believing in reincarnation. Forced pills on him. Yet here Renee Nichols stood.

Down the alleyway, two homeless men circled a fire burning up from a rusted garbage can. Tristan stared at the fire. A smoky cloud hung over their heads. A bird swooped down through the smoke and winged its way through the alley.

Yes, reincarnation. Reborn in fire.

"Hey, buddy. You getting on or not?"

Tristan flashed the bus driver a glare. He saw the man blanch.

Fear. Somewhere in the portion of the brain that warns you not to walk in dangerous neighborhoods after dark, the bus driver saw the danger in Tristan and understood he was more god than man.

The door quickly closed. The bus belched exhaust and pulled away.

There in the window. The girl. She saw Tristan staring and averted her eyes before the bus disappeared down the street.

Tristan's eye twitched. In his coat pocket, he felt the pill bottle rolling between his fingers. How long had it been since he'd taken his medication? The confusion was less pronounced when he regularly followed his prescription. Still, the pills made him tired and irritable, and he couldn't run a business with his eyes drooping shut all day.

Besides, if he allowed the medication to weaken his inhibitions he might slip up and tell someone what he did to those girls in Westland. Smart men didn't get caught, and he was smarter than any of the miscreants he met every day. The poor old souls whose pensions he saved, the sociopaths who eschewed proper investing for credit card debt and lived beyond their means.

But lately, he'd begun to make mistakes.

Michael Tompkins, that sniveling coward, heard Tristan confuse Marissa's name. That was a problem because Michael wouldn't hesitate to drive a wedge between Tristan and Marissa. Tristan noticed how she drew Michael's eyes, knew he'd steal her away like Jimmy Rodgers stole Jess during high school.

His beautiful Jess.

Yet it was Tristan who had the last laugh. Jess was his again, reincarnated in Marissa.

He thumbed the safety latch on the pill bottle, felt the plastic scrape at his skin.

Michael Tompkins would wreck Tristan's plans… oh, yes, he most certainly would if given the chance.

Tristan rose from the bench. The slats squealed in relief. Crumpling up the ticket, he tossed it into a garbage can and stared off to the east. He could catch Renee in Saratoga Springs. In his Camaro, he could easily close the distance on the bus and pass it by. Maybe he'd wait in the shadows at the next stop, see if she remembered him after so many years.

Not today. The opportunity to see the girl would come again, as surely as the great wheel in the sky kept spinning.

It was time he paid an old friend a visit.

CHAPTER NINE

I Know Your Name

Blurred by tears, it was hard for Marissa to see the notes, let alone read them.

The wash cycle had long since ended, and she sat shivering on the cold floor with her arms wrapped around her knees, crying into the crook of her arm.

The sun was gone from the windows. Darkness pressed against the panes.

Minutes passed before she bit back tears. She was angry.

Sorting through the scattered notes, she pulled one from the pile and opened it. The envelope was addressed to Tristan. The woman had the gall to mail it directly to their house, though there was no return address in the corner. Strangely, the letter lacked postage.

She braced herself and read the note.

They'd known each other since high school, stayed in touch for decades while planning this affair.

Marissa stopped reading when she reached the part where the woman began to describe in detail what she would do to Tristan behind closed doors. The bottom of the note was signed *Alisha M*. Whoever she was, the whore had terrible handwriting.

The thought struck Marissa as funny. She was a

mix of tears and ironic laughter in the seclusion of the basement. Alisha M might have been sexier than Marissa, but her penmanship was ghastly.

A car drove past the house. Probably Alisha M.

She reached for another letter lacking a stamp or return address, tore it open and read this one from start-to-finish. She imagined Alisha slipping a letter into their mailbox under Marissa's nose. How brazen.

Marissa froze at the letter's end. Alisha had signed her full name and included her address. *Alisha Morgan*. Medford, Massachusetts. Marissa knew Medford but didn't recognize the street. Odd the woman included her surname and address. Perhaps she'd moved recently and wished Tristan to know.

Another two dozen notes covered the carpet. Marissa wasn't sure if she should burn them or throw the notes in Tristan's face.

Neither.

More than ever she wanted to know who Alisha Morgan was. She wanted to catch them in the act.

Obviously, Tristan knew she'd found the letters and tried to cover his tracks by hiding them elsewhere and filling the box in the attic with Marissa's own notes. He was playing on her fragility and confusion. If Marissa encountered him, Tristan would switch the notes again and claim she was losing her grip on reality.

Bastard.

Alisha spoke of Tristan as if she knew him intimately, knew his secrets and everything about his past.

In the stifling silence, she heard the clock ticking from the upstairs hallway. Leaves crawled toward the window and scratched at the glass.

The pungent bluefish hung in the air, their dinner certainly cold now. She couldn't stomach the thought of food, and he could starve for all she cared.

She resolved to open one more envelope before

concealing them under the sofa. Let Tristan think he'd fooled her, that she wasn't onto him and Alisha Morgan.

Tearing open the letter, she noticed this one was printed whereas the others had been written in cursive. The handwriting was still terrible.

It wasn't until she reached the bottom that Marissa realized this note was from a different lover.

Son-of-a-bitch!

Krista Steiner, Binghamton, New York.

The remaining envelopes became confetti as Marissa tore through them with desperation and growing dread. Two more women.

The basement lurched toward her and spun on an imaginary axis.

The fight had gone out of her. She leaned back against the couch, sucking broken-glass breaths into her lungs, listening to the empty house. She was aware of two children laughing from a few yards away and someone dragging recycling bins to the curb.

Then she fell unconscious.

Marissa remembers when she dreams. The breath is harsh in her lungs. When she is at the gym for Krav Maga she knows only one speed.

The man who circles in on her is young and strong. His face holds a vague hint of contempt; he refuses to accept a woman can put him down.

Class rules state only soft contact is allowed during sparring, yet he takes liberties. An attempt at a leg sweep clips her shin hard, and he doesn't pull back on the jab which whistles past her head.

His scowl grows to one of derision. She can hear two men, friends of his, snicker as they watch him circle in and close on "the tough girl," cutting off the mat.

A roundhouse kick screams over her head. If he connects, he'll knock her unconscious. The instructor is somewhere across the mat and unaware of his brutality.

She backs herself into another sparring couple. A jab flicks out and catches her ear. Stinging pain and more laughter. Nowhere to go now.

As she counter-punches to back him off and give herself room, he flicks aside her extended arm and grins jagged, yellow teeth back at her.

The unwanted memory of her near-rape whispers from the back of her mind. Freshman year at Brown. An unlit path between the dormitories after midnight. A dark shape lunging out of the bushes and catching hold of her jacket. The fabric tears, the only thing that saves her from being pulled into the shadows. Her scream brings forth shouts of alarm as window lights flicker on and other students run to help. The rapist is gone. Dumb luck and a cheap coat are the only reasons she is safe.

A gloved hand clips her earlobe and shocks her back to the fight. A hook kick backs the man off of her. He's surprised by her flexibility. Yet he doubts her strength, questions her willingness to fight back once he hits her hard.

He's confident.

He's a dead man.

The young man lunges forward and grabs her shoulder. She brings her elbow down hard onto the bend in his arm. As he falters, her free arm snakes under his.

He gasps as she twists his arm and forces his face into the mat.

Before she can lock the arm, he rolls free and bounces back to his feet.

A sane man would respect her by now. He doesn't. The young man is too angry to think.

His defenses are down. He wants only to hurt and humiliate.

He throws a hook punch intended to take her head off. She blocks it with one arm, knocks him backward with a front kick to the chest.

Furious, he wheels back for another punch as though this is a street fight and not a supervised martial arts class.

She sees his eyes grow wide, seeing too late what is about to happen.

Marissa's roundhouse kick strikes flush against his temple. His legs go out from under him, and he collapses to his knees.

Realizing their match has gotten out of hand, the more experienced class members rush to separate the young man from Marissa. He feigns at going after her, but she can tell he's letting the others hold him back. She'll kill him if he charges.

Marissa's eyes popped open.

Twilight blues dripped against the basement window. Her head was swimming distractedly as if floating in a distant ocean.

Seeing the notes ripped and scattered across the carpet brought her back to reality. She kept quiet and listened.

No, Tristan hadn't returned.

Marissa steadied herself against the sofa and caught her breath. Wanting to keep up the appearance of normalcy, she moved the wet clothes into the dryer and set them spinning.

Nothing to see here, Tristan. Just your loving wife making sure your clothes are clean and the house spotless.

The stairway to the kitchen appeared to stretch for miles. In the kitchen, she grabbed the keys and shoved them into her pocket. She left a note on the table.

Dinner is in the fridge. Went to visit an old friend.
Be back tomorrow.
Marissa

If there was a God, Tristan would choke on his dinner.

In the entryway, she leaned against the frame, feeling the October evening bite at her face. The cold invigorated Marissa and got her moving.

One of her neighbors, Keiran Blakely, was two driveways away, rushing to polish his Range Rover before it got too dark. He was always at their house, asking Tristan if he could borrow a tool or if Tristan might want to meet him at The Golden Caribou for a drink. An insolent little puppy.

Keiran waved. As she climbed into her car she could see him cross the lawn with concern on his face. The whole neighborhood knew about the accident. Tristan wouldn't approve of Marissa driving on her own, and surely Keiran knew this.

Marissa backed out fast. The underside scraped blacktop at the bottom of the driveway. Keiran had his arms raised in question as she threw the car into drive and squealed away.

She put Alisha Morgan's address into the GPS and headed for Route 6.

CHAPTER TEN

Alisha Morgan

The moon was out and the stars bright when Marissa left the Cape. By the time she reached Braintree and began to skirt greater Boston's heavy traffic, the clouds thickened and turned the sky black above an endless sea of shining lights.

She stopped for gas in Medford and bought herself a large coffee. Then she climbed a steep and narrow grade into Morgan's neighborhood, where vehicles lined both sides of the street, leaving barely enough room for her to drive.

A group of teenagers wearing hooded sweatshirts watched her climb the hill. Two of them broke from the pack as she passed and strode arrogantly toward her car. Marissa hit the gas and got around them. She could see them in her rear view mirror, standing in the middle of the road watching her.

A few hairpin turns brought Marissa to Collier Avenue. According to her note, Alisha Morgan's address was 17 Collier. The street lights didn't do much to break the darkness spilling down from the trees. She drove the entire length of the street and came to a dead end before determining on which side of the street the odd-numbered residences sat. On the return trip, she finally saw the house. It was a big paint-chipped duplex with a porch light on. A staircase climbed into darkness behind the door, ostensibly leading to separate apartments.

"Shit," she said, leaning her head out the car window.

Marissa didn't know which apartment was Alisha's or what the woman looked like.

Her breath formed little clouds in the cold night air. It was easily ten degrees colder in Medford than it had been on the Cape.

She started to get out of the car and thought better of it when another group of teenagers came walking down the sidewalk. The street was too dark to make them out.

Closer now. Heading straight for her.

She gripped the steering wheel. Knuckles white, heart hammering to a dangerously fast beat.

She was ready to turn the key in the ignition just as they broke out of the gloom. They crossed through a mottled pool of light below a street lamp.

False alarm.

The four teenagers turned out to be two couples. The boy and girl in front draped their arms over each other's shoulders. The two in back walked a few paces behind, whispering to one another and giggling.

Marissa slunk down in her seat so they wouldn't see her. From this position, she stared up into a tangle of tree branches and power lines.

They were close now. Voices and the scrape of shoe soles against pavement traveled from just outside the car.

The sounds trailed away.

Motors gunned from a few blocks in the distance. Shifting winds pulled the echo of the occasional car horn from the city center.

Hiding beneath the steering wheel stirred her paranoia. The dashboard clock read midnight.

A dark thought gripped her. What if she saw Tristan

staring at her through the window?

Impossible? Not if he'd come to Medford to visit Alisha Morgan and found his wife's car outside the apartment.

Yet the street was quiet and empty.

Her nervous laughter was loud inside the car.

Marissa sipped at the gas station coffee, bitter but warm. The duplex lights were on upstairs and downstairs. The second-floor window was too tall to see into unless someone looked down at her. She couldn't see anything through the translucent curtain covering the downstairs window. Now and again a shadow passed over the glass. She could see a television glowing inside.

Sitting low in her seat so as not to attract attention, she drank her coffee and watched.

A little after one in the morning, the front door opened. She hid beneath the wheel as a middle-aged man in a hat and winter jacket hurried down the stairs and into a pickup truck. The motor growled. The red eyes of his brake lights flared at her. The truck pulled away and grew smaller as it disappeared down Collier Avenue.

Marissa wondered if the man knew Alisha. Maybe he was another one of her lovers or her husband.

The cold crept into the car. She could see her breath again. The windows started to fog up.

No amount of patient waiting could force Alisha Morgan to appear. For all Marissa knew, Morgan was curled under the covers and sound asleep.

Marissa yawned. She hadn't stayed up late in months.

A few minutes later her eyes began to droop. Finding Alisha could wait until tomorrow.

She found a Hampton Inn a few miles outside of Medford. Though she expected a slew of messages from Tristan demanding to know where she was and who she was visiting, no messages waited on her phone.

After locking the door and throwing the bolt, she peered out through the peephole. The hallway was empty. Two potted plants framed the elevator doors. The scent of carpet cleaner was cloying.

The room was clean and the bed soft. She collapsed onto the bed without removing her clothes and stared at the ceiling's rough contours, following their lines the way a child imagines pathways in the sky. She cleared her throat and coughed. She'd overdone it tonight, pushing her weakened body beyond its limits.

She lay awake, wondering what to do about Tristan. He was anathema to her, a poison she needed to expel.

Two decades of her life wasted.

Yet she had to know why. Knowing why began with learning more about Alisha Morgan.

CHAPTER ELEVEN

Jimmy Rodgers

The light through the window was too fucking bright.

Jimmy Rodgers reached across his nightstand and ripped down on the shade. The entire apparatus crashed down and spilled the alarm clock onto the floor.

"Shit."

Sitting on the edge of the bed, he rubbed at his temples. The clock read seven. Too late to eat if he planned on making it to the highway on time. His crew was repaving one of the westbound lanes on I-90 outside of Worcester today, and the foreman would kick his ass to the curb if he was late again.

From the drawer, he pulled a half-full bottle of whiskey. He removed the cap and took a whiff, the liquor strong enough to bring tears to his eyes.

The prospect of a hangover while tractor trailers thundered past at 70 mph made his head hurt worse.

He needed something to take the edge off, but the last thing he needed was to show up at the repaving site baked and smelling of reefer.

He'd had the dream again last night. Fire spreading up the barn walls. The door locked from the outside. An explosion along the roof, then the boards caving in as the inferno's roar drowned out their screaming.

It didn't make sense that he should see the barn burning in his dreams, as he hadn't seen the fire, only arrived when the last charred embers were put out by the fire crew.

No survivors.

Jess.

He started to cry and whipped the whiskey bottle across the room. Glass shattered. Another hole in the plaster he'd need to fix.

Twenty years. Twenty goddamn years and the dream wouldn't leave him the hell alone.

To make matters worse, someone had called him in the middle of the night. No voice on the other line, same as it had been twice last week. Kids, probably.

Jimmy staggered into the shower and ran the spray long enough to wash away the stink of last night's drinking. On his way out the door, he snatched a granola bar, one of those rice, nut, and oat concoctions that was supposedly good for you but tasted like cardboard sprinkled with bee pollen. His Ford pickup, pocked by rust blotches, its back bumper sagging like a broken jaw, was one of the only vehicles on the road. Westland, Massachusetts had always been a dingy offshoot from the healthy roots of Worcester, rarely able to attract industry or keep it for long. The vacant shells of departed plants and factories sagged to either side of the road. Here was where the old Smith Corona typewriter plant once stood, and a few blocks ahead loomed the deserted IBM facility where his father had worked. Gone twenty years and still empty.

Battling the sun and a five-alarm migraine, he checked the mirrors and saw a car a few blocks behind him. No big deal, except he swore the same car had followed him out of the trailer park. The glare prevented him from making out the driver or the vehicle, but it appeared to be a sports car, slung low and effortlessly hugging corners. The brights flashed twice.

He turned at Main Street and passed The Blue Dragon tavern. *Hair of the dog that bit me*, he thought, eyeing the beer bottle rolling around on the floor.

The road was empty behind him now, not unusual for early morning in Westland. Running late, he pressed the gas pedal and bent the city speed limit between downtown and the interstate.

As he crept the car past the toll booths and accelerated onto I-90, he glanced up and saw the sports car behind him again. No question it was the same car from Westland. He watched it weaving around traffic as though the driver meant to keep Jimmy in his sights, but always staying far enough back that he couldn't get a good look. The car flashed its high beams. Jimmy's stomach dropped. An unwelcome memory returned to him—his old buddy, Tristan, showing up in the dead of night and blaring the high beams into Jimmy's bedroom window, the boy incessantly flashing the headlights at a car that cut him off, following the driver as Jimmy begged him not to do anything crazy.

But Jimmy hadn't seen Tristan since the barn fire stole Jess away from him, along with four of their friends.

No, it couldn't be Tristan. The boy had moved on to an Ivy League school and never returned to Westland except to visit his bastard father on holidays. Good riddance. Jimmy remembered Tristan skipping the funeral and community memorial services, and that never sat right with Jimmy.

Last Jimmy heard, Tristan was into stocks or something and living down the Cape.

Jimmy's work site was only five miles up the road. He pushed the truck to 75 mph and watched the sports car lurch ahead to keep pace. He cut in front of a slow train of vehicles, then zigzagged into the speeding lane. A horn accosted him; a man in a BMW shot his middle finger out the window. Another hair-raising cut through congestion brought forth more horns and flashing headlights.

He was nearly hyperventilating as he accelerated out of the traffic glut at 85 mph.

The sports car was gone again.

Spotting a state trooper in the median a half-mile up the road, he tapped the brakes. He knew the stench of alcohol was still on his breath and doubted he'd pass the Breathalyzer test six hours after his bender. If not for the prospect of another DUI, he wouldn't have minded the trooper pulling him over. Especially with someone following him.

As he pulled into the work site, the black sports car slowed along the concrete barriers before disappearing down the interstate.

CHAPTER TWELVE

Tristan

Clambering out of the car, Tristan shook with tension. The razor sharp acuity of his senses stood in stark contrast to his thoughts, which lay submerged below a black morass of unplaced anger and confusion.

He'd followed someone he once knew. Jimmy… yes, Jimmy was his name. Attempts to clear his racing mind failed. There had been a betrayal once. A long time ago. So long ago that it felt like another lifetime.

Something rattled in his coat pocket. Removing the pill bottle, he looked at it curiously the way a spelunker would an odd gem collected from the bottom of a deep, dark cavern. He recognized his name on the bottle, the medication, recalled its purported benefits. In actuality, the medicine was meant to blind him to reality.

The corner of his mind, which had warned him he wasn't sticking to his medicine, seemed to drift farther and farther away until he couldn't hear its warnings. The medicine was meant for the weak and delusional, neither of which described Tristan. He'd seen the Phoenix. Yes, he had.

Tristan's grandmother, the last person who'd shielded the young boy from his abusive father, had died when he was six. The night of her death, he'd looked out the back window and watched a bonfire burning from the neighboring yard. Something rose out of the flames. At first, he'd thought it shadow or smoke. Then the wings became apparent. A bird larger than any he'd seen before. The Phoenix. His grandmother, who'd sworn to Tristan she'd always look after him, had been reborn.

The medicine made him believe he hadn't seen the Phoenix, which was a bad thing. It robbed him of a life-defining experience. Perhaps it was jealousy on his doctor's part. The man would never witness what Tristan saw because he wasn't worthy.

Tristan opened the passenger door, tossed the bottle into the glove compartment, and slammed the door shut.

He was outside a pastry shop, he realized, somewhere between Worcester and the Cape, though he couldn't recall pulling off the interstate. Acoustic guitar, piped out from the shop via external speaker, mingled with the din of highway traffic behind a row of trees. Six tables circled the outside of the pastry shop, where Tristan sat upon a metal chair and gazed up into a fitful sky that couldn't decide if it wanted to shine or storm.

One thing of which he was certain—Marissa had begun to stray from him just as Jess had, and this only convinced him more that they were one in the same. Jess reborn. Exactly as he'd envisioned the night of the fire.

Marissa needed guidance. No, correction.

The scrape of chair legs over concrete spun his head around. An obese woman trailed by a young, greasy-haired girl of slight build shuffled between the tables toward the shop door. The woman's hip struck the table and drove it into Tristan's belly. She huffed as though the obstacle was to blame and shambled into the shop without issuing an apology.

Tristan squeezed his hands into fists until his knuckles cracked. Gluttony. One of the seven deadly sins. Removing the woman from her pitiful existence would do the world a favor, make it a better place for enlightened ones such as him. What did she know of rebirth through fire, of his power over life and death? If she knew she would quake in his presence and offer the deference he deserved.

He was so lost in his thoughts that he jolted when the door flew open. The woman returned carrying a grease-stained, white paper bag. He barely noticed the intoxicating scents of cinnamon, sugar, and baked bread, so intent was he on observing the glutton.

The girl dolefully followed her mother. Though she was thin and frail, Tristan knew she'd one day be fat like her mother. The girl had a fat droop to her eyes, a fat, lazy gait that was almost elephantine in her plodding, disinterested manner, and a softness to her bare thighs, devoid of muscle, which would one day fill with cellulite like water gushing into a balloon.

The glutton plopped down into the chair and began ripping at the bag with an animal's desperation. It was like watching a lioness tear apart a fleshy carcass.

The woman shoved a turnover into her mouth. Bit down. Dark, cherry juices like blood sluiced down the sugar-flecked dough and sullied her sausage fingers. She moaned, a sound of ecstasy. This was the closest she would ever come to sex again, Tristan thought.

In silence he observed the girl shyly awaiting her mother's frenzy to abate. He sensed the girl required permission to nibble on the scraps, lest her hand be chewed off at the wrist. She was attractive in a submissive, pathetic way, a girl he would have pursued in his youth for no other reason than to dominate her.

The turnover already consumed, the glutton groped the interior of the bag and came out with a raspberry tart. This, too, she crammed into her mouth. Two enormous bites nearly finished the tart. She put it down with derision—the treat didn't adequately fill the glutton—and slurped the filling off each finger. Though repulsed, Tristan found himself strangely drawn to the display, perhaps due to the girl's submissive capitulation. He couldn't take his eyes off of her. She wouldn't eat until the glutton allowed her to.

"Hmph," the glutton groaned. Crumbs spit from her mouth.

Taking this as a signal she could now eat, the girl jammed her hand into the bag and fished out a blueberry-stained tart before her mother could change her mind and snatch it away.

There was something familiar about the girl's sheepish mannerisms. Tristan recalled a girl from high school. Ina. Shy and destitute, her family too poor to properly clothe her. Ina wore the same unlaundered jeans and threadbare sweatshirt to school every day whether in the suffocating heat of June or the gelid freeze of February.

Under the dusty clothing and greasy hair was a pretty face, but that wasn't what had attracted Tristan to Ina. Rather it was the way she walked the school hallways, cowering at sniffs and taunts, with her eyes always fixed to the floor and unwilling to meet her classmates' eyes. This was a girl Tristan could use for his own purposes. Control. Dominate.

And she would never tell because he was stronger-willed than she. Who would believe Ina if he pitted his word against hers? He, the prodigy student with the athlete's physique and teen idol's face, or the dusty, foul-scented girl?

Yet he saw too much risk. He needed leverage, something he could hold over her head.

Tristan was a smart boy, and a smart boy intelligently assessed a dangerous situation. He didn't walk in blindly. Ina needed money. Money to feed her emaciated body, money to purchase new clothes, apparel which wasn't falling apart at the seams. Clothes which didn't give off the stench of juice eating away at the bottom of a fast food restaurant's garbage can.

Tristan grinned inside when Ina was charitably selected to serve on the spring fund raising committee for the local food bank. Some principal or teacher had taken pity on her. Of the ten-student committee, mainly comprised of the popular and entitled, Ina was the only student deemed desperate enough to pilfer the money.

Patiently concealing himself inside his locker, the door open just a crack so the lock wouldn't engage, Tristan waited until the school cleared out after six o'clock. Except for a lone janitor mopping the corridor around the corner, no one was present to see Tristan slip into Mrs. Tinelli's room where the funds lay hidden in an envelope inside the desk—she routinely locked her desk, but Tristan had stolen the key off the ring before lunch hour, raced downtown to duplicate the lock at Morgan's Hardware, and replaced the key before Tinelli noticed—and remove the contents of the envelope. He was tempted to whistle. Over three hundred dollars was concealed in the envelope. The next day would bring frenetic accusation and an administration-led witch hunt, and Tristan would be the first to come forward with information implicating Ina if she didn't obey his every wish.

So it was during his sophomore year that Tristan followed Ina out of school on a warm May afternoon. He'd watched her for weeks, knew the route she took home, the field she cut across behind the abandoned corset factory.

She'd been easy to persuade when he came from the opposite direction and met her in front of the building. Tristan put it succinctly so even a dullard like Ina would understand. He would plant the key in her locker and tell the principal he'd watched Ina sneak into Tinelli's room after school. But if she kept her mouth shut, if she went willingly to the abandoned warehouse with him, Tristan, the beloved student, would keep Ina's name out of the investigation. In fact, he promised her, he'd point the finger at Wendell Reyser. Pretentious little prick.

Tristan even claimed he would let her keep the money, a vow he had no intention of keeping.

The first day in the warehouse carried strange and powerful magic. Sharp strands of sunlight cut through breaks in the walls and open windows. Sparkling dust particles stirred with their presence. The smells were a combination of dry, baking wood planks and the sweet meadow scents hustled inside by the spring breeze. And something dark and decaying under the floorboards.

He tied her ankles together and roped them against the leg of a chair he'd found. She sobbed when he tied her wrists behind her back. He liked it when she cried, relishing in the frightened-fawn look of Ina's eyes as her master controlled her. The way her feet pathetically kicked and wiggled with no hope of defeating the bindings. She writhed her hands—that was hopeless, too—and Tristan was convinced she struggled for his delight. She knew it got him off.

Perform for me, you little…

Sometimes he gagged her mouth, reveled in the terrified rictus the cloth shaped. Most of the time he left her mouth uncovered so she could plead and whine.

For two weeks she obediently followed him into the warehouse, where he touched and groped, fingered her nipples, slipped his hands inside her shorts. While these violations excited him, it was his domination of the girl which generated the most arousal. When he felt so hard he might burst, he retreated to the shadowed corner and slid his hand into his pants. Afterward he always felt dirty. A bit disgusted with himself. Not for what he'd done, but whom he'd done it to. Yet the memory of Ina and the warehouse would stick with him for decades, invading his dreams, stoking the flames of his innermost fantasies. Oh, to have violated Jess in this fashion.

Or Marissa. There was still time for that.

Yes, the girl before him was so much like Ina. The things he could do to her if he—

"Do you mind?" The glutton glared at him. "The rudeness of some people…you can't go out for a bite to eat without some sicko leering at you. You're lucky I don't call my husband. Keep staring and I'll see that he thrashes you."

The contemptuous flare of her words temporarily set Tristan on his heels. Then he recovered. Grinned at her the way a wolf does a legless rabbit.

"You want me to give you a show?"

She slipped one enormous leg out from under the table, pulled up on her skirts, revealing a blue-veined leg that was more relief map than flesh.

"Like what you see, sicko? There's more where that came from, but it takes a real man to win that prize. Get out of here before I sic my husband on you."

Tristan smiled at the woman, then shifted his focus to the girl, squirming in her seat. So much like Ina.

"Are you deaf and dumb?"

Jelly dribbled off the fat woman's lip. She trembled with rage. He wondered if she might explode, spraying the walls with cellulite, intestines, and confectionery powder. The girl's eyes had gone wide. She sensed in Tristan what her mother was blind to. The power he commanded over life and death. The fire burning inside him.

The girl pressed back against the chair as he rose to his feet. He took his time, locking eyes with the fat woman until she flinched. Tristan was more than a man. He was a god capable of dealing death and restoring life.

He'd seen the Phoenix, unlocked the secrets of reincarnation.

Now the glutton was pressed back along the rail dividing the parking lot from the tables. Her eyes were twin moons of fear. How easy it would be to take her life: one swift swipe of the blade in his jacket pocket, then grab the girl and drag her into the car. Find an abandoned building and have his way with her.

"A good day to you, madame. Remember to feed your kin first, lest they wither away to nothing."

He gracefully bowed without losing eye contact. As the woman stared in slack-jawed horror, he walked past their table.

Back to the car.

Time to correct Marissa.

CHAPTER THIRTEEN

Ghosts

It was nearly eight when Marissa's eyes popped open. Her body argued for more sleep as she dragged herself into the shower. The continental breakfast was stocked full of comfort foods she normally avoided: french toast, sausage, sugary cereals, home fries. After eating her second helping of berries and fruit, one of the few healthy choices available, she gave in to her screaming belly and tore into three slices of french toast and a bowl of oatmeal. Then she found herself back in the buffet line for seconds and thirds.

The heavy food cramped her stomach. She couldn't recall the last time she'd eaten so much. Sitting near the back of the room, she clutched her gut and doubled over. An elderly couple noticed, and the man asked if she needed help. The cramping subsided, and she waved that she was fine.

Marissa checked out and climbed into the car with a big cup of coffee. She kicked the vehicle into drive and felt the car lurch forward. Slamming the brakes before she drove into a parked car, she came to a stop. Her strength was coming back. For the last several months, every mundane task had been a struggle.

She made it back to the duplex after nine. The sun was bright and hot, requiring her to roll down the windows. The smell of dried leaves pervaded the wind, the blue sky dotted with cumulus clouds. Halloween decorations adorned houses up and down the street, which looked far less nefarious in the light of day. Mountains of raked leaves blocked most of her parking options, but she found a good spot a few doors down from Morgan's house that gave her full view of the front door.

Cars came and went without anyone giving her a second glance. A woman trailed by a small child on a Big Wheel walked past. Morgan's residence was quiet. Maybe Tristan's lover was at work.

Or screwing Tristan in her bed.

Regardless, Morgan needed to come home eventually. Marissa had all day and night to wait.

After ten, Marissa stepped from the car and stretched her legs. Tristan still hadn't called or messaged her. Obviously, he didn't care where she was or if she lay alone and dying on the side of the road. He had to know she'd discovered the notes. With any luck, the son-of-a-bitch would pack his bags and leave before she returned.

No, he wouldn't. The house was his, paid for with his money and maintained by Marissa to his exact specifications. All aspects of her life revolved around Tristan. He planned vacations where his clients resided, often leaving her alone for several hours so he could fit an important investor into his daily plans. Two summers ago, she'd spent the day sunning herself on a St. Augustine beach while he was supposedly meeting with a client, then ate dinner by herself at a food shack overlooking the ocean, sipping wine alone as other couples held each other close and watched the tide slide out into the Atlantic.

The possibility that Tristan had been in bed all day with a *client* made her wonder how she hadn't seen signs of his infidelity.

She weaved between leaf piles and strode toward the house. A black metal mailbox was affixed beside the door. A quick look would tell her which apartment Morgan occupied. If the woman was home Marissa had a bevy of questions for her.

She looked behind her to make sure no one was watching, then she cut hard up the concrete pathway and climbed the steps.

As quiet as she tried to be, the old steps squeaked and gave her away.

After looking behind her one more time, she bent over in front of the mailbox and read the names.

No Alisha Morgan.

She bit her tongue in anger. Not ready to give up, she pulled out her phone and photographed the mailbox. One of the names was scratched out. It was hard to make out, but it definitely wasn't Alisha Morgan. It appeared to read Marie Emerson. Enlarging the photograph on the computer would tell her for sure.

"Hey!"

She jumped.

"What do you think you're doing?"

A figure rounded the house and cut across the lawn. He wore a leather jacket that had seen better days. His face was unshaven, his jeans muddied to the cuffs and torn at the knees.

She recognized him as the man who'd driven off in the truck last night. He looked angry.

Marissa stammered.

"You better answer before I call the police. You're trespassing."

He gripped a phone as he climbed the steps.

"Well?"

"I'm looking for an old friend," she said.

"Bullshit. It looks like you're canvassing the house. I recognize you, you know? Saw your car out here last night and watched you pull up a half-hour ago. Maybe I should phone the cops right now and let you explain to them why you've been watching my house. Not that I believe you, but who exactly are you looking for?"

"A woman named Alisha Morgan. We went to high school together."

"Now I know you're bullshitting me." He grinned through brown-stained teeth. The stench of his breath made her flinch. "There's no one here named Alisha Morgan. You wanna try another name, or should I start dialing?"

"It's been a long time." Marissa felt her skin prickle with heat as he pressed closer. Sweat ran down her back. "She probably married. Her last name might be different."

"As far as I'm concerned, you don't have the right to know the names of my tenants, present or past, but there isn't anyone here named Alisha. And before you change your story, I've owned this house for seventeen years, and nobody named Alisha ever rented from me."

He stepped toward her. She inched back and immediately felt ashamed for allowing the man to intimidate her.

"But this was the address I was given—"

"Even if someone gave you bad information, it doesn't explain why you were watching the house in the middle of the night. You may think I'm an asshole, lady, but I'm protecting my property the way anyone else would do. How would you react if you saw someone parked outside your residence at two in the morning and watching your windows? I bet you'd call the police. Lucky for you I'm feeling charitable this morning. Here's the deal. Get in your car and drive back to your precious mansion and I'll forget I ever saw you. Don't come back, or the next time I won't be so forgiving."

An older couple stopped to watch from across the street. The man was pleased with himself for the way he browbeat her.

Humiliated, Marissa lowered her head and started

down the steps. A final desperate thought gripped her at the bottom, and she pulled out her phone.

"I thought I told you to get the hell out of here."

"Just give me one second. Please."

Quickly scrolling through old photographs, she found a vacation picture of her and Tristan from a few years ago.

"You're still on my property," the man said.

"Just look at this picture," she said, climbing up the steps.

"I'm not interested in looking at your pictures."

"Please, it will only take a second."

He sighed.

"Make it quick."

"The man in the photograph."

"What about him?"

"I think he's visited your house over the last several years."

"Never seen him before."

He started to walk away. She grabbed his arm and pulled him around. He was furious now, a split second from striking her if her intuition was correct.

"Look closer," Marissa said. "If you've owned this house for as long as you say you have, you've seen him."

He scowled and ripped the phone from her hand. For a moment, she believed he might toss her phone into the street or crush it under boot. Instead, he brought it closer to his face and studied it. His eyes changed, widening for a moment. Unless Marissa was imagining things, she thought she recognized fear. Then the man's face was hard and disinterested again.

"He's never been here. Now get off my—"

She pulled the phone out of his grip. He looked stunned by her quickness.

"You've seen him. Tell me when he was here and

who he was with. It was Alisha Morgan, wasn't it?"

"For the last goddamn time, no Alisha Morgan lives here. But if she ever shows up, I'll be sure to send the bitch your way."

He turned and slammed the door behind him before she could protest. Glass rattled in the pane. The elderly man and woman across the road started to walk away, flashing concerned glances over their shoulders.

The man recognized Tristan. There was no doubting it. He must have been lying about Alisha Morgan.

Not to be deterred, Marissa climbed back into her car and drove down the block. When she was out of view of the duplex, she pulled over and brought out her phone. A quick Internet search was all it took to locate the county records office.

She spent the rest of the morning pouring through records and searching for anyone named Alisha Morgan. Certain the duplex owner had lied, all Marissa discovered was Alisha Morgan was a ghost. Not only couldn't she prove Morgan had ever lived in the duplex, Tristan's lover didn't seem to exist at all.

Clouds smothered out the sun by early afternoon as Marissa began her drive back to the Cape. Raindrops pattered against the roof when she merged onto the highway.

Marissa kicked the accelerator and raced southward, desperate to record his lovers' names and addresses before Tristan figured out what she was up to.

She prayed he wouldn't be home waiting for her.

She knew better.

CHAPTER FOURTEEN

I Don't Believe You

Storm clouds over Medford trailed her back to the Cape. Rain slapped against the car like a cold ocean spray.

On a normal day, Tristan would be home by now, yet his jet-black Camaro wasn't in the driveway when Marissa pulled into her neighborhood at four o'clock.

Her legs trembled as she half-ran, half-stumbled from the car to the front door. The mailbox was jammed with magazines and bills. Wrestling the key into the lock, Marissa shot a look across the lawn. No sign of Keiran Blakely watching for her. Life would be so much calmer, she thought, if Michael lived next door instead of Keiran.

She rushed inside and shut the door as rain lashed at the windows.

Only two hours remained until sunset. Already the living room appeared dark and threatening.

Although his car was nowhere to be seen, Marissa wasn't taking any chances. She called out to Tristan. The clock ticked from the dining room.

She spared a glance into the kitchen and saw the floor glistening next to the sink. The leak from the filter was getting worse.

Rushing down the basement stairway, she almost tripped and tumbled forward. That would be ironic, she thought, to break her neck trying to escape.

She shoved aside the couch. Thunder shook the walls and rolled toward the sea.

The notes were torn and splayed out as she'd left them. Even with the light switch thrown, Marissa could barely see what she was doing as she knelt down and shoveled the notes into a shopping bag. Every time the wind gusted, it sounded as if someone opened the front door.

She struggled up the stairs, grabbed hold of the threshold, and stood panting in the kitchen.

Remembering the cold bluefish, she opened the refrigerator and stared. The leftovers were gone.

She wheeled around and saw the plate in the sink.

Her note was missing from the kitchen table.

Tristan had come home last night.

Marissa grabbed an apple off the counter and stuffed it into the bag. Lightning lit the windows as she turned to leave.

She saw him in the doorway and screamed.

It was Tristan, but it didn't look like him at all. Pale, disheveled, danger in his eyes.

"Where have you been?"

Marissa's throat went dry.

He stalked into the kitchen, a dark silhouette in the deepening gloom. She'd never thought him dangerous before. Not until now.

Another burst of lightning flashed into the kitchen.

"Answer me, Marissa. I want to know where you were last night."

His shoes dragged over the linoleum. Even in the dark, she could see how tired he looked. His face was unshaven. Black spiraled around his eyes.

"I told you in my note," she said, her voice barely more than a whisper. She took an involuntary step backward as he loomed closer. "I went to see a friend—"

"Who?"

She paused and spit out the first name that popped into her head.

"Kari."

"Kari. As in Kari Sherman? From Brown?"

"My old roommate."

She saw in his eyes that he didn't believe her.

"You haven't spoken with her in twenty-five years, I'd say. What made you reconnect after so many years?"

"We ran into each other on Facebook. It turns out she lives nearby."

"How wonderful."

His grin showed plenty of teeth.

All the better to eat you with, my dear.

"All this time you lived so close," he said. "It's almost tragic you didn't know."

"Yes…yes it is."

He pressed the light switch. She suddenly felt exposed in the brightness. Her eyes squinted, temples pounded.

"Kari was always such a pretty woman. I can't imagine her unmarried."

"Divorced."

"Such a shame."

"Yes."

"Children?"

"Excuse me?"

"Does Kari have children? Divorce is such an ugly thing, especially for the kids."

"No…I don't believe so."

"But you'd know, wouldn't you? You would have seen them running about the house, no?"

"I don't know, Tristan."

His grin widened. He had her now.

She backed into the counter. Trapped.

The bag hung off her hand. If he looked down he'd recognize the notes. She moved it behind her.

"So where is the mysterious Kari Sherman keeping herself these days?"

"Near Boston."

"In Boston or near Boston?"

Medford, you son-of-a-bitch. She's probably neighbors with Alisha Morgan.

"Quincy."

"Ah, quaint little old Quincy. I have clients in Quincy. I wonder if she knows them. Affluent neighborhood?"

"I don't…"

"Does Kari Sherman live in an affluent neighborhood, Jess?"

"Did you just call me Jess?"

He shook the cobwebs from his head.

"No, no I didn't.

"You did. Who the hell is Jess?"

"You never let me finish. I said *just*."

"You didn't."

She tried to turn away and he grabbed her shoulder, dug his fingers into her muscles.

"Ow, you're hurting me!"

"Don't fight me."

"Let go."

He stood tall over her. His eyes were sunken and sick-looking. Something was wrong with his face. It kept twitching below the eye. Fury was the only thing which kept her fear in check.

"I don't think you visited Kari Sherman at all."

"What are you saying, Tristan? That I'm lying?"

She wanted to blurt out all she knew of his affairs. She didn't. She was too terrified to move.

"We could settle this quite easily, you and I." He

reached into Marissa's pocket and fished out her phone. "Call her. I'd love to say hello after so many years. Kari Sherman from Brown. Had I not found you I might have pursued her myself."

"I don't have her number."

"You drove all the way to Quincy in a sickened state and didn't even have her phone number? What if you got lost or fell ill?"

"We messaged each other. Like I said, on…"

"On Facebook. Yes, I remember."

He started to open her messages. She snatched the phone back from him.

"That's enough. You can't bully me into showing you my messages. Do I badger you for details when you're away for days meeting with strangers?"

Anger burned momentarily in his eyes and was gone.

"I'm not bullying you," he said. "I was awake all night, worried sick over whether you were safe."

"Why didn't you call me if you were so concerned?"

"You know you shouldn't be driving in your condition," he said, continuing as if she hadn't spoken. "What if you fainted and got into another accident? What if it happened on the highway?"

He touched her face. She shivered.

"I couldn't live with myself if I lost you."

She turned her face away.

"Marissa…please."

It was damn paradoxical what he was doing to her. Accusing her of…something. Did it matter what? She could have slapped him until he saw stars. Better to bide her time and discover the truth about his affairs.

She leaned woodenly against him and stared off at the window so he couldn't see her face. He stroked her hair.

"I love you," he whispered. "You were always the

only one for me. Always and forever. You know that."

Oh, the things she could have screamed in that moment.

"I…love you, too."

The words tasted acrid.

"You act as though you don't want to touch me."

It took effort to move her hands along his back. She might have caressed a centipede. The bag of love letters dangled from her hand, swaying and brushing the backs of his legs.

How long he held her she didn't know. A few minutes in his arms felt like hours.

"The storm's letting up," he said.

"What?"

"The rain ended."

The kitchen was brighter even though the sun was almost down. Streaks of water blurred her view out the window.

"Please don't run off again without telling me," he said. Gently, he turned her face toward his. "If you need to see a friend, if you just need to get out of the house and get fresh air, tell me. I will take you."

"You don't need to do that, Tristan."

"Don't I? You could have been killed the other day. Have you forgotten the accident already? You were lucky. We both were."

Tristan almost looked himself again. It was difficult for Marissa not to lose herself in his eyes. This was the beautiful man she'd fallen in love with so many years ago.

"The time away did me good, Tristan. I'm starting to feel a lot better. Maybe I needed to get out of the house and see what I've been missing."

He studied her face. His eyes interrogated hers. Almost with desperation, she thought, as if the improvement in her health raised his anxiety.

"You *do* look better. Oh, hon, this is what I've wished and prayed for all these months."

"I'm going to be fine. Thank you for taking care of me."

That was a laugh. All those days she lay in bed, wasting away and slowly dying for all she knew, and Tristan was nowhere to be found.

"This is wonderful. We should celebrate tonight. Just the two of us."

"Yes, that would be nice."

"My goodness, you are beautiful."

He kissed her forehead.

"But if you don't mind me saying so," he said, reaching into the cupboard for a glass. "You're dehydrated again. I can see it in your face, and your skin is dry."

As he reached for the faucet, she grabbed his arm.

"No, don't."

"You have to drink."

"The leak, Tristan. It's gotten worse. I wouldn't use that faucet if I were you."

"Nonsense, hon. One glass of water won't cause a disaster. If it leaks, I'll clean it up and fix it first chance I get over the weekend."

Tristan mentioning the repair made her remember the appointment with Michael. The microwave clock was over Tristan's shoulder. Michael was past due and would arrive at any second.

"I already made the call to get it fixed."

"You called a repairman?"

"Of course. Michael Tompkins."

"Tompkins is a fool. Call him back. I can fix the leak immediately, Marissa."

"I can't call him now. He'll be here at any second."

"Any second? This is ridiculous."

He yanked open the cabinet doors and craned his

head underneath. He was angry again. About what she could only guess.

"Be a dear and grab my toolbox out of the garage. It's on the shelf next to the lawn mower."

Water dripped onto his forehead. He brushed it away.

"I know where it is, Tristan. But Michael can—"

"Get me the fucking toolbox!"

The kitchen still held the echo of his outburst as she backed away. Teeth clenched, she turned and ran down the hall. A moment later, she returned with the toolbox and dropped it at his feet. The racket of tools smashing against the linoleum was louder than his curse, but not nearly as harsh.

He glared at her and snatched a pipe wrench out of the box. Water fell in progressively larger drops as he struggled with odd desperation to loosen the connection. A torrent crashed over his face and shoulders, drawing a curse.

"Get a pan or a bucket. Anything to catch water with."

"If you'd just let the repairman handle this—"

"I told you to cancel the appointment, goddammit. I know what I'm doing."

From the cupboard, Marissa grabbed a wide sauce pot.

"Here," she said, handing him the pot.

Cursing again, he slammed down the wrench and ripped the pot from her. The handle caught her hand and cut her.

"Jesus, Tristan. Slow down. You'll make the mess worse if you break the pipe."

The bottom of the cupboard was a swamp. Water spilled over the edge and ran around her shoes.

A clang came from behind the pipes. He dropped the wrench again.

"Christ!"

Tristan licked away blood where he'd sliced his hand on the fittings. Rather than stopping to bandage the wound, he picked up the wrench and worked with even more desperation.

The longer she watched the more confused she became. It seemed he was more intent on removing the filter than fixing the leak.

She was about to yell at him again when the doorbell rang.

"Marissa!"

She was already running to the door before he could order her to send away Michael, who was standing on the top step when she pulled open the door. She knew he'd worked all day—he looked exhausted, face drawn and arms hanging as if attached to his shoulders by thumbtacks. His toolbox appeared twice as large as he could handle.

"Sorry," he said. "The Sanderson job took longer than expected. It isn't too late, is it?"

"No, I'm just glad you're here."

Marissa stood back to let him by. Tristan swore from the kitchen. She could see Michael's eyes shift down the dark corridor to the kitchen.

"You didn't tell me Tristan was here. I didn't see his car in the driveway."

She disgustedly blew the hair out of her face.

"*Tristan* is trying to fix the leak. Save my home before he floods us out the door."

Laughing nervously, Michael followed her down the hall toward the kitchen.

"How goes it, Tristan?" Michael asked.

When they turned the corner, Tristan was gone. Simply vanished.

The pot was fixed under the filter and catch pipe. Water drizzled from above.

"Tristan? What in the hell?"

She massaged her forehead.

"And you said he was fixing the pipe?" Michael asked.

She looked at him levelly. No, she hadn't hallucinated her husband's repair attempts. The open toolbox and dripping mess were ample evidence.

"Fair enough," he said. He knelt down and pushed Tristan's toolbox aside. Opening his own, he wiggled into the cupboard and shined a flashlight at the pipes and fittings. "He ever do anything like this before?"

"You mean try to fix a plumbing issue?"

"No, like disappear without telling you where he was going."

Yes, she thought. He did that quite often lately.

But not like this. Not when company visited and his presence was expected.

She hadn't even heard him leave.

"I don't mean to keep prying, Marissa. But with you not feeling yourself these last months, Tristan shouldn't leave without telling you first."

"He probably ran out to buy a different tool."

"No reason to." Michael slid out from under the cabinet and nodded at Tristan's cache of tools. "He's got everything he needs."

What Marissa couldn't decide was why Tristan rushed off and left the leak to slowly fill the pan.

"What I don't get," Michael said, "is why he was screwing around with the pipes and fittings to begin with. They aren't leaking."

He tested the fittings and verified they were snug. Then he used a stained cloth to rub down the pipes.

"Should I turn on the water?"

"Yep. Turn the knob slowly and let's see what we're up against."

"If you say so," she said.

Apprehensively, she turned on the faucet and progressively increased the flow.

"Don't be bashful. The pipes aren't leaking."

The faucet blasted out hot water. Steam rose out of the basin and wet her face.

"Okay," Michael said. "Turn her off."

The silence turned heavy without the water running. He struggled halfway out from under the cabinet and groaned.

"Damn back could use a rest." Michael looked embarrassed for swearing.

"What did you find?"

"You feel strong enough to wrench yourself in on the other side of the piping?"

"Sure."

"Okay. Watch your head."

When she was underneath and looking up at the small maze of pipes running to the sink, her hand brushed with his. He smiled, a tight-lipped, sheepish expression that said, *I'm sorry.*

She didn't mind the contact. In fact, she realized it was the first time today a man had treated her with kindness. She felt relieved he was here.

Michael cleared his throat and pointed to the where the fittings around the water filter had been loosened.

"Run your finger along that pipe." She did as he asked. The pipe was warm but dry. "That pipe isn't leaking. Feel dry to you?"

"Yeah."

"Here's the part I don't understand." He swept the beam from the fitting above the filter to below. "Why was he trying to remove the water filter?"

A drip of water fell onto his forehead. He wiped it away with the cuff of his sleeve.

"Where did *that* come from?"

"I thought it was from the pipes like Tristan said."

"Not from the pipes." He turned the light and ran his hand along the water filter. "Weird. I've never seen anything like this before."

"So it's the filter that's leaking."

"Yeah, but how? I checked and rechecked. It's as snug to the pipe as I can get it." He kept rubbing his thumb along the side of the filter. Putting the flashlight aside, he reached into his shirt pocket for his reading glasses. "That's better."

Michael's face was right up against the filter. He kept working his fingers along what appeared to be an imperfection in the housing.

"You think the filter was damaged during shipping?"

"No way. I'd have noticed it during the install and sent it back to the factory. You think I'd stick you with a cracked filter?" He removed the glasses, rubbed his eyes, and put the glasses back on. "If it didn't sound so crazy, I'd swear someone cut into the housing and tried to weld it back together. Was the filter ever removed?"

"I don't see why it would be."

"It looks like it was dropped. But if you crack the housing, you swallow the cost and get a new filter. You don't try to fix the casing. Anyhow, that's where your leak is coming from."

"Just remove it then."

"Definitely. Otherwise, one of these mornings you're gonna wake up and find the Atlantic flowing into the hallway. If you want a new one, I'll place the order right now...now what the hell is this?"

Michael shifted the light toward the housing's center. She couldn't make out what he was looking at. Another imperfection, a shadow, this one inside the housing.

"Is something inside the filter? Can you tell what it is?"

"No. If the filter was dropped there might be a loose part jostling around inside."

"But how could it have been dropped? We never removed it."

"Maybe you banged it while shoving the garbage basket under the sink."

He shut off the water supply and loosened the filter. When it was removed with a short length of pipe connected in its place, he held the filter up near the light and gave it a shake. It sounded as if a hard object was lodged in the filter's belly. The most logical conclusion was a loose part lay broken inside.

"Whatever it is," he said, "it's not your problem anymore."

He collected his tools and closed up the box. The filter was under his arm as she walked him to the door.

"My daughter wants me to take her to Provincetown this weekend." An ironic grin curled his lips. He shook his head. "You can guess how much I *love* that place. So much for my Patriots tickets, but kids are worth it. When I get a chance, I want to get a better look at this filter and see what's going on inside."

"Don't worry about the filter. Order a replacement when you get the chance. Spend time with your daughter. You're a good father, Michael."

"Could have spent time together at the game."

He hesitated at the door.

"Will you be okay alone, Marissa?"

She told him she'd be fine. Yet as he hobbled to his Ford pickup and pulled out of the driveway, she began to miss his company. He beeped and she waved. From a break in the living room curtains, she watched his truck turn into the driveway of his modest two-story at the end of the neighborhood. A couple of kids were throwing a baseball in the twilight.

No sign of her husband.

She called Tristan's phone. It rang several times and went to voice-mail.

What the hell are you up to?

Tristan was right about one thing. She was teetering on the brink of dehydration.

Marissa poured herself a glass of water. It tasted cold and refreshing.

And somehow different.

Before the filter had been removed the water carried a strange aftertaste.

Picking up her bag, she sifted through the notes until she found Krista Steiner's. After entering the woman's Binghamton, New York address into her phone, she went back to the window and made sure no prying eyes watched her house. The sun was on the horizon. The neighborhood appeared gilded and ablaze.

She guessed the trip would take five or six hours. It might be after midnight by the time she found the address. Better to grab a hotel on the way and get an early start in the morning.

She'd paid for the Medford hotel with her credit card. It suddenly occurred to her Tristan could see the transaction and know she'd lied about Kari Sherman and Quincy.

To hell with it. He already knew she was lying.

But she couldn't let Tristan track her movement.

Marissa stopped at the bank and withdrew enough cash to pay for a few days' food and lodging. Then she aimed the car into the setting sun and drove west.

West toward Krista Steiner.

CHAPTER FIFTEEN

Phoenix in the Woods

Bitch!

Tristan slammed his fist against the seat back.

Marissa had brought Michael into Tristan's home, an inexcusable betrayal.

It was happening again, just as it had in Westland. First Jimmy stole Jess, then the college boy took Jamie away from him.

Then the attack, the humiliation. Tristan stripped of his clothes, displayed by the side of the road for the world's amusement.

Tristan made them pay dearly, and he would again.

Michael had the water filter. That was a problem.

Tristan drummed his fingers on the steering wheel. He had to get the filter back. The little prick would get the police involved.

He wasn't careful enough. He hadn't properly sealed the leak, and now the secret was out and the filter was in enemy hands.

Even worse, Marissa's health was improving. She'd stray, just as Jess had. It was already starting again with Michael. Marissa was Jess after all, prone to make similar mistakes, even though she didn't recall her past life or believe in reincarnation. Tristan knew, if given enough time, she would remember her past life. He simply needed to remind her. And that's why he wanted to keep her home. Making her sick was simply a means to an end.

A way out of this mess existed.

The Camaro sliced through the rain. He'd driven without stopping since late-afternoon, and now the distant lights from Burlington blazed from the other side of the dark forest. The car cornered hairpin turns with slick precision. It wasn't safe to drive this fast through the woods. He didn't care.

Tristan needed to see Denise again, had to set things straight before he lost her. Denise was Jamie. He was certain. It had taken Tristan so long to find her. The facial recognition software never found a match for Jamie, despite months of arduous searches. Simple fate, a chance meeting at the bank in Burlington, brought them together. Fate. He couldn't let Denise go. Not now.

Tristan prayed she wasn't the same monster who'd humiliated him in Westland. He didn't want to kill her.

Reborn in fire.

If she forced his hand, if she wronged him as she had in high school, he'd burn her again. Make her see the error of her ways.

A gush of water from the overhead tree branches splattered the windshield. The wipers swept it away.

The pill bottle rolled around inside the glove compartment. He punched open the compartment and slung the bottle against the door. He should have thrown the medication out the window. Only a god possessed the power to kill and restore life. These were powers no doctor could conceive of, so they strove to make him as ignorant as they were.

Lightning exploded off the road. He slammed the brakes.

The car fishtailed along the shoulder. Tristan desperately worked the wheel to keep the car from rolling.

He brought the Camaro to a stop on the rim of a steep ditch choked by rushing water. The car had spun nearly 180-degrees and was pointed at the forest. Smoke floated wraith-like through the trees where lightning struck. The air smelled of ozone and smoldering wood.

Tristan stopped and stared as flames flickered on fallen branches.

He caught his breath.

There amid the blaze was an orange and winged form, rising up through the trees.

He rubbed his eyes and looked again. The Phoenix was gone.

His temples throbbed as water gurgled down the roadside creek.

He righted the Camaro and slammed it into drive. Tires screeched and tossed back water.

He trembled with anger as he drove into Burlington.

CHAPTER SIXTEEN

Cold Rain

Denise Moretti rushed from the car to the house, narrowly beating a gale-driven rainstorm that chased her home. The freezing spray whipped at the backs of her skirted legs as she fought with the door lock. Shutting it behind her, she leaned against the door and caught her breath.

Warming scents from the Crockpot wafted from the kitchen to the foyer. It was after eleven, and she hadn't eaten since lunch. Tuesdays were always busy with her hurrying from the bank to the children's hospital where she volunteered twice per week.

She flicked on the entryway light and started toward the kitchen. One light over the stove shone weakly. The rest of the downstairs was cloaked in shadow.

The feeling that someone was behind her had been with Denise the entire ride home, and now it followed her into the kitchen. As much as she valued her volunteer work and making a sick child smile, she hated driving home from the hospital this time of year, when it was always dark by the time she walked from the lobby to the car.

Twice tonight she'd noticed a stranger watching her. The first time she saw him he was at the end of the hall, a pedestrian where only hospital personnel were allowed. When she turned to get a good look at him, he disappeared through a pair of swinging double doors. The second time occurred on her way out of the children's ward. She turned the corner into the parking garage and heard a door echo shut above her. He was standing in the shadows, staring over the rail. Always just beyond the light so she couldn't see who he was.

The first encounter she might have brushed off. Maybe it was a lost visitor. Seeing him a second time was no coincidence.

The drive home took Denise through three miles of winding forestland. Usually, she was the only person on the county road after dark. Tonight, she'd seen a pair of high beams trailing from a half-mile behind. The vehicle, itself, didn't faze her, rather it was the way the car kept lurching closer only to fall back and disappear behind a bend whenever she checked the mirror.

The ordeal recalled to Denise her junior year at Tufts. Her housemate, Evelyn, had been stalked for several months. Evelyn knew it was her old boyfriend from high school and reported him to the police, but she had no proof that he endangered her, and the cop's interrogation only served to make the boy more dangerous. Sometimes Denise came home at night to find an open window, the curtains swaying in and out. Items went missing from the house, including Evelyn's purse. The phone rang incessantly, often in the dead of night. There was never a voice on the other end, just the sound of someone breathing. Sometimes Denise wondered if the boy, now a man, was still following Evelyn.

She'd never felt so relieved to break out of the forest into the well-lighted outskirts of Burlington suburbs than tonight. As though the lights kept unseen demons at bay, the road behind her emptied, then filled with traffic along the main thoroughfare. Big box retailers and chain restaurants sprang from the ground like invasive plants.

Repeated checks of the mirror showed no sign of the car following her.

Now in the kitchen, Denise pulled a chair across the floor and stood on the seat, reaching for the bowls on the top shelf of the cupboard. She faltered climbing down and almost dropped the bowl.

She found herself looking warily at the windows. The panes were a smear of rain and darkness.

The man at the hospital left her spooked. She imagined turning off the lights and seeing his face at the window.

A quick check confirmed the Pendleton's lights were on next door. Sometimes she wished she lived in the country with several acres of land between her and the closest neighbor and enough darkness to see the stars. Tonight, she thanked God for closely cramped houses, streetlights, and a police station only a few miles away.

She sat down at the table and pulled off a chunk of baked bread to dunk in her chicken cacciatore. The wind kept rattling the panes. Somewhere, a loose shutter banged angrily with each gust. Soon it would be winter, and when winter came to Vermont it stayed until April, sometimes longer. Half-a-year of monster nor'easters and below-zero-wind chills made her wish she'd booked a vacation someplace warm for a few weeks this winter.

Denise finished her meal alone, mechanically washed her dishes, and listened to the building storm. Somewhere on the west side of Burlington, her ex was putting his children to sleep and going to bed with the woman he loved. Her stomach clenched with jealousy, not for the man she lost but what he gained. She caught her reflection in the mirror—a youthful-looking 35, still as pretty as she'd been through her college years. She pulled the curly blonde locks off her shoulders and sighed.

Just then something whacked against the pane.

She backed away from the window. Probably just a tree branch caught in the fury of the storm. The lights were off at the Pendleton's now. She felt isolated, as though a black craggy wall cut her off from the rest of the world.

Denise nervously dried the dishes and put them away, giving the window a wide berth as she crossed the kitchen.

A knock on the door made her flinch. Who would be out in this weather?

Digging her phone out of her purse, she started to type 911.

A more insistent pounding at the door got her heart racing.

She approached the door, the phone in her hand. The closet door off the entryway was open a crack. It reminded her of a horror movie she'd watched as a teenager—a babysitter alone in an unfamiliar house heard a knock at the door in the middle of the night, but when she opened the door the front steps were empty. It was a trick. The killer was already inside the house.

Outside, the rain fell in sheets.

Another pounding on the door, furious this time.

She backed away and thought again about calling the police.

"Who's there?"

No answer.

The lights were off in the den and living room. The shadowed lamp standing in the corner looked like a man holding a knife.

So idiotic to let her imagination get the best of her. Her neighborhood was too populated to worry about a killer breaking down the front door. In fact, the person at the door was probably one of her neighbors. Maybe someone had lost power or couldn't start the car.

A fist slammed hard against the door. Again.

"I'm calling the police. Who's at the door."

"It's me. Open the goddamn door."

The man's voice sounded familiar, but it was too difficult to hear over the storm.

"Who the hell is *me*?"

"Dammit, Denise. It's Tristan."

Tristan? What was he doing at her house this late?

She unbolted the door and threw it open. A waterfall of rain poured off the porch roof behind him. He was soaked to the bone, shivering in the doorway like an abandoned dog.

She reached to unlock the storm door and stopped. His face was pallid, eyes bloodshot and sunk deep into his head. Tristan might have crawled out of a crypt, he looked so sickly. Something else about his eyes —unfocused and darting from side-to-side as if he expected an attack to come from the shadows—made her pause.

"What do you want, Tristan? You can't show up at any hour of the night without telling me first."

"I just wanted to see you again."

His hair was matted to his forehead like black leaves. The overcoat poured water as if he'd stood in the rain for hours.

"Then you should have called or messaged me first."

"Why should I have to call my girlfriend if I want to see her?"

His words struck her.

"Girlfriend? Tristan, we had two dates together. The way you left things the other morning, I didn't expect to ever see you again."

"The way *I* left things? That's a laugh. You think I wanted to hurt you the way Jess hurt me? It's true what Jimmy said about you."

He moved threateningly close to the storm door. His breath fogged the glass.

"Jimmy? I don't know who you're talking about. This is starting to get too weird. I think you should leave."

"You're fucking that college guy. Don't tell me you aren't."

"You're scaring me."

"How the hell do you think I feel? Everyone's always looking at me and whispering into each others' ears about what a fool I am. If you think you can cross me and get away with it, you can't. I don't think you have the slightest idea what I'm capable of."

"Tristan—"

"All of you. Every fucking one of you will burn for this."

She slammed the door in his face.

CHAPTER SEVENTEEN

The Death House

Marissa awoke before the break of dawn. The tiny motel, about an hour outside of Binghamton along I-88, was cold and dingy, and the desk clerk hadn't asked any questions when she handed him cash and checked herself in as Kari Sherman.

Her phone was conspicuously quiet. No messages or missed calls from Tristan. She figured he would have tried to contact her by now, at the very least to explain why he ran off when Michael arrived.

She grabbed bagels and coffee from the lobby and stepped out into the early morning darkness. Ice plated the car windows. It was too black to see into the meadow across the road. She smelled manure from a nearby farm.

As she drove along I-88 the sun ascended from back near the Cape, where all she loved had turned out to be a lie. She wondered where Tristan was, if he was home or in another woman's bed. The prospect of finding him at Krista Steiner's house turned her skin clammy.

Despite a night of fitful, truncated sleep, she didn't feel exhausted. If Marissa's imagination wasn't fooling her, the brittleness that made her fear all her hair would fly off in a stiff breeze seemed to be softening. It was like watching the dead old stalks of her perennials disappear into soil and be replaced by new growth after a long winter.

Road construction brought her to a crawl a few miles outside of Binghamton. From the highway, she could see the old city, dormant, its old world factories and smokestacks ugly blemishes against a somber gray sky.

An angry horn brought her up from her thoughts. Traffic was moving again. She followed the train of vehicles to the first city exit and took the ramp.

Canisteo Street was hidden inside a maze of side streets in the city's more upscale western end. Young, exhausted-looking children climbed into a school bus. *I know how you feel*, she said to herself and fought back a yawn. Parents in robes and winter coats hopped and shuffled, willing the children to hurry so they could get out of the cold.

Twenty-seven Canisteo Street, Steiner's address, was a brown ranch with a cherry-red door. The frigid morning kept the walkers inside. With any luck, she could watch the house without attracting attention.

Marissa parked two houses away. As was the case with Alisha Morgan's neighborhood, Krista Steiner's was engulfed by leaf piles. Their scents were already drifting into the car.

Steiner's driveway was empty. She imagined Tristan's car parked here, her husband following the winding path from the driveway to the porch. He'd ring the bell and she'd let him inside. Then sex, of course. Yet Marissa's instincts told her there was more to these visits than a cheap affair.

So far to drive just to cheat on her.

The ranch couldn't have been worth more than a hundred grand. A fine home, but not what she'd expect from a woman with a sizable brokerage account. Now that she thought about it, the Medford duplex didn't fit with Tristan's clientele. No, these women weren't wealthy investors. If not through his business, how did Tristan find them?

The mirror caught movement. A police cruiser crawled between the leaf piles. She reached for the ignition and thought better of it. Fleeing would raise suspicion.

The car closed the distance between them. It was close enough for her to see the officers—a heavyset woman behind the wheel and a stocky man riding shotgun—scanning the street. The man raised a coffee cup to his lips. The woman had her eyes dead set on Marissa's car, the Massachusetts plates drawing too much attention.

The cruiser slowed as it crept up on her.

Shit. The lights flashed.

With a brief scream of its siren, the police car came to a stop behind her. The lights lit up her mirrors.

She saw them climb out of the car. Neither drew a weapon, but the man's hand was a few inches away from his holster.

Marissa was so busy watching him round her car that she jumped when the woman knocked on the window. The female officer looked even bigger up close, blotting out Marissa's view. The woman made a turning signal with her hand—she wanted Marissa to roll down the window.

Her hands shaking, Marissa motioned that she needed to turn on the ignition. She worried about misunderstandings and inadvertent shootings. The woman nodded and took a step back from the door, her eyes fixed on Marissa's every movement. The engine fired. Marissa rolled down her window.

"Turn it off," the woman said. "Remove the keys from the ignition."

The man stood back. She could see him in the mirrors writing down her plate number. He brought a radio to his lips and spoke into it.

"License and registration."

Digging into her handbag for her wallet, Marissa moved slowly so as not to appear threatening.

She touched her phone. The wallet wasn't there. Her heart raced as she imagined the wallet in the frozen mud outside the motel.

A thousand explanations the officers wouldn't find satisfactory flew at her. She laughed nervously as the woman officer's eyes bore holes into her.

Then her hand closed over the leather wallet.

She opened the wallet and displayed her license.

"Ma'am, you need to remove the license from the wallet."

Marissa pulled the license from its sleeve, fumbled it into her lap, and picked it up. As she handed the woman the license it occurred to Marissa the picture was three-years-old, taken when Marissa looked fifteen years younger than she did now. The woman kept comparing the license photo to Marissa's face.

"Have you been sick, Mrs. Carrington?"

"Yes."

Taking the car registration from Marissa, the woman handed the two cards to the male officer, who took them back to the police car. Marissa saw him talking into his radio again.

"What's your business in Binghamton, Mrs. Carrington?"

The bitch in the ranch is sleeping with my husband. I'm canvassing her house.

"My husband…Tristan…and I run a Massachusetts brokerage firm. Carrington Associates. Maybe you've heard of us? He's been on CNBC."

The woman never blinked.

"One of our clients lives on this street. I was just waiting for her to come home."

The officer ran her eyes over the residences. A few of the homes passed for upscale, but not Steiner's. Most of the neighborhood was middle class at best.

"A neighbor saw you pull up a half-hour ago. Says you've been sitting in your car watching the house the whole time."

Marissa's pulse beat faster.

"That's not quite true, officer. Yes, I've been out here for about that long, I suppose. I rang my client's doorbell when I first arrived but no one answered. We had an appointment. Since the drive back to Massachusetts is a long one, I thought I'd better give her time to arrive."

No response. Just a hard stare made of ice and switchblades.

"You can ask her yourself, officer. Mrs. Krista Steiner. Just tell her Tristan Carrington's wife is waiting to discuss her…situation."

"Krista Steiner, did you say?"

"Yes."

The officer pointed at the ranch house.

"Twenty-seven Canisteo Street?"

"Yes, officer. That's the address I have on file."

The woman shared a look with her partner back in the car. He shook his head.

"Nobody with the last name of Steiner lives in that house. Perhaps you have the wrong address."

"No, I don't believe so. We receive regular correspondence from Mrs. Steiner. Her return address is twenty-seven Canisteo in Binghamton, New York."

There was that stare again.

After a moment, the woman ordered Marissa to wait while she spoke with the male officer. Through the mirrors, Marissa watched them confer. They kept looking at her.

When the woman returned the other officer was by her side. She handed Marissa the license and registration.

"Is there something wrong, officers?"

"We confirmed your identity, Mrs. Carrington. Sorry for the confusion. We've had issues with reporters harassing the homeowner."

Reporters?

"Harassing Mrs. Steiner?"

"That's the issue. Nobody by the name of Krista Steiner lives at twenty-seven Canisteo Street. You're positive of the address?"

Confusion swan-dived over Marissa.

"Mrs. Carrington?"

"She has to live here. This is the address my husband has on file. I've seen it myself."

"We checked, Mrs. Carrington. We can't find anyone by the name of Krista Steiner in the city. There must be some mistake. Perhaps she lives in one of the satellite cities around here—Vestal, Endicott, Johnson City…"

The woman's voice trailed off.

No laws had been broken, yet the stern glances from the two officers convinced Marissa to leave and never come back.

The bag of notes lay on the passenger seat floor. If Marissa started driving now by lunchtime she would reach Syracuse, where Monica Leigh, another of Tristan's lovers, resided. There was no reason to rush. She already knew what she'd find—another house with no record of anyone named Monica Leigh ever having lived there.

After the officers let her go, Marissa circled the block and parked at a gas station down the road. The tank had plenty of fuel, but she topped it off and waited until the police cruiser turned out of the neighborhood and headed downtown.

Checking one last time to ensure the police were out of sight, she returned to Canisteo Street and parked behind a rusted pickup truck, large enough to hide her car from prying eyes.

She stepped out of the vehicle and into the autumn cold. Much too cold for a week before Halloween. A gusting wind bit her ears and made her nose run as she walked down the sidewalk. Clutching her coat around her, she wished she'd worn something warmer.

Now and again the wind shifted and pulled city sounds into the neighborhood. All around her the air was redolent of wood stoves and leaf mold. She kept watch of the houses, searching for someone peeking between the curtains. Whoever had phoned the police would report Marissa again. She knew she'd never talk her way out of it if the two officers returned and found her here.

A few houses later she passed an elderly man in a black overcoat shuffling in the opposite direction. His face didn't appear friendly, and she had to round the sidewalk and crunch through leaves to give him room. Across the street, a boy hunched over a black Mustang's grill. The hood was up. The ping of metal and a curse word broke the windy desolation.

He grasped his hand and rubbed the combined pain and cold out of it. She guessed he was in his early-twenties. Not the type to phone the authorities upon seeing a stranger.

She could see him watching as she cut across the street. Leaves swirled around her ankles. Her sneakers scratched along the blacktop.

"Good morning," she said.

"Morning."

He gave a wary look and turned back to work on the Mustang. It seemed nobody in Binghamton trusted her.

"Cold enough for you?"

"October is way too early to be dealing with this shit."

He squinted at the gray sky. She half-expected

117

snowflakes to begin falling.

"I was hoping you could solve a mystery for me," Marissa said.

He was back under the hood, avoiding her, and working on an iron-willed, corroded bolt with a socket wrench.

"What paper?"

"Huh?"

"What newspaper do you write for?"

"Oh. I'm not a reporter."

"Uh-huh."

The boy looked grim-faced and distracted. He exhaled and aimed an anti-corrosion spray at the offending bolt. As he waited for it to eat at the rust, he wiped his hands on an oily rag and leaned against the grille.

"Then what's the name of your blog?"

"I don't know what you're talking about. Why are you convinced I'm either a reporter or a blogger?"

"Only two types of out-of-towner's come into this neighborhood: reporters and looky-loos."

"How do you know I'm an out-of-towner?"

He nodded toward her car, nearly invisible behind the truck.

"Massachusetts plates."

"You can't see my plates from here."

"Saw you about an hour ago. You parked down near Annie Wallace's old place. Left after the cops chased you out and circled back after they took off."

"You see a lot."

He shrugged.

"Not a whole hell of a lot happens around here." His eyes traveled to the dead end and stopped on the brown ranch where she'd expected to find Krista Steiner. "At least, not usually. So who are you really?"

"Marissa Carrington." She wasn't sure why she

offered her name so willingly. The boy seemed trustworthy if overcautious.

"Pat Bradley. I'd offer to shake your hand, but…" he said, turning over greasy palms.

"Nice to meet you, Pat. That's a nice Mustang. Are you a mechanic?"

"What, me? No. I'm just trying to keep this baby on the road. Not having much luck lately. That's cool that you know your cars, Mrs. Carrington. So what brings you to Binghamton?"

"My husband runs a brokerage firm in Massachusetts."

"So he's like a banker?"

"Stocks and options, mutual funds, retirement stuff."

"Hmm."

She was losing him again. He attacked the bolt and grinned when it finally popped free. Pat tossed the corroded battery cable aside, slipped a new cable into the car, and smiled to himself.

"That ought to do it," he said. "Hold on a second."

Opening the driver side door, he turned the ignition. The motor turned over and growled. He cut the ignition and tapped the hood twice as he circled back to the front of the Mustang. There was a big grin on his face.

"Sure you aren't a mechanic? You seem to know a lot about cars."

"I'm just a car buff. Your husband is a stockbroker, eh? What's that have to do with the *death house*?"

She stopped in mid-sentence and stared at him.

"Did you just call it the death house?"

"Yeah, that's the name people around here call it. Kinda stupid, right?"

"Why in the world would you call it that?"

He set down the wrench and wiped off his hands

again. The boy banged the hood shut and pushed himself up to sit on it.

"Nothing good happens there," he said. "That's why."

"I'm not following."

"When I was in grade school, the Marsten's lived there. I used to race go-karts with Tommy. When Tommy was about ten, I guess, his dad died of a heart attack. Only forty-seven, can you believe that? 'Course he smoked like a chimney and drank pretty hard, so maybe he stacked the cards against himself. Still, that's pretty young for a heart attack."

"It seems a little extreme to come up with a name like the death house just because someone had a heart attack."

"There's more to the story than that. The Barton's moved in a few years after, but they didn't stick around long. No kids, and Lockheed Martin kept moving the guy all over the country. Two weeks before they were set to move to Dallas, the wife tripped taking the laundry down to the cellar and broke her neck."

"That's terrible."

"Yeah, pretty sick stuff. Then Annie Wallace moved in."

He averted his eyes from the ranch and stared down at his shoes, as though the rest of the story was tied in with the laces.

"Pretty girl…well, woman," he said.

His cheeks turned pink. Marissa didn't think the wind caused it.

"She landscaped the place real nice. *Like putting lipstick on a pig*, my Dad used to say, but she was out there all spring and summer planting flowers and keeping the hedges trimmed just so." He jumped down from the hood, kicked at a stone, and looked off at the ranch. "I could see her from here, ya know? Out working on my car like today, I could see her in the yard."

The boy saw Marissa studying him and said, "I didn't spy on her or nothing if that's what you're thinking."

"No, you don't seem like the voyeur type."

"You don't know a thing about me."

"I trust you. Tell me more about Annie Wallace."

"You sure you aren't a reporter?"

"I have my husband's business card in my wallet if that will help. You wanna see?"

"Nah. I believe you I guess. So you really don't know anything about what happened, do you? To Annie Wallace, I mean."

"How could I?"

"The death house got her, too. A year ago this November. The police found her in her bed, all cut up with a red rose laid on her chest. Sick stuff. The story was a big deal in the papers. It's all we ever heard about on the evening news, but I guess it wasn't exactly national news, so you wouldn't have known about it in Massachusetts."

"Did the police ever catch the guy who did it?"

"No. Annie had a lot of boyfriends. I don't mean she was sleeping around with every guy in town, just that when you are as pretty as Annie was, a lot of guys are gonna notice."

"You did."

Marissa reached for her phone and found the vacation picture she'd shown the duplex owner.

She moved close to Pat and held the phone up for him.

"You ever see this man hanging around Annie's place?"

He took hold of the phone and studied the picture. His eyes stopped on the young, vigorous Marissa then traveled back to Tristan. Marissa held her breath.

After a long interrogation, he shook his head.

"Sorry. I've never seen him."

Thank God.

"I take it that's your husband. How old is the picture?"

"Just a few years. I look a lot older now."

"Not so much."

She caught him stealing a quick glance and sniffing at her perfume. It was the first time, she realized, that another guy had taken an interest in her since she'd gotten sick. Unless she counted the shared touch with Michael, which was too innocent to consider.

"Yeah," he said, changing the subject. "That's three deaths in the last ten years. That should answer your question as to why everyone calls Annie Wallace's place the death house."

He sighed and stuffed his hands into his pockets.

"Hey, Pat," Marissa said. "Do you remember a Krista Steiner living in that house?"

"No."

"You absolutely positive about that? I have her name listed at that address."

"Must be a mistake. I've lived in this house since I was five. Nobody with that name ever lived there."

Marissa leaned closer to him.

"Think real hard. Did Annie ever have a girlfriend visit or move in for a little while? And maybe a man came around to visit Annie's friend?"

"No. I would have noticed."

"Hold on for just a second."

She dug a pen out of her pocketbook and wrote her name and number on the back of Tristan's business card.

"You trying to sell me a mutual fund, Mrs. Carrington?"

There was a sardonic arch to one of his eyebrows and the hint of a grin. It was the second time Marissa had seen Pat smile. He was a good-looking boy, she thought.

"This is my name and mobile number," she said, handing him the card. "Ask your neighbors when you get the chance. If Krista Steiner's name rings a bell with anyone, or anybody saw an older male, maybe a boyfriend who drives a black Camaro, hanging around Annie's apartment, could you give me a call? "

The boy said he would, but after Marissa thanked him and began the bitter walk back to her car, she knew not to expect a call. No Krista Steiner lived in the death house. Like Alisha Morgan, Steiner was a phantom, an urban legend which only existed in the hidden notes of an unfaithful husband.

CHAPTER EIGHTEEN

Stranger in the Rain

Something pressed against the window. Marissa awoke screaming.

She was parked at a rest stop on a hill just south of Syracuse. It was late afternoon with night closing in fast. The sky was a black veil draped over the hills. Dark claws of rain raked the valley below. Spinning in her seat, she looked out the windows. She'd dreamed someone was jiggling the handle and trying to break into the car.

Two tractor trailers with out of state plates slept dormant near the back of the rest stop. Another vehicle was wedged between the two trucks, yet all she could see was the bottoms of two front tires. Rain kept lashing against the car, obscuring the service plaza.

She'd slept for too long. Her back was cramped, her legs a prickling mess of pins and needles.

Each breath clouded the windshield. Marissa turned on the ignition and threw the heat on high but couldn't stop shivering.

Alisha Morgan, Krista Steiner. Who were these women, and why couldn't she find them? If Monica Leigh proved to be just as much of a mystery, Marissa's only recourse would be to follow Tristan the next time he left the house. Trail him to the Boston suburbs, to New York, to wherever he hid his lovers and catch him in the act.

The car shook.

Marissa whipped around. It felt as if two strong hands had grabbed hold of the bumper and given it a shove.

The windows were a blur of rain, the service plaza and the hills warped beyond recognition as the squall struck the car from all angles. When the wind briefly abated she saw one of the tractor trailer's doors push open. A pair of work boots descended from the cab, and then a graying, middle-aged man climbed into the rain.

He walked toward Marissa's car.

She slid beneath the seat back and watched him through the window. He was hunched over with his hands in his pockets.

Closer.

Now the rain fell in black sheets. She lost view of the man in her mirrors.

She touched the gearshift. He was gone. Simply vanished.

Marissa watched the service plaza. Nobody came in or out.

She exhaled when the truck driver appeared walking out from the men's bathroom a few minutes later. He cut across the parking lot and ran headlong into a storm which kept trying to throw him backward. His sweatshirt and jeans were soggy and stained dark by the elements. Marissa found herself willing the man back to the truck. Finally, he climbed into the cab and slammed the door shut. The parking lot was empty and safe again.

Except for the other figure in the rain.

He disappeared in the downpour and reappeared back by the trucks.

She blinked and the shape was gone.

Another glance over her shoulder confirmed no one was standing back near the trucks. At least no one she could see.

The sky turned darker. It was after six.

Waiting any longer meant she'd be searching for Leigh's address in the dead of night.

Something scraped the door as she reached for the radio.

She screamed.

The storm screamed back at her.

Marissa was frozen, her breath like razor blades through her lungs.

Nothing in the mirrors. Only an empty lot over her shoulder.

Yet something was out there. She'd heard it.

She leaned over the seat. If a man was crouched below the passenger window, she couldn't see him from here.

Marissa yanked the car into drive and slammed hard on the gas.

Something pounded against the door panel.

Hard and heavy.

The back end fishtailed in the deluge. She turned the wheel and brought the car under control. All she saw was black rain.

A pounding struck the car from behind.

The tires caught blacktop, and the car jumped forward.

Marissa could have been driving straight at a guardrail or the service plaza and wouldn't have known.

Then the ramp sprang out of the gloom. As she angled toward the exit she heard footsteps racing at the car.

She hit the on-ramp at forty mph and accelerated around the bend. She almost took the car over the embankment coming out of the curve. The lonely highway appeared in her windshield while she pushed the car up to seventy. Her breath caught in her throat when she felt the tires hydroplane and saw the car sliding toward a rock wall. Spinning. She saw the precipitous drop into the valley several hundred feet below. The guardrails weren't going to save her.

The rock wall again, the chasm, back to the rock wall.

The car began to tilt. Then the tires caught the blacktop and the frame bucked. Marissa gripped the wheel as the car skidded to a stop in the middle of the highway.

Her chest heaved, heart thundered.

The storm crashed all around her. Only a few feet of blacktop lay visible before the rain swallowed everything. Anything could have been in the road: a stalled vehicle, a rock slide, the man who chased her from the rest area.

Her hands trembled on the steering wheel as she got the car moving again. She wasn't even sure she was driving in the right direction until she barely discerned the speed limit sign off to the right.

Marissa was still shaking as she took the exit and crept into the Syracuse suburbs.

Outside, the storm had given way to a cold drizzle. Seeing people hustling to get out of the weather calmed her down. Still, she swung the car into the first busy parking lot she saw. The way things were going she was more likely to get herself murdered than find Monica Leigh.

She glanced at her phone. A green light blinked indicating a message had arrived. Her stomach rumbled. She'd forgotten to eat again.

Clicking on her messages, she saw an unknown phone number. When she opened the message, she realized Pat, the young man from Binghamton, had written her.

I did some asking around. A buddy from up the street said he didn't recognize anyone by the name of

*Krista Steiner, but he told me he used to see a black
Camaro with Mass plates in the driveway.*

*It got me thinking about you showing me that
picture of you and your husband and wondering if I'd
ever seen him over at Annie's place. I think I know what
you are suggesting. If he drives a black Camaro…well,
all I can say is I'm really sorry.*

The night closed in around her. She knew where
this path led: someone murdered Annie Wallace.

Not Tristan. He was an adulterer, yes. But she
couldn't accept he was a killer.

Marissa couldn't deny how crazed Tristan had
looked in the kitchen.

How well do we truly know the ones we love? What
black secrets lie under the surface, rooting and
spreading tendrils under layers of dirt?

The lights of the supermarket appeared to shine
from a million miles away. Nothing but darkness lurked
between the car and the entry doors.

As Marissa climbed down from the car and hurried
across the lot, she checked her voice-mail and saw an
hour-old recording from Michael.

The warm blowers of the entryway thawed her and
threw down scents of baked bread.

Michael's voice was jittery, perhaps scared.

*"Hey…Marissa. It's Michael. Look, I really gotta
talk to you about the filter. I found something."*

His voice went quiet. She expected to hear a
crowd of people talking and laughing in the background.
There was only the polite silence of his workshop.
Immediately, she knew Michael hadn't taken his
daughter to Provincetown and felt terrible.

*"Truth is, I'm not sure what I found. But I think you
should have somebody look at it. A doctor, maybe. Or the
police."*

Marissa's fingers went cold.

"I don't want to talk about this in a damn voice-mail…sorry about the language again. When you get this message you need to call me, okay?"

The message seemed to end. As she removed the phone from her ear he started talking again.

"And one more thing…Christ, I don't know how to say this, Marissa…until you get this thing looked at, I don't want you anywhere near Tristan. I know how crazy this sounds. I hope to hell I'm wrong. Just call me back as soon as you can. And don't tell anyone about what I said, especially Tristan. I gotta go."

The message ended. She stood in the produce aisle with no memory of how she'd gotten there. An old woman impatiently pushed a shopping cart around Marissa, muttering to herself about young people and their goddamn phones as she stuffed lettuce into a plastic bag.

Marissa's fingers trembled. Barely able to hold on, she stared at the phone. Then she felt her stomach give way and ran to the restroom, where her dry heaves echoed out to the store.

CHAPTER NINETEEN

Night Calls

The phone wailed at three in the morning. Jimmy Rodgers fell out of bed and knocked over the nightstand trying to reach it, the bedroom as dark as a tomb. He'd missed the call. Rubbing the blur from his eyes, he saw the time and groaned.

Wonderful. He had to be to work in five hours.

An unlisted number perched at the top of his phone log, probably the same caller that had badgered him in the dead of night over the last few weeks.

He struggled through the trailer, stumbling into the walls until he made it to the kitchenette. Though he wasn't particularly hungry, Jimmy couldn't stop himself from milling through the refrigerator and tearing off a slice of cold pizza.

His stomach burned, something else he'd put off—calling the doctor. That was how the problems always started—you went to the doctor about indigestion and the next thing you knew you were hooked to a monitor with a tube blasting barium up your ass. He popped two antacids and limped back to the bedroom.

Sitting on the edge of the bed, the tight fit between the walls making the bed space seem cave-like, he turned on the light and rubbed his eyes. On the floor lay a capped bottle of bourbon and a twelve-step card stained by a beer ring. A bitter drop of irony. He fixed the nightstand and put the clock, bourbon, and AA card on top, then he grabbed the bottle and swirled the golden contents. A drink would help him get back to sleep, but he'd pay for it in when the alarm woke him for work. Not a good idea.

Maybe he should call her. It was late. She might not like it if he called now.

Then again, his sponsor told him to call whenever he needed to talk. Valorie, though she insisted he call her Val. She thought Valorie made her sound too much like somebody's great aunt.

Val was a blonde with better legs than the girls he'd dated in high school, which was why he'd chosen her as his sponsor in the first place. So much for working the program or letting the program work for him. Two months of meetings and he hadn't made it through three days without drinking.

He grabbed the card and turned it over to where she'd written *this too shall pass*, with her phone number right below.

This too shall pass. Easier said...

Tapping a finger on the card, he couldn't decide. She had a husband, a big guy with a military crew cut and muscles ripping out of his sleeves. Jimmy had seen him parked down the street, waiting for Valorie.

Anonymity. What a crock of shit. As if twenty coffee drinkers filing out of the First Methodist Church with pamphlets tucked under their arms didn't attract attention.

Jimmy punched Val's number into his phone, erased it, then typed it again. Now the hard part—hitting *send*.

Three in the morning. She'd kill him. Or he'd kill him.

Send.

The phone rang too loudly in his ear. He willed it to

be quieter as if doing so would ensure she didn't answer.

Two rings.

Three rings.

Still time to hang up.

Four rings.

Five rings.

He prayed she turned her phone off at night so he wouldn't have to face the discomfort of talking with her. At least he could say he tried.

Six rings.

She answered.

Her voice was groggy, her head submerged in the bog of sleepiness. If he hung up now she'd fall back to sleep, maybe forget his call. Except his number would be in her log. Jimmy was trapped.

"Who is this?"

"Hey…Val, it's Jimmy."

"Jimmy?" It took a while for the wheels in her head to start turning. Christ, it was late. "Oh…hi, Jimmy. Hold on a second."

He heard the mattress springs creak, then a door opened and softly closed.

"Sorry about that," she said. "I didn't want to wake Danny."

Danny? That was her husband's name? He looked more like a Rocky or Butch.

"I shouldn't have called so late."

"No, no. You call me anytime you want to talk, understand?"

"Okay."

"Haven't seen you at the meetings lately."

A lie tried to pry past his lips. He could have told her he'd been attending meetings across town.

"Right. Work has been ridiculously busy, and I've got this thing going on with my family—"

"Stop, Jimmy. I can't go to your place and drag you to the church. That's up to you. Take responsibility."

"I know."

"When you least want to attend is the time you most need a meeting. My own sponsor told me that eleven years ago when I was in your position."

Eleven years. Decent odds said he'd be dead in eleven years. How much of his remaining life did he want to devote to steps scrawled on a note card?

"When did you have your last drink?"

He almost said he hadn't. Val wouldn't have believed him.

"About six hours ago."

He braced himself for a scolding. It didn't come.

"So you are six hours sober."

"What?"

"One step at a time. Congratulations on six hours of sobriety."

"You get one of those coins for six hours?"

She giggled. At least she had a sense of humor.

"No, but the next coffee is on me. You got booze in the house, Jimmy?"

He glanced over at the bourbon. The way the light hit the bottle made the liquid look like honey.

"Yeah."

"Let me hear you pouring it down the sink."

"Come on, Val."

"Do it," Val said. "It's like ripping off a bandage. You'll hate me every second of the way, but once those bottles are empty you'll feel better."

"Doubtful."

"Jimmy."

"Okay, okay."

Jimmy grabbed the bourbon and walked it to the kitchen sink, where he poured it down the drain. Each *glug-glug* tempted him to open his mouth under the flow. He half-considered pouring water down the sink. She would have known. Valorie could read his mind...or maybe she'd seen every trick in the eleven years she'd worked the program. When he finished, she told him to scour the refrigerator of beer and check the cupboards.

"It's all gone," he said, lying and feeling horrible about it.

"You only had one bottle of booze in the house?"

"Yeah, bourbon. I do most of my drinking at The Blue Dragon."

"I see." Her skepticism was a knife in his belly. "You're having the dreams again."

It wasn't a question.

"Almost every night this week."

"God, Jimmy. Have you talked to anybody about them?"

By *anybody*, she meant a shrink. No way he was going to lie on a couch and pour his heart out to a stranger.

"No," Jimmy said.

"It doesn't have to be a psychologist. Ever thought of telling your physician about the dreams?"

"No pills."

Another golden nugget of irony. He didn't trust prescriptions, but he happily poured any liquid down his throat if it made the dreams stop.

"I never mentioned pills. A good doctor respects the value of nutrition and exercise. Look, Jimmy. I can't do it all for you. Get yourself to tonight's meeting. A lot of the weight you carry around will come off once you learn to let go."

Jimmy didn't realize he was crying until he heard himself echoed in the receiver. Jess, his beautiful Jess and their friends—gone forever. A tragedy he could have prevented.

Since the fire the scent of anything burning made his mind rush back to the rescue team pawing through the still-burning embers, Jimmy knowing no one could have survived the fire, the police pulling him away from the wreckage as he screamed for Jess.

He needed to talk to someone about what happened. Not a shrink, but maybe Val. If he didn't the memory would consume him.

"I'll come tonight."

"Promise me," said Val.

"Yeah…I promise."

Ending the call made him feel alone. It was too quiet in the trailer.

The half-eaten slice of pizza lay on the counter. After a moment of consideration he bit into the food with mechanical indifference. Food was food. All he needed was a little energy to make it through what was shaping up to be a very long day.

The last bit of pizza swished around inside his mouth when the phone rang again.

Thinking it was Val calling him back, he answered. Quiet.

Then the dark susurrus of breathing.

"Whoever the fuck this is, you're starting to piss me off."

No reply.

"I got a cousin who works at the F.B.I. That's the Federal Bureau of I'm Gonna Kick Your Ass. One call and he'll trace your number, hotshot."

The bastard kept breathing into his ear. He thought he heard a car engine in the background.

Jimmy hung up and threw the phone on the counter just as a car motor rumbled down the street.

Enough of this shit. After work he'd change his phone number. God, he needed a drink.

As he turned toward the back of the trailer the

phone blared again.

He stood staring at the phone. On the third ring, he snatched up the phone and screamed at the caller.

The man on the other end—he strongly sensed it was a man—didn't reply. Running through a mental inventory, he tried to think of who might be harassing him. Jimmy hadn't had more than two dates in the last year, and neither led to a relationship. That ruled out a scorned lover. His instinct insisted it was a man.

"Come on, friend. Who is this?"

Nothing.

It wasn't smart to show weakness and Jimmy knew this. He'd only embolden the man.

The call went dead.

He glanced at the clock. It was almost four.

The floor was freezing beneath his bare feet. He walked slowly to the front window and looked between the blinds. The other trailer windows were dark, while one light burned from a porch up the road.

Blinding light blazed into the trailer. A motor thundered. He hadn't seen the car hidden in the darkness across the street.

Jimmy stepped back as the car lurched forward, the engine growling.

The grille emerged over the curb. The car was in his yard now, tires digging fissures into the soil and spraying turf and rock into the street. For God's sake, he thought the driver meant to crash through the door.

Jimmy always saw things better when he was afraid. The lights were too bright to make out the car or driver, but he could see it was a sports car, knew it was the same maniac who'd followed him from Westland to his work site.

The car thundered forward. The bumper was almost to the porch steps.

The car abruptly reversed. It jounced over the curb,

then tires squealed as the driver wheeled around and raced up the street. Staring out from the corner of the window, Jimmy watched the car's progress until it disappeared around the corner. He heard the engine as the car raced toward the town center. Then it was gone.

Twin gorges were dug into the yard. The smell of burning rubber came into the trailer.

Jimmy slumped down against the wall. The sins of his past had finally caught up to him.

CHAPTER TWENTY

Jamie Bracket

Marissa punched the steering wheel.

No one named Monica Leigh lived in Syracuse. Her body was stiff and trembling with cold after sleeping in her car.

Now she sat with black circles under her eyes, staring at the pile of love letters on the floor.

Pulling out the bag of notes, she sifted through the letters and found the one she sought.

Jamie Bracket. Burlington, Vermont.

It was a three-hour trip down the thruway and up I-87 to Burlington. Marissa crumpled up the note and threw it down, knowing she couldn't go home until she spoke with Michael.

A thinly veiled sun crawled out of the horizon behind an overcast sky as Marissa resumed driving. Halfway to the interstate, she felt herself nodding off.

She swung the car into a parking space in front of a defunct cinema where a torn poster for "Wolf Creek" hung in the window. The trash can in front of the theater emitted a spoiled meat scent.

After sleeping for an hour, Marissa left Syracuse at eight. Along the way to Vermont, she perceived more changes inside of her. She felt ravenous. After six months of being too sick to eat and losing an unhealthy amount of weight, it seemed she was making up for lost time. She stopped twice for food, once at a Dunkin Donuts and another time at a service plaza deli. Both meals settled into her stomach without issue. Her thoughts came with full clarity, and gone was the lingering sensation that her brain was trapped in fog. Her body felt anxious, as if pent-up energy was building toward an explosion. What she saw in the mirror shocked her—not the dead, gray strands of hair lying across her shoulders, but how dark the roots were underneath. A snake shedding skin, she thought.

The mid-morning sun burned through the clouds by the time Marissa pulled into Burlington. She picked up the phone and dialed Michael's number. The call went to his voice-mail.

Thirteen Maplecrest Drive lay a mile from Burlington's center.

Marissa breathed a sigh of relief upon entering Bracket's neighborhood. The yards were large and well-manicured, the homes a rustic mix of Colonial, Greek Revival, and Victorian, a far cry from the black darkness of Monica Leigh's apartment. As with the other neighborhoods she'd visited, Halloween decorations adorned the houses. A group of children played bike tag in the crisp autumn air, while a yard sale drew a throng of neighbors to a beautiful brick-faced residence with flower-lined pathways. Several cars were parked along the curb.

Indeed, it felt no less impossible Tristan had visited here than he'd stepped inside Monica Leigh's apartment, one door away from the bad man. Tristan's darkness didn't fit here. The sky couldn't have been a deeper blue, and everyone in Bracket's neighborhood smiled, making the most of a picturesque New England Saturday morning.

Even the temperature, much warmer than it had been yesterday, made the day seem spring-like.

Turning the radio off, Marissa stopped the car outside of Jamie Bracket's residence, a historic Colonial with a white picket fence and red barn that glowed under the golden sun. A silver BMW sat in the driveway.

A knock on the window made Marissa jump in her seat. A beautiful woman with curly blonde hair falling out from under a sunbonnet smiled through the window.

"Here for the yard sale?" the woman asked after Marissa rolled down her window.

"Of course, the yard sale," Marissa said.

"The sign says *no parking*, but don't pay it any mind. It's not like the police are going to ticket anyone. Hey, are you sure everything is all right?"

"Yes. For a moment, I couldn't remember if I'd forgotten my wallet. But it's right here."

Marissa smiled and patted her handbag.

"Good. You don't want to be caught short on cash at the annual Maplecrest tag sale and wine soiree."

"I guess I wouldn't."

A golden locket of two dolphins kissing, similar to a necklace Marissa wore as a child, slipped out of the woman's shirt as she bent forward.

"Denise Moretti," she said, offering her hand through the window.

"Marissa…Marissa Carrington."

Again, Marissa was surprised when she gave her name to a complete stranger. She trusted this woman on some deep, intrinsic level, the way she had Pat from Krista Steiner's neighborhood, though she couldn't say why.

Marissa caught Denise eyeing her neck. She glanced in the mirror and saw a purple bruise had formed where Tristan grabbed her.

"How'd that happen?" she asked.

"What?"

"Your neck. Did somebody hurt you?"

By *somebody*, Marissa knew Denise meant her husband. A cross between a stern parent and concerned friend, Denise studied Marissa's eyes for a truthful answer.

"Yes, somebody did. But he's not a part of my life anymore."

Denise nodded, satisfied. Marissa felt happy to finally say something truthful.

"Good for you."

A Subaru packed with a man, woman, and three young children parked in front of them. The kids burst laughing from the doors as their parents trailed behind with reusable shopping bags.

"Come on before the vultures pick the place clean," said Denise.

Marissa climbed from the car and followed the woman, watching her locks, doused orange by the morning light, swing from shoulder-to-shoulder.

It wasn't until Marissa started up the driveway that she noticed neighboring garages yawning open, the entire community coming to life as more cars streamed into the neighborhood.

At the first home, a Greek Revival which seemed to stretch to the sky, Marissa found a garage stocked with barely worn furniture, antique tables with matching chairs, three sizes of microwaves, and a master bed set. Outside stood paintings Marissa felt sure would fetch a pretty penny on the auction market. She recognized a Jackson Pollock and a Martin Johnson Heade set among lesser-known pieces. Thumbing through a crate of vinyl albums, Marissa discovered Elvis' Christmas album and The Beatles' Abbey Road stacked between various pop rock from the 1970s and 1980s.

Happy murmurs drifted among the visitors and became one with a gentle wind pulling leaves through the grass.

Denise must have glimpsed Marissa's mood

swings, for she pulled her aside when the crowd thinned.

"Are you okay?" Denise asked.

"It hasn't been a good week."

"Whatever this man did to you, you need to let it go. You're the survivor, and he's not worth your worries."

They walked the block, visiting yard sales all morning. Denise, who didn't buy anything except for a Smiths CD Marissa once loved during college, seemed content to browse and chat with Marissa. Where was Marissa from and what brought her to Burlington? How long did she plan to stay?

Denise had taken note of the Massachusetts license plate, Marissa knew. It wasn't likely Marissa had driven several hours to grab good deals on bedding and toaster ovens.

"A friend of mine from high school is a professor at the University of Vermont," said Marissa, feeling guilty for having to lie again.

"Oh yeah? A Vermont professor lives at the end of the block. I should introduce you. Maybe he knows your friend? What's her name?"

"Kari Sherman."

Though Marissa did her best to steer the conversation toward other topics, she couldn't skirt the unmissable. Even if Denise bought Marissa's story about visiting a friend—and something told Marissa she didn't —how did she know about the yard sales?

Finally, Marissa rolled the dice.

"Actually, Kari told me one of her good friends lives nearby. I think this is the neighborhood."

"Oh? Do you remember her name? I'll introduce you if I know her."

"Jamie Bracket."

Denise thought about it for a moment and shook her head.

"Sorry. That name doesn't ring a bell."

Of course, it didn't.

When lunchtime rolled around, Marissa said her goodbyes and thanked Denise for showing her around.

"Don't go yet," Denise said. "I want you to stay for lunch. Please tell me you'll do that."

"I really should be on my way. I've taken up all of your morning as it is."

"Nonsense. As much as I love Burlington, I'll be the first to tell you the restaurants are overrated and overpriced. I bet you haven't had a good meal in days." Denise leaned close and whispered. "Besides, I was a nursing assistant for three years. I'd like to take a closer look at that bruise."

Curious eyes watched, wondering who Denise's friend was.

"Thank you, Denise."

It was probably for the best, Marissa thought. Jamie Bracket's name had proven to be another dead end despite the address on Tristan's note, and Marissa didn't relish the long drive back to the Cape. Denise and Pat had been the only people to show her kindness since this journey began. What harm would a warm meal and good conversation do?

They walked in the direction of Marissa's car, boxed in by a jam of curbside vehicles, some of which blocked driveways as shoppers tried to find space to squeeze into. The disco beat of Earth, Wind, and Fire pounded from a garage up the street.

"How far down is your house?" Marissa asked.

"Right here."

The Colonial with the red barn. Jamie Bracket's house.

Marissa stopped at the curb.

"Something wrong?"

"No," Marissa said. "Nothing."

"You look like you just woke up from a nightmare."

A million questions swarmed inside Marissa's head. Denise must know Tristan's lover. The coincidence was too strong for happenstance.

Maybe this was a mistake. Before she could decide, Denise opened the door and walked Marissa in.

After being out in the sun, the inside of Denise's home felt cool and looked shadowed.

A black-and-ivory area rug lay at the entryway. An archway to the left framed the living room, and to the right stood a den with a computer desk. Shelves held framed degrees and photographs of Denise with friends and an older couple, probably her parents.

"Make yourself at home. Coffee?"

"Please. That would be nice."

The curtains were drawn and the room shadowed. Denise pulled open the curtains to let the light in before disappearing around the corner.

Marissa sat on the living room couch. From the kitchen came sounds of cupboards opening and closing, then water percolating. Additional pictures of Denise and her parents were scattered throughout the living room on walls and on tables. A picture of a younger Denise hugging a big German Shepherd with a lolling tongue made Marissa smile.

But no pictures of kids or a husband.

It started to make sense, didn't it? Denise was beautiful, vibrant, and apparently single. The perfect woman for Tristan to have an affair with. Marissa didn't want to believe it—she already liked Denise a great deal —but this was thirteen Maplecrest Drive, the address from the love note.

"Cream or sugar?"

Marissa jumped. She hadn't seen Denise poke her head around the corner.

"What?"

"Do you want cream or sugar in your coffee?"

Marissa shook her head. Denise gave her a concerned look. "I'm happy to look at your bruise, but if you don't trust me, there's a good walk-in clinic just up the road."

"I trust you. It's not that bad. Is it?"

"It's not good." Denise stood considering and put her hands on her hips. "Okay then. If I can't convince you to see a doctor, I'll see what I can do."

"That's very kind of you."

The mug smelled wonderful.

Denise sat one chair over, shapely legs crossed with a sundress kissing her thighs. The sunbonnet removed and her hair pulled back by a sea-blue headband, Denise was stunningly beautiful.

"Do you like The Smiths?" Denise asked.

Denise slid the CD into her stereo.

"Well, I used to have a thing for Morrissey."

"Oh my God, yes!"

With that admission, the two women started giggling before Denise excused herself. She returned from the kitchen with an ice pack tucked under one arm. Marissa flinched when Denise prodded at the bruise.

"Sorry," said Denise. "Did somebody hit you?"

"No, he didn't."

"I see. Well, it's just a bruise, but it's going to hurt for a while. Hold this to your neck."

Marissa gingerly pressed the ice pack to her neck.

"Be careful. Try not to overexert yourself. You sure you don't want to see a doctor?"

"No, it feels better already."

They met eyes in the mirror. Denise stood behind Marissa, looking worried as she stared over Marissa's shoulder. If this was one of the women Tristan cheated with, Marissa didn't think she could bring herself to hate her, but that nagging feeling that Marissa was missing something important returned.

Denise threw a shrimp and brown rice meal

together, apologizing the entire time for not making a lunch fit for guests. The aroma alone was enough to make Marissa's mouth water. After eating, Marissa helped with the dishes.

"What's next? Are you visiting your professor friend?"

Confused, Marissa faltered momentarily. Too many lies to keep track of.

"Oh, no. We already visited. I was about to drive back to Massachusetts."

"And you just happened to stop by our not-so-famous neighborhood sale? What a strange stroke of luck that we should meet." Marissa nodded, seeing Denise's doubtful expression. "I apologize. Your reasons for visiting Burlington aren't my business. I'm just happy we met."

"Me, too."

Something changed in Denise's eyes. Loneliness? It was like seeing a campfire's final embers die off.

"If you don't mind me saying so, you look like you could use rest even more than you needed food in your stomach."

On Denise's insistence, Marissa napped in the upstairs guest room. She awoke with the last vestiges of day painted against the bedroom window. It was late. If she left now, it would be after ten o'clock before Marissa made it back to the Cape.

A gentle knock on the door brought Marissa's head up.

"Yes?"

"Can I come in?"

Denise pulled a chair over and sat bedside. Marissa could tell something had upset her.

"It's nothing," Denise said. "Just this creepy guy I made a mistake with keeps messaging me."

"What kind of mistake? You slept with him?"

Denise shrugged and looked out the window.

"Yes, I did, before I found out he's not such a nice guy after all. He showed up at my house two nights ago, acting really strange."

"Was he drunk or something?"

"No, nothing like that. He seemed confused, even dangerous. He wouldn't take no for an answer."

"You didn't let him inside, did you?"

"Of course not. After I shut the door in his face, I figured that was the last I'd hear from him. But now he keeps sending texts, and they're getting disturbing."

It was Marissa's turn to console. She made room on the bed. Denise, eyes red, sat next to Marissa with her knees drawn to her chest.

"Is he threatening you? If he is, you need to call the police," said Marissa.

"No, he didn't threaten me. But I worry he will come back. I don't want to see him again."

"This is a tight-knit neighborhood. Everyone was so happy to see each other today. You have to let your neighbors know you have a problem with this guy, that he might come around and cause trouble for you. Ask someone you trust to keep an eye on the house and check on you if a strange vehicle shows up in the driveway."

Denise grabbed a tissue off the nightstand and dabbed her eyes.

"It's so humiliating. First my failed marriage, and now the first guy I meet turns out to be some kind of stalker."

"Don't look at things that way. Your friends won't judge you. If this guy causes you any problems, promise me you'll call the police." Denise nodded resignedly. Marissa draped an arm around her shoulder. "And I want you to call or text me anytime, day or night. You don't have to do this alone."

Denise broke down and cried on Marissa's shoulder. When they'd first met, Denise seemed so strong and confident. Marissa knew everyone had a bogeyman hiding in the closet.

"I don't want you driving after dark," said Denise. "I'd like you to stay the night. Maybe a little longer if I can convince you."

Though she barely knew this woman, Marissa felt a warm comfort whenever Denise was near. The two might have been sisters in a second life, Marissa thought, perhaps long lost friends, and she wouldn't abandon a sister in need.

"I'm imposing. Really, you've done enough already."

"What if I said I wanted the company? Would you stay then?"

There was that despairing look Marissa had seen from Denise earlier.

Marissa agreed to stay.

The music from across the street stopped after sunset. The sales were over and the last of the visitors drove off. A hushed loneliness settled over the neighborhood.

They spoke over the quiet of the big Colonial, a quiet not unlike that of her home on the Cape, Marissa thought. Too many nights spent alone, worrying and wondering, never aware of Tristan's indiscretions. Seeing no harm in divulging a few truths, Marissa told Denise her husband was cheating on her, though she held back Tristan's name.

Smothered his name in a rotting trench was more like it. Had she divulged his name, *Tristan* would have rolled off her tongue like a fungus.

The conversation led to Denise's divorce.

"Ben and I married straight out of college," Denise said. "Really, I think we didn't love each other so much as we loved the idea of *us*. It was a mistake. My sister had seen as much and suggested we give it a few more years before tying the knot. But I was headstrong, stubborn."

"What happened?"

"It was as if we woke up one morning after three years of lying about love and realized neither of us was happy. The separation and divorce were amicable. I got the house in lieu of alimony, but I didn't want anything. Ben insisted. He's a good man, my ex. We still talk now-and-then. He's remarried and happy now, you know? I've met her. She's quite beautiful and perfect and altogether impossible to hate."

"Does he still live nearby?"

"Unfortunately, yes. Ben and Erin have a gorgeous old place in the country just outside of Burlington. That means I end up running into them where I least expect—the grocery store, the mall, the wineries. It always makes for an awkward situation."

Denise sipped at a glass of wine and glanced over at the wall of pictures. Marissa wondered anew about Denise's relation to the name on Tristan's note. *Jamie Bracket*. Did Tristan insist his lovers use fictional names so they couldn't be traced? No, that couldn't be. Marissa had watched Denise closely when she used Bracket's name. Denise hadn't reacted at all.

"What about you?" Marissa asked. "Aren't you happy?"

"I have good days and bad days. Sometimes I wonder if Ben and I should have tried harder, waited a little. Mostly I kick myself for not getting out of this house once in a while. Can't find Mr. Right when I never leave the neighborhood." Denise nervously tapped a nail on her lap. "Funny, me telling you my life story when we only just met."

"Are you uncomfortable with me staying the night? It's not too late to grab a hotel room."

"Don't be silly. I like you, Marissa. And if you

decide to go home tomorrow, I want you to keep in touch. Will you do that?"

"That would be nice."

***

Leaving the following morning was like saying goodbye to long-lost family. After exchanging phone numbers, Marissa gathered her belongings and said her farewells before she could convince herself to stay. A young couple, the man and woman who'd sold Denise the Smiths CD, waved as she drove past. She would miss Maplecrest Drive.

It was past due that she confront Tristan.

She turned onto the interstate and headed south.

She only made it to Concord.

CHAPTER TWENTY-ONE

Malice

The sun was a glare against the windshield, the cars on the highway a confusing assemblage of colors cutting her off and shooting by. Marissa was ten miles north of Concord when the phone rang.

Michael.

She swallowed hard and answered.

"Michael…I was just about to call you."

"Where are you, Marissa?"

"Returning home after visiting a friend in Burlington."

He was quiet for too long. She didn't like it.

"Are you stopped?"

"No, I'm on the highway."

"I think you should pull over before you hear me out."

Marissa's heart thundered as she took the next exit. Palms sweaty, she drove around the back of a McDonald's and pulled into a parking space. That moment would forever be ingrained in her memory—the greasy scents, a female teen employee rushing a bag of food out to a car two spaces away, poplar trees bending in the wind. An elderly woman in the next car kept looking over at her.

"I don't know how to tell you this. I found a vial

inside the filter."

A vial?

Marissa turned away from watchful eyes and leaned over the seat compartment.

"Marissa?"

"Yes. I'm here. Go on."

"The vial contained a liquid. Two tiny holes were made in the ends—I wouldn't have seen them without a magnifying glass. Whatever was inside was leaking into the filter."

She tried to answer. The words wouldn't come. Instead, she sat and listened while incongruously happy children crawled over playground equipment on the other side of the fence, and the world spun off its axis.

The phone was pressed to her head and digging a crevice into her ear. Michael kept talking. She didn't hear much of it.

"Are you still there?"

She nodded, only partially aware Michael couldn't see her.

"Just stay where you are. I'll come get you."

The idea of Michael driving up to Concord snapped her back to reality.

"That's not necessary," she said. "I'm fine, really."

"You sound like you shouldn't be driving if you don't mind me saying so."

"I can drive, Michael!"

She felt him flinch through the phone.

"Either way," he said. "I think the police should take a look at the vial."

"You don't know Tristan was the one who put the vial inside the filter."

Yet she did know, and from the silent pause on the other end, she could tell Michael knew, too.

"What would you like me to do?"

"Yes, call the police," Marissa said. "I'll be back in

two hours."

"You don't plan to go home first, do you?"

The parking lot filled with the lunch hour crowd. This wasn't the place for a private conversation.

"I'm getting back on the road right now. I'll call you as soon as I check on a few things."

"I can meet you at your house if—"

"No. I'll call you soon. I promise."

He was still talking when she ended the call. Behind her, a voice on the intercom droned as a customer argued over his order, and a horn honked as two vehicles vied for the last parking spot. It was all white noise to her.

Marissa hit the interstate and pressed hard on the accelerator. Her hands trembled on the steering wheel.

The hospital doctor's concerns over drug abuse began to make sense. So did six months of sickness.

The hair loss, fatigue, nausea, and clouded thoughts—Tristan had poisoned her, for Christ's sake. It occurred to her he drank water from the faucet upstairs and insisted she use bottled water for cooking. Clever. Her being bedridden must have been convenient for Tristan. He could come and go as he pleased, cheating on Marissa while she was too drugged to notice the signs.

The son-of-a-bitch.

She forced herself to lower her speed from 80 mph down to the highway limit.

Marissa didn't remember passing Medford. The trip was a dream sequence of ill-defined shapes deformed by a furious sun. It was a shock when Boston appeared in her windshield and she started passing familiar landmarks.

Her intuition kept assailing her that there was more to Tristan's affairs. It was right under her nose.

One man could offer insight into Tristan and why

he'd done this to her, but just thinking his name made the hairs on the back of her neck stand on end.

Keith Carrington.

Tristan's father was 74 now. Years of alcohol abuse had taken their toll, landing him in an assisted living center outside of Worcester.

He was still a monster.

Marissa couldn't bear the thought of seeing Keith again. She'd breathed a sigh of relief when Tristan demanded his father move to the center. No more frightening Christmases with Keith, no liquor bottles smashing through plaster.

Turning west on I-90, Marissa wondered aloud why she was putting herself through this. Keith had always despised her. He practically spat Marissa's name and thought she would make his son weak. Two decades of marriage failed to soften his stance.

Marissa pulled into the assisted living center parking lot at mid-afternoon. The autumn sun had started its slow descent in the western sky, while a group of seniors meandered outside on the promenade overlooking the Blackstone River as she stepped from the car. After a hasty examination of the crowd, she determined Keith wasn't part of the group. Not surprising. The bastard was never one for being around others.

Her thoughts turned to Tristan as she approached the double-door entryway.

We're all capable of many things, she thought, our hopes and fears precariously lined up like dominoes. Then someone comes along and sets into motion a chain reaction of events that change lives forever.

All fall down.

Inside, the splash of color from potted flowers and a corner fern did little to offset the all-encompassing whiteness. All that white strangely consumed more light than it reflected, as though the walls sucked the light inward.

The receptionist took her name and directed her to take the first left and proceed to the end of the hall. The stench of urine and disinfectant pervaded the air as sad, desperate eyes watched her from the rooms. She felt a pang of regret as she passed by and wondered how often patients received visitors.

Deeper down the hall, Marissa closed her ears to the incoherent babbling for her attention, though she felt their cries prickle the atmosphere with tension. The stench grew more fetid and, juxtaposed against the white, it somehow made the home feel dangerous.

Keith's room was the last at the end of the corridor. It was the size of a typical bedroom, the curtains drawn and blinds closed, making it seem like night inside. A small dresser with a television on top stood against the near wall. In the opposite corner was a single bed with antiseptic white sheets and a matching white blanket. Keith sat on the edge of the bed with his back to her. An assault of wiry gray hair spilled from the back of his head, his skin peppered with clumps of age spots where his hair had fallen out.

As she stood in the doorway, she realized he hadn't seen her yet. There was still time to turn and leave.

"Come to watch me die?"

Marissa's skin crawled. Keith sat looking at the closed curtains, staring at nothing. She stepped inside.

"Why are you here?"

His speech was choked with phlegm and slurred as if someone had sneaked Keith a supply of liquor. Joints crackled like little firecrackers as he pushed himself up from the mattress. With considerable effort, he shuffled to the other side of the bed, his socked feet making swishing noises.

Marissa gasped when he sat down. A crone's face glared back at her. Keith Carrington appeared twenty years older, a shell of the man she'd seen earlier this year.

"Sick, are you?" A grin curled his lips.

"I'm doing all right for myself," Marissa said.

"Chasing me to the grave is more like it. Couldn't happen to a better person. Where's my prick of a son?"

"Tristan is...away."

"Away." With that word, a knowing smile spread his mouth wide. His lips opened to a disheveled mess of yellowed teeth. "I'll bet you wonder where Tristan goes when he is *away*. Is that why came to see me?"

A groan twisted her head around. The door had drifted closed so that only a sliver of light knifed into Keith's room.

"I'm not sure I know what you mean."

"Ever since he was a child, Tristan loved to wander," he said. "Do you know, Marissa, that my son rode his bicycle from Worcester to Spencer when he was only seven? Said he wanted to see the airplanes again. I'd taken him there once, and somehow the little son-of-a-bitch remembered the way. One of the workers found him looking at the runway through the fencing. Tristan was lighting matches and tossing them onto the concrete. Guess he wanted to see if there were enough fumes to get a good fire going. Blistered his backside for that one, I did."

The blackest eyes she'd ever seen bore into her.

"Book smart," he said, nearly puking on the words. "Feeble-minded, otherwise. And always slipping away when no one is looking. Where do you think Tristan goes when he wanders?"

She forced herself to meet his glare.

"Stop beating around the bush, Keith. Just tell me what you know."

"Oh, there are many things I could tell you about bad, little Tristan. You must have some idea what he's up to, especially with all the time he's had on his hands with you being so…sick."

"I'm not sick anymore."

His grin grew again. The fetid stink of his breath reached her.

"Good. Terrible thing, being sick. Reminds me of Mrs. Carpenter, Tristan's tenth-grade geometry teacher. Pretty little thing. Such a shame she became so ill. Tristan, you see, barely earned an A in geometry even though he was an honors student and a genius at mathematics. He scored 100 on all his exams, but that bitch lost his homework assignment and gave him a zero. Not a wise move on her part. Tristan was quite upset over that, but I bet you know what his favorite class was. Chemistry."

His words hung in the air.

"What made his teacher sick, Keith?"

She already knew the answer. It felt as if she watched a fatal car wreck in slow motion.

He shrugged.

"No one ever determined the truth. But I do know one thing for certain. Mrs. Carpenter always brought bottled water to school, and every day after lunch she'd fall ill and vomit in the bathroom, or the hallway, or right on her desk. Why she left her lunch unguarded in the staff room is anyone's guess. You'd think a mathematics teacher would be intelligent enough to put two and two together."

"Are you saying Tristan poisoned his teacher?"

"You know exactly what I'm saying, Marissa. Don't play stupid."

Marissa fell back against the door, shutting it with a click. Gulping air like a fish out of water, she couldn't catch her breath.

Keith Carrington started to push himself off the bed.

"Don't come any closer, Keith."

"Now, now," he said. He grabbed hold of the mattress and struggled back to his feet. "A man's home is his castle, and you're a guest in my castle. Mind how you speak to me, you whore."

He stuck one unsteady foot out and started wobbling toward her. Gnarled claws for hands extended toward Marissa like the movie monsters who'd terrified her as a child.

"Tell me what Tristan did to me, Keith. Did he poison me like he did his teacher?"

"Why should I tell you? So you can ruin his life just like the others? Filthy whores, all of you."

Keith Carrington tottered halfway across the room. In the darkness of the closed room, he was a shadowed nightmare.

"He's a very bad boy, my Tristan, but he's too smart to get caught."

She grabbed hold of the doorknob.

"He'll pay for what he did to me," Marissa said.

He was almost to her now, close enough to rake his filthy nails across her face if he desired.

"The only one who will pay is you. Just like the others. You're no better than that whore, Alisha Morgan, who swore she loved him even while she was fucking his friends."

Marissa froze in place. The room turned darker, a fun house trick her mind played on her.

"What did you say her name was?"

"Who?"

"Alisha Morgan. How do I find her?"

Keith laughed.

"That might be rather difficult."

"Why would it be difficult? I need to speak—"

"Have you checked the cemetery in Westland?" He was frenzied now. Phlegm oozed over his lip as he yelled. "They all lied to him. Krista Steiner, Monica Leigh,

Jamie Bracket. And that bitch, Jess Martin. She was the troublemaker, the one who tore his heart out and then convinced Alisha to leave Tristan."

The names flew at her from all corners of the room. She was drowning in the darkness, drowning and grasping for a way out of this nightmare.

Jess Martin. Hadn't Tristan called her Jess?

"They all found out what happens to whores who cross Tristan Carrington. They paid the ultimate price. Burn in hell, they all can. You will pay the price, too, Marissa. You will pay the price for crossing my Tristan."

She burst from the room. The hallway light was blinding, confusing. She could hear him laughing behind the door.

Three nurses glared accusingly at her as they hurried toward Keith Carrington's room. Marissa stumbled into a male nurse who gripped her by the arms. As he tried to calm her down, she tore free and ran for the exit.

Keith's lunatic laughter followed her out the door.

CHAPTER TWENTY-TWO

Back to the Cape

The radio, the cars darting around her, were a boundless undertone like faraway waves crashing along the coast as Marissa drove back to the Cape.

Alisha Morgan, Krista Steiner, Monica Leigh, Jamie Bracket. What had Tristan done to them? How could they be tied to the addresses in the love letters if nobody in those neighborhoods had ever heard of the four women? And now a fifth name, Jess Martin, was added to the puzzle.

Marissa sensed clues existed somewhere in their house. On Tristan's computer?

As she slalomed through the early evening she dialed Michael's number. No answer.

Her skin prickled when she pulled into her neighborhood, and she'd have given anything to be back in Burlington with Denise. Here, the high-end real estate seemed cold and cruel, not inviting like Maplecrest Drive.

She waited at the top of the cul-de-sac. Nobody was out in their yards as night thickened and the temperature turned frigid. Between two perfectly-pruned hickory trees, she spied her house.

Dark windows. No sign of Tristan's car.

Shifting into drive, she coasted out of the shadow of an old oak.

Two over-sized vehicles—a 4x4 and an SUV—
were parked three houses down from hers. She slipped
her car in between them and checked the mirrors. The
cul-de-sac was quiet. Almost dead.

When she stepped from the car the wind howled
and tried to crush her legs between the door and frame.
She shoved the door open, slammed it behind her, and
engaged the locks. The twin beeps of the car alarm
seemed unusually loud.

She followed the curb, passing under the low
hanging branches of a maple tree. Looking over her
shoulder, she felt eyes watching, enough to make
goosebumps spread down her back. After she emerged
from the shadows, she rushed up the length of the
driveway and unlocked the door.

The house was dark and had a musty smell.
Passing through the kitchen, she saw the cabinet doors
hanging open below the sink.

She pulled open the basement door. The steps
descended into a deeper darkness.

"Tristan?"

A scratching noise came from the basement. It
might have been a tree branch brushing a window pane.
Or something else.

"Tristan, you home?"

Marissa shut the door and latched the hook-and-
eye, then hurried down the hallway and back to the
stairs. The upstairs seemed much too dark for nightfall.
The shades had been pulled, the curtains drawn.

Flicking on the lights, she crept up the staircase,
wincing when the stairs squeaked.

"Tristan, it's me. Are you up here?"

The silence of the upstairs turned heavy. A living
thing.

At the top of the landing, she made quick glances
into the bathroom and master bedroom. Above the final
flight of stairs stood the attic door.

The hallway was quiet. It should have set her mind at ease. The silence was all wrong, like the sound the night makes when a shadow passes by.

She fought down a shudder and turned toward Tristan's study.

It was too gloomy to see inside, so she turned on the overhead light. Shelving took up one wall. His finance books were stacked here, efficiently organized by subject and author. Framed diplomas and awards freckled a second wall.

He doesn't keep a picture of us, Marissa realized.

When she sat down at the desk and turned on the laptop, the computer awoke from sleep mode. A long time had passed since she'd last used his computer, making her surprised it wasn't locked with a password.

Searching through his file folders, she had no idea what she was looking for. Anything to link him back to the five women.

His expanding clientele took up one subdirectory. Names, addresses, bank accounts, ages, risk profiles. Looking made her feel seedy.

Opening his master client spreadsheet, she sorted by address. There were no matches for the residences in the love letters.

Marissa's heart stopped when she found a woman named Denise. False alarm. This Denise was a seventy-two-year-old client outside of Myrtle Beach.

The poisoned school teacher gnawed at her thoughts.

Tristan's high school yearbook.

Marissa closed out the spreadsheet and shut the laptop. The memory of Keith Carrington's insane screaming followed her through the dark hallway as she raced up the landing and opened the attic door.

A wasp angrily buzzed along the joists as she climbed the steps. Her old wedding dress slithered in the wind.

Boxes were stacked upon boxes. Too many to search. Tristan's dogged insistence on organization was a blessing this time, as most of the boxes were labeled in black marker. Eliminating containers of clothing and old photos, she whittled the search down to a dozen boxes.

Throwing open the first container, she found his college textbooks and a stack of worn notebooks. The next box held her own high school yearbooks and photographs of friends she hadn't seen in more than two decades.

She shouted upon finding Tristan's high school yearbook in the next box. Westland High School. Class of 1990.

Certain she'd find pictures of the five girls, Marissa thumbed through the pages.

A door slammed. The floor shook.

Tristan.

Marissa eyed the open attic door, knowing she was cut off. If Tristan started up the staircase, he'd see.

"Marissa."

She shrank back into the shadows. The yearbook was closed at her feet, one page dog-eared where she'd last searched. She tucked it back into the box and listened.

He wasn't moving, just standing in the entryway.

She crept to the top of the attic stairs. The planks were gritty under her sneakers.

"Marissa!"

She flinched.

A part of her wanted to scream back at him, confront him. She didn't. His fury terrified her, made her wish she'd never come home.

When he stomped toward the kitchen, she exhaled and crept down the staircase. It was quiet again. Tristan knew she was home.

Approaching the attic door, she expected him to

leap out at her.

He threw shut the cabinet doors below the sink. The blasts echoed like gunshots.

Knowing where Tristan was now, Marissa edged around the corner and peered down the stairs, her heart a jackhammer shattering her courage. It was too far to the doorway. Too many steps. He'd catch her before she made it to the door.

Then what?

Yes, Marissa. Then what? Do you truly believe Tristan would hurt you?

The Tristan she thought she'd married would never hurt her.

But the man downstairs was someone entirely different. Dark. Cold.

One hand gripped to the banister, she took the first step down the staircase. Still quiet. No Tristan.

She took another step. Then one more.

Marissa paused halfway to the landing. Her shadow preceded her down the staircase, stretched long by the upstairs light. Another step and Tristan would see her shadow from the hallway.

As the wind moaned through the eaves, she heard him climbing the stairs.

A moment of frozen indecision cost her. She was caught between fleeing upstairs or making a dash for the front door. As if he sensed her, he quickened his pace.

Tristan was almost to the kitchen when she ran down the steps and sprinted for the door. He heard her as she ripped the door open.

"Don't you leave me, you bitch! You do as I say, Jess!"

Jess. That name again.

His voice was a razor against the back of her neck as she burst off the porch. He was coming for her now. Her legs pumped and carried her ahead of him. She felt the old Marissa awakening from hibernation, muscles taut and fueled by terror.

She could see his shadow stumbling through the doorway as she climbed into the car. Shifting into drive, she had a momentary sensation that it wasn't Tristan's shadow but Keith Carrington's. A walking cadaver.

Tires squealed. She accelerated out of the cul-de-sac, narrowly missing an oncoming car.

She felt Tristan's eyes burn into her back as she turned out of the neighborhood.

CHAPTER TWENTY-THREE

The Blue Dragon '

Marissa was furious as she raced down the interstate. She was nearly hoarse from arguing with the police officer who'd said he'd pay Tristan a visit but couldn't arrest him. Tristan had done nothing wrong, hadn't struck her, and there was no mention of the poison vial.

Marissa knew she could never go home again. Tristan was dangerous, unhinged.

Knowing he'd poisoned a teacher over poor grades and drugged Marissa for half-a-year, she didn't want to think what he'd done to the five girls who'd somehow wronged him. Kicking herself for leaving Tristan's yearbook in the attic, she pressed the accelerator and raced for his hometown.

The Westland Public Library locked its doors moments before Marissa drove into the parking lot. She'd hoped to dig through newspaper archives for mention of Tristan's former lovers. The library wouldn't open until tomorrow at eight.

She couldn't wait that long. The fear that she was out of time scuttled around on insect legs inside her head.

Westland, Massachusetts, a tiny village on the outskirts of Worcester, appeared asleep for the night.

Though she couldn't say why, Marissa sensed tragedy as she turned out of the lot and headed uptown. The commercial district, what little there was of it, appeared commonplace. Convenience stores, fast food restaurants, taverns, a boarded-up movie theater, and a post office lined Main Street. The strip continued for another mile before stabbing into faraway darkness.

Her phone rang. Seeing it was Michael's home number, Marissa grabbed the phone and answered.

"Marissa, it's Jennifer…Jennifer Tompkins."

"Yes, Jennifer. I'm glad you got hold of me. I'd been meaning to return your father's call."

"That's what I wanted to talk to you about. My Dad was supposed to pick me up from soccer at six but he never came. It's okay because Julie's mom drove me home."

"Are you alone, honey?"

"Yes."

A street lamp flickered overhead and went out.

"I'm worried," Jennifer said. "Dad texted me from the hardware store after school and said he'd be back in time to pick me up. It's not like him to forget."

Marissa felt as if a dead hand touched the back of her neck.

"He didn't say anything about stopping by my house, did he?"

"No," Jennifer said. "Did something happen to my Dad? Maybe I should call the police."

"Are you positive he wasn't called away to another job?"

"He gets emergency calls all the time, but he always lets me know. Something is wrong, Marissa. I can feel it." Jennifer's voice broke. "What should I do?"

"Stay calm. It's probably nothing."

"It doesn't feel right."

Marissa brought the car to a halt at the street's only

stoplight as a 4x4 pulled up behind her. The lights ignited her mirrors and left a red imprint on her eyes. She turned down the mirror and tried unsuccessfully to ignore the hulking vehicle bearing down on her.

"Jennifer, do you have time to run out back to your Dad's shop?"

"Sure. Why?"

"There should be a broken water filter on his desk. Tell me what you see."

"What's all of this about?"

"Please, just do as I say."

Marissa's heart hammered as she listened to Jennifer run through the house. She heard the back door open and click shut, then the sound of shoes swishing through grass.

Outside the car, two couples walked hurriedly down Main Street. Huddled inside their coats from the autumn chill, they lowered their heads against the wind and disappeared into a bar.

Marissa heard the door to Michael's shop slam shut.

The sound of glass smashing.

Then nothing.

"Jennifer?"

The traffic light swung in the wind like a hanging man.

"Oh, God. What happened? Talk to me."

"I'm here," Jennifer said. Marissa fell back against the seat, relieved. "I broke one of his projects."

"Do you see the filter?"

The light turned green. Marissa moved through the intersection with the 4x4 right on her bumper, listening as Jennifer searched Michael's shop. Keys jangled. A drawer slid open and closed shut.

The truck swerved around her and tore down the road, coughing black fog from the exhaust pipe.

Marissa turned into a parking spot in front of a darkened mobile phone repair shop. The Blue Dragon bar sat kitty-corner to her.

She began to worry. She hadn't heard Jennifer in a while.

"The filter isn't here," Jennifer finally said.

Of course, it isn't. Smart bad boys never get caught.

"I don't understand any of this, Marissa. Why do you need me to find a broken water filter? Wouldn't Dad just throw it away?"

"Jennifer, go across the street to the Benoit's house."

"Why?"

"Just do it, please."

"You're scaring me."

"Tell Mr. Benoit to call the police and say your Dad never picked you up."

"Did someone hurt my dad?"

"Do as I say. And when you hear back from your dad, have him call me immediately."

But Jennifer wouldn't hear from Michael. Never again. Tristan had covered his tracks well.

"Okay, Jennifer?"

Jennifer hitched and sobbed as she rushed across the street. Marissa didn't breathe until she heard a doorbell ring. Then Mr. Benoit let her inside.

"I'm safe now."

"It's going to be okay," Marissa said.

"Promise me nothing bad happened to Dad."

"I promise."

It was a lie.

When Jennifer was off the phone Marissa bundled her coat and stepped into the night air. The wind shoved her with cruel intentions. A paper bag crawled down the sidewalk.

This morning she'd left Burlington convinced Tristan was unfaithful. In the hours that followed she'd learned he was poisoning her, exactly as he'd done to a former teacher. He'd somehow hurt five girls from his past—four of their names on his love letters, a fifth name, Jess Martin, one Marissa had never heard before—but was he capable of murder?

Inside The Blue Dragon, the lights would be bright and there would be safety in numbers. Jingling the keys, she decided. The smell of beer was strong and the music loud when she stepped into the bar. A jukebox pumped out Black Sabbath's "Paranoid." The bass thumped through her legs, and under the alcohol stench drifted the scent of grilled pizza, savory enough to make Marissa's mouth water.

A sign on the bar announced restrooms were for paying customers only. Behind the counter, a dark-haired man with a Ramones tattoo on one muscular forearm dried a glass, then filled a second with beer and slid it deftly down the polished surface to a man at the end of the bar. A scattering of lonely drinkers sat upon stools. The most action appeared to be taking place at the back of the tavern, where a small dance floor was cluttered by tables and a glut of patrons bobbed to the music.

The couples she'd watched enter the bar were in the back, pulling off their coats and choosing seats across from each other. Marissa took an open seat at the bar, leaving considerable room between her and the drunk man ogling her from a few seats away.

The bartender noticed her and came over. Up close she discerned the first spots of gray dotting his sideburns.

"What can I get ya?"

"A root beer," Marissa said. She saw him grin and added, "I've got a long drive ahead of me tomorrow."

"Fair enough. How about something to eat?"

Several eyes inside the bar watched her. She was

a foreigner in this small world.

A leggy waitress passed behind, carrying a pizza.

"I could go for one of those pizzas," Marissa said to the bartender.

"Coming right up."

He shouted to another waitress, who jotted down the order and disappeared through a pair of swinging doors at the back of the room. Greasy food scents blew out at her.

The waiter plopped a foaming mug of root beer on the bar.

"Thanks," she said. "I guess you can tell I like to party hard."

He laughed and placed a bowl of salty snacks in front of her. Famished as she was, Marissa stuffed a handful in her mouth. The drunk guy was looking at her again, staring as if he knew her. He wore a dusty jean jacket and a baseball cap turned backward.

"Pay attention to your beer, Jimmy," the waiter said. "Leave the nice lady alone." Jimmy turned back to his drink. She could see him casting sidelong glances as she talked with the barman. "Sorry about that. Jimmy's about reached his limit for the night. If he bothers you again I'll see that he leaves."

There was a longing in Jimmy's eyes. Not sexual but rooted in a desperate need to speak with her. He wasn't an ugly man, she thought. Around the same age as her. His cheeks and nose were peppered red, the result of decades of alcohol abuse.

"Don't worry about it," said Marissa. "I don't think he means any harm."

The waiter nodded but shot another warning glance in Jimmy's direction.

A few minutes later, the waitress slid the pizza in front of her. The dough was thin and perfectly browned, the aromas wonderful.

When she was halfway through the second slice, she saw Jimmy leaning over his drink. Had his hands not supported his face, she thought his head might break off and tumble over the bar. If her intuition was correct, his beer was dinner.

Marissa tore off a slice and slid it to him on a napkin.

"You hungry?"

Jimmy looked down at the pizza.

"I might be a drunk, but I'm not a beggar. Keep it."

His face was back in his hands, fingers massaging his forehead.

"Suit yourself. More for me then." She pulled the napkin back. "Nice to meet you. I'm Marissa, by the way."

"Jimmy Rodgers."

"Sure you don't want that pizza?"

He grunted to himself and went back to studying his beer, as though an answer to a pressing question floated within the golden liquid.

"Why don't you slide over and tell me a little about this town?" Marissa asked. "I've never visited Westland."

He shifted his eyes in her direction.

"Never visited? You sure look like you've been here before."

"I haven't."

"Then I must be drunker than I thought."

Before he turned away she saw his eyes glisten. To her, Jimmy didn't look like a hapless drunk. He looked haunted, perhaps even frightened.

From the back of the room, she noticed a heavy-thighed waitress glaring at her. The waitress leaned over and whispered into the ear of a man wearing a Carhartt vest. He vigorously shook his head as if in disagreement. The waitress insisted he look again and pointed at Marissa.

Counting Jimmy, three patrons were watching

Marissa now. Marissa focused on her food, hurrying so she could get out of The Blue Dragon. Coming here was a bad idea.

"You don't have any idea why they're looking at you," Jimmy said. "Do you?"

Marissa jumped. Jimmy had slid into the next seat without her noticing. The barman saw and hurried over.

"It's okay," Marissa said, waving the barman off.

The barman nodded and gave her a meaningful look. If Jimmy made her uncomfortable, he'd step in.

"I noticed you staring at me," Marissa said to Jimmy.

"You're related to her somehow. A cousin, maybe. You'd have to be or I'm hallucinating. I'm drunk, but I'm not *that* drunk."

"Related to who?"

"You're really not from Westland?"

"No. I told you that."

"Your family is then."

"Not that I'm aware of."

Hidden beneath the pounding music, a murmur spread like a wave through the tavern.

"I think I want to leave."

"No worries. I'll walk you out."

"That's not necessary."

Before she could protest, he straightened his back and threw a twenty dollar bill down on the bar. Placing his glass on top of the twenty, he waved to the barman and put a hand on her shoulder. She shrugged his hand off and he glared at her, a stare which said *you won't get out of here without me*.

They were all looking at her now as she pushed through the crowd, closing in like a mob desperate to get a look at a sideshow freak. Jimmy led her toward the door, his legs shaky and gait erratic.

"What the hell was that about?" Marissa asked,

pushing open the exit door.

Jimmy tottered and caught his balance.

"Like I told you, you look just like her."

"Like who?"

"Jess. You look just like Jess."

CHAPTER TWENTY-FOUR

Fire

So cold.

The snap of a finger brought Michael Tompkins awake. His head felt crushed inside a vise, everything blurry. He could tell by the crisp chill to the air and the scent of ryegrass that he was outside, somewhere in the countryside.

A slap rang his eardrums. He winced and shook his head. A strand of bloody drool connected his lip to the cold earth.

Michael was propped up in a sitting position, feet bound by a zip tie and wrists locked behind his back. Wiggling made the sharp plastic bite into his flesh.

A second slap clipped him under the chin and bent his head backward. Spittle flew across his forehead.

"Wake up, sleepy head."

That voice. It was familiar to him, but his head was too muddled to make a connection.

Michael blinked until the scene slowly revealed itself, initially in vague shapes and shades of darkness. He was in a field on a hill. Looking around, he didn't see a nearby residence. Far below lay a town where lights winked on-and-off like a Christmas tree.

The man was behind him. Michael tried to twist his head around but couldn't move.

"You've been a bad boy, Michael. Should have stayed out of my affairs."

"Who is that? My girl," said Michael. "I want to see my girl."

"Your girl can't protect you from me, Michael. You always had eyes for Marissa. Don't think I didn't notice. I see all."

Tristan.

Michael's breaths quickened, his head swimming.

"Tristan…why the hell are you doing this?"

Maybe this was a dream. He tugged at the zip ties and tried to push himself up from the ground. The stinging pain in his wrists felt too real to be a dream.

Tristan kicked him in the back and drove the wind from his lungs. Michael's neck was folded over, his head between his knees as the cold dug at him. High above the unknown town, the wind was unrelenting, sending the tall grass into a frenzy.

"I took back my water filter. You really shouldn't have opened it. Trying to play the hero and win her affection?"

"Win who's affection?"

Stay calm. He's not going to kill me.

There was a way out of this. He only needed to keep his wits until he figured it out.

"Do you know how long I waited to have her for myself? Away from Jimmy, away from all of them."

Jimmy? Who was Jimmy?

Michael thought back to the strange encounter outside of The Golden Caribou. He'd called Marissa by a name Michael didn't recognize that night. The possibility that Tristan was losing touch with reality drove a cold lance into Michael's chest and got him tugging at the zip ties again.

Michael heard dead grass crunch as Tristan circled around from behind. He stood before Michael now, a dark statue puffing out frozen clouds of disdain as the night grew colder.

"Please," Michael said. "Whatever you believe, you're wrong."

"You tried to take her from me. Came into my house—twice in the last year alone, wasn't it? Once for the upstairs window, and then to stick your pig nose under my kitchen sink. You told her I wasn't good enough for her, tried to convince her to leave me."

"No, never."

"Liar."

Tristan stomped Michael's head and crushed his nose. Blood sprayed under Tristan's heel.

"Lying to me will only prolong the pain. Tell me the truth, Michael. Did you tell the police about your little discovery?" Tristan dropped down to one knee and ripped Michael's head up by the hair. "Look at me, you insolent little dog. Did you talk to the police? If you lie to me, I will know."

"No."

"I don't believe you."

"I swear…I swear I didn't tell anyone about the water filter."

Ashamed to hear himself grovel, Michael turned away. Tristan snatched him by the hair and turned his head up to where Tristan's face was an inch from Michael's, eyes burning and interrogating.

"She wasn't like the other girls. Nothing like Alisha."

Another name which meant nothing to Michael.

One thing was certain in Michael's mind. He was going to die. Die at the hands of a lunatic. He would never see his daughter again.

"You have no concept of what you discovered. You think you know, but you are not capable of understanding."

"I don't want to know."

"Oh, but you do. Tell me. In your expert opinion as a master tradesman, what was in the vial, Michael?"

"I don't know what it was."

"But you have an idea. Tell me honestly. I promise not to laugh."

Michael shook his head.

"Some type of drug…a poison."

Tristan sneered.

"You make it difficult for me to fulfill my promise. Do you know about chemistry, Michael? I would suppose not. They don't teach such things to future home repairmen. Attend, and I will do my best to explain. You see, Jess always loved me."

Jess. That was the name Tristan used outside The Golden Caribou.

"She didn't believe herself worthy of me, which is why she settled for Jimmy. I noticed how she looked at me, perceiving what I would become, the greatness I would achieve. I see all, Michael. Yet she didn't understand what it is to be a god and have power over life and death."

"I don't know what you're talking about."

"Because you aren't paying attention. Listen. The time would come for me to reveal who I truly am to Jess, but she turned on me. They tried to hurt me, Michael. Did you know that?"

When he spoke, Tristan's coat rippled in the wind like the wings of a great predator.

"Do you believe in life after death, Michael?"

"I don't know."

"You don't know? It's a simple question."

"I believe in God," said Michael.

"Does he believe in you?"

Tristan was gone again. Somewhere behind him. The pop of a car trunk opening.

This was Michael's opportunity. He leaned back so his fingers brushed the frozen ground, feeling the cruel, frosty grass and a clump of mud and stone. And something sharp.

A broken stick. Small, but maybe enough to free him from the zip ties. He snatched it with his forefingers and wrenched his wrists backward until the stick sawed at the tie.

It snapped in his fingers and was lost to the dead strands of grass. He desperately felt around for the stick but couldn't find it.

The trunk door slammed shut. He could hear Tristan coming again, the swish of shoes through the field as the wind wormed into Michael's ears.

"You never answered my question," Tristan said.

"I told you I believe in God."

"I specifically asked you about life after death."

"Heaven? Yes, I believe in heaven." *Keep him talking. He won't hurt you if he's talking.* "What about you, Tristan? Do you believe in Heaven?"

"I don't have to *believe* in anything. I'm a scientist. *I shall multiply my days like the Phoenix.* Do you know from where that quote originates, Michael?"

"The Phoenix…it's a bird, right? A mythological creature."

"Mythological? I don't think so. That quote comes from the Hebrew Bible. Perhaps the creature itself is mythological, much the way the bible employs legends and stories which are meant to educate rather than be literally interpreted. Like Jonah and the whale. Jonah was not swallowed by a whale. Only a fool believes such drivel. The lesson is that we cannot escape fate…or God's plan, if you prefer to interpret it so. Shakespeare and Dante refer to the Phoenix. Similar beliefs are held by the Arabians, Hindus, Slavs, and Japanese. The Chinese call the Phoenix the Fenghuang. Call it myth if you will, but the process of being reborn, reincarnation…

those are very real things, but not all people are worthy of reincarnation."

Reasoning with Tristan was folly. Michael knelt before a madman.

"You kneel on hallowed ground. A magnificent fire once burned here, an inferno which could be seen across the world." Tristan swept his hand over the town. "We are reborn in fire. Like the great Phoenix, the worthy rise again and realize their potential."

"You're out of your mind."

"Jess believed I meant to hurt her, but like you, she did not understand. I helped her to understand, just as I will do for you very shortly. Jess rose from the ashes like the Phoenix. It was up to me to find her, to discover her new form, which I quickly did."

Tristan gazed into the sky as though considering.

"Jess was reborn, yet she didn't recall who she was. I knew in time she would come to understand, but I couldn't risk her wandering off before she realized we were destined to be together. Though it may seem a cruel thing to do, I forced her to rest until she remembered. You call it poison, but you don't understand. Realize the process of re-creation and reincarnation is eternal and ongoing. We don't reemerge without flaw. Sometimes when we are reborn, our imperfections are too extreme to overcome. I've come to understand Jess isn't destined to meet her potential in her present form as Marissa. She is too weak, too prone to wander. And so the process must begin anew. In fire, we shall be reborn. The wheel always turning. As for the other girls…they were not worthy for reincarnation, yet somehow they returned the way maggots emerge from carrion. I found them, just as I discovered Jess, and rectified the issue. I wonder, Michael. Are you worthy of rising again?"

Tristan reached into his coat pocket. Michael tore at his bindings, thinking the next thing he'd see was a knife in Tristan's hand. Instead, the man pulled a phone from his pocket. He typed a password which Michael couldn't see and opened a folder of photographs.

Tristan shoved the phone in front of Michael's face.

Michael saw. He wished he couldn't.

"Monica Leigh," said Tristan. "I found her in Syracuse, New York."

The woman's hands were tied above her head and hanging off a bedpost, her neck split open by a jagged slice, the sheets sprayed with blood. The woman Tristan called Monica Leigh stared into the camera, stared straight at Michael, with dead, open eyes. A doll's eyes.

"She did not deserve to be reborn, so she is dead forever, the cycle ended."

He swept a finger across the screen.

"Krista Steiner. She hid from me in Binghamton, not far from Syracuse and Monica Leigh. It's interesting how they gravitated toward each other in different lives. Do you think they knew each other, Michael, as they did in Westland?"

Michael couldn't answer. The woman lay on a bed soaked in blood, a single red rose laid upon her chest. Crimson gorges where a knife had pried and scraped the eyes from their sockets peered lifelessly at the ceiling.

Next photo.

"Alisha Morgan. Medford, Massachusetts."

The photograph was dark, but Michael could see it was taken in a forest. As with the woman Tristan called Krista Steiner, this new woman bled out from a gash across her throat. She lay splayed beneath a tree, her stomach punctured by dozens of stab wounds. Blood soaked her shirt. Beneath the cloth, the woman's breasts were visible.

"Do you know what they did to me, Michael?"

Tristan's face changed, parrying with rage.

"Please, Tristan. I don't want to see anymore."

Another photograph. A beautiful woman with blonde curls.

"Jamie Bracket. She is very beautiful, don't you think?"

"Please."

Next photograph. Marissa.

"And my beautiful Jess."

Tristan lingered on the photograph for a long time before he shut down the phone and stuffed it inside his coat.

"Let me go…let me go, and I won't tell anyone what you showed me. You can trust me, Tristan. Did I tell the police about the water filter? No, I didn't, and I won't tell the police about the girls. Please, just let me go home to my daughter."

"Maybe you will see Beth-Anne as well as your daughter in your next life. That is not for me to decide, for I can only send you through the portal. You will reemerge if you are worthy. Like the myth of Jonah teaches us, we cannot escape our fate."

The night turned a shade darker. Tristan rounded Michael and disappeared into the night. For a long time, Michael couldn't see or hear him. The plastic chewed into his wrists as he struggled to free himself. Warm blood trickled off his fingertips.

Then Michael heard Tristan coming again, thundering through the grass and weeds like a mythological god seeking vengeance.

Michael smelled the gasoline before he heard it sloshing around in its container. Tristan threw it on the ground. A drop splashed Michael's face.

"I apologize if gasoline seems crude. The ends justify the means. It is time to discover if you are worthy, Michael Tompkins."

Tristan lifted the container. Michael screamed as fuel soaked his clothes.

He ripped harder against the ties, deepening the wounds. Gasoline dribbled hot agony into the gashes.

"Please don't do this…please, Tristan."

"You are not worthy in your present form and must be reborn."

"I don't want to be reborn."

Tristan emptied the fuel container over Michael's head, burning his eyes and choking him.

As Michael screamed, Tristan turned to survey the town from the hilltop. His eyes were closed, and when he breathed in the fuel scents he smiled as though a savory meal lay upwind.

A match flared.

Michael flailed violently against the ties and fell forward into the grass, his nose and mouth buried in a pool of gasoline. He gagged and choked. He inhaled. Fuel rushed into his mouth and down his throat.

Something dropped onto his back. The lit match was a stinging wasp. A whoosh ripped across his back. Agony spread across his body, caught the pool, and ignited his face. At once, his flesh blistered and popped mountains of bloody pus.

Tristan smiled down at Michael, then looked out over the lights of Westland.

"I've come back for you, Jess."

CHAPTER TWENTY-FIVE

Westland

"Where are we going?" Jimmy asked. He turned in a circle as if lost.

A crowd had gathered in The Blue Dragon doorway. The heavyset waitress was staring at Marissa.

"*We* aren't going anywhere," Marissa said, unlocking the car.

"I thought you wanted to hear about Jess."

Before she could argue, he slipped into the passenger seat.

The beer on his breath smelled overwhelming inside the car. Marissa pulled out and drove until Main Street was several blocks behind her.

Jimmy's head seemed too heavy, wobbling with each acceleration and turn. He stared glassy-eyed through the windshield. Every so often Marissa caught him glancing at her, scrutinizing her as the people inside the Blue Dragon had.

When she found a 24-hour gas station, Marissa steered in and let the car idle.

"This is ridiculous," she said. "Why do you keep staring at me?"

"Sorry. I don't mean to. It's just that you look like Jess."

A police car blazed past with flashing lights. She

heard a dog barking from a nearby neighborhood. The dog could have been on the other side of the world, she was so lost in thought.

"Jess Martin—does she still live in Westland? There's something I need to talk to her about."

"What is this? Some kind of sick joke? Ain't anything funny about it." He was suddenly angry. "Maybe you ought to let me out right here."

"It's not a joke. Just tell me how to get a hold of Jess—"

Jimmy shot her a furious glare.

"You show up out of nowhere looking just like Jess and claim you want to speak to her. What a laugh."

"If I said something wrong, I'm sorry—"

"Said something wrong? Oh, that's the understatement of the century. How anybody can make a practical joke over what happened is beyond me. I guess some people find humor in the sickest shit."

"You think I'm lying, Jimmy, but I'm not. I know something happened to five girls in Westland and Jess was involved."

He gazed up at the starless sky.

"Tell me what happened," she said. "Please."

She took one of his hands in hers. Jimmy appeared too pained to look Marissa in the face.

"Whatever you heard, it wasn't Jess's fault," he said. "Maybe it was the other girls' faults, or maybe it was mine." It took him several deep breaths to regain control of his voice. "Jess and I had gone together since sophomore year." He shook his head. "We used to go up to the old abandoned farm on Holly Hill and drink inside the barn. All of us did—our whole crew. Sometimes we'd smoke a little pot, ya know? All of us did—Monica, Alisha, Krista, and Jamie."

The four names on Tristan's love letters. Marissa felt her pulse quicken. Her grip tightened on his hand.

She was only aware when he grimaced.

"I'd known Jamie since the first grade. My buddy used to go with her, so we did a lot of double dating. Me and Jess, Tristan and Jamie."

Marissa felt faint.

Now it was Jimmy looking concerned.

"I'm okay," she said.

"You feel all right? You aren't sick, are you?"

"No. Not anymore."

He gave her a confused look.

Black shadows crawled off the trees and doused portions of the sidewalk in darkness.

"Tristan loved Jamie," Jimmy said. "But he *really* loved Jess even though she was with me. Talked about her so much that he was obsessed. Jess and Tristan went together for two years before they grew apart, you know? Nothing unusual about that. They were just kids. But it was Jess who wanted to move on. Tristan never got over her. When he and Jamie started dating, I started to worry."

"How so?"

"Talk about a desperate rebound. Tristan was ready to marry Jamie. Not even out of high school, and he already wanted to put a ring on her finger. But Jamie was playing with Tristan. I knew it. Jess knew it, too. Friday nights we'd go up to Holly Hill to party and make out, and Jamie would be all over Tristan, going far enough that Jess and I were embarrassed sometimes. It was one thing to fool around in front of each other, but Jamie acted like they were alone in a hotel room. I'd look over, and she'd be nude from the waist up and unzipping his jeans. It got so heated a few times that Jess and I went outside in the cold and waited until they finished."

The wind crawled up the windshield and over the roof. It wanted to come inside.

"After Jamie got what she wanted out of Tristan,

she'd go cold on him and take off. Wouldn't even let him drive her home. That's because Jamie wasn't going home. She had a college guy on the other side of town, a rich, snobby type from one of those schools like Tufts or Amherst, I forget. Tristan found out about a month before prom. He turned real dark. Wouldn't even talk to me about Jamie. Tristan was always a little scary to be around, but after the breakup, I didn't want to go near him."

"How was he scary?" Marissa asked.

"He blew up over the littlest things, and he always had a look in his eye like he knew more than you and could hurt you if he wanted. I can't blame him for the way he was, to be honest. His father was the nastiest son-of-a-bitch you ever wanted to know. He beat the hell out of his boy until Tristan got too big to slap around."

Marissa shifted uncomfortably in her seat. The heater didn't halt the chill working through her bones.

"What about Jess? Did she have something to do with Tristan and Jamie breaking up?"

Jimmy's eyes glazed over again. He looked down at his hands until he was composed enough to talk.

"Boy, for someone who didn't know Jess, you sure know a lot about the rumors."

"What rumors?"

"All lies, pure bullshit. Jess knew the college guy Jamie was hooking up with. A friend of the family, I guess. Jess still cared about Tristan, but she didn't trust him to be around Jamie because of how angry he got when things didn't go right for him. One day we drove out to Sturbridge, and this asshole in a Jeep cut us off and nearly drove Tristan right into the ditch. So Tristan followed the guy, and I kept thinking Tristan just wanted to scare him, that he wouldn't actually hurt anyone. At the next stoplight, Tristan jumped out of the car before I could stop him and dragged the guy out of his Jeep. Tristan just about killed him. He would have, I think, if I hadn't dragged him off. The guy could have wrecked us, but he didn't deserve to get beaten so badly. His face was a mess. Tristan's clothes were covered with blood. I still get the creeps thinking about it. You never knew what you were gonna get with Tristan. That's why none of us trusted him. But Jess didn't make Jamie break up with Tristan, even though Tristan was convinced it was her fault. No, Jess thought Jamie was good for Tristan. The real troublemakers were Alisha, Monica, and Krista."

"How so?"

Another car pulled into the abandoned lot across the street. A boarded up coffee shop stood behind the car. Marissa twisted around in her seat.

High beams flared into the car, the mirrors burning as though a thousand suns set behind her. The car lights were too bright to make out the vehicle.

Jimmy was antsy. He kept fiddling with one of the buttons on his jacket and looking over his shoulder.

"What the hell is he doing?" Marissa asked. "Do you know who that is?"

The twin beams stayed fixed on them. It had been almost a minute now.

A motor roared from across the street. Jimmy opened the door and stepped outside.

"Jimmy, get back in the car."

But Jimmy was too scared to hear. In her mind she pictured the mysterious vehicle crashing out of the darkness, the brights turning Jimmy into a ghost before the grille cut him in half.

"Jimmy, let's go!"

He jolted and climbed back inside.

"It couldn't be him," he said.

"Who's back there?"

"Nobody...nobody. Just drive."

She angled across the gas station lot and turned left. The other car wasn't moving, just sitting there with its beams locked on where they'd parked. As Marissa turned down another side street, the offending headlights went out. She could see the car creeping out of the lot with its lights dimmed.

"You sure you don't know who that was?" she asked. "Tell me the truth."

"Just someone screwing with me, probably the same as you are."

His face pale, Jimmy kept sneaking glances at the mirrors.

Marissa took three more turns down sleepy residential streets, not knowing where she was until she noticed the public library up the road. They weren't far from downtown. Several glances at the empty stretch of road behind her showed no sign of the car.

Turning on the radio, Marissa scanned through stations until she found an all-news radio station. She didn't care what was on the radio as long as the clamor provided a distraction.

As she passed a row of churches, her phone rang. Denise Moretti's number.

"Sorry, Jimmy. I need to take this."

Jimmy didn't appear to hear. He was too busy looking over his shoulder.

Denise was crying when Marissa answered.

"Calm down. Tell me what happened."

"That guy won't stop calling, and now he just told me he is gonna come here tonight."

"You need to call the police," Marissa said.

"It won't make a difference. He hasn't done anything illegal, he just won't leave me alone."

"Is he stalking you, Denise? Think about it. Has anyone been hanging around your work or the neighborhood, someone your co-workers or neighbors didn't recognize? Be honest with me."

The other end of the phone was quiet. Marissa

could tell Denise was thinking hard about it.

"Maybe," said Denise.

"Maybe?"

"There was this guy at the children's hospital two nights ago. I saw him once in a restricted corridor and then in the parking garage."

"Who was he?"

"He was too far away for me to tell."

"But you think he was following you."

"No…well, yeah. I mean he never came after me or anything. He just kept showing up wherever I was."

"Denise, isn't it possible the same man who keeps bothering you followed you home from the hospital?"

Denise started crying again. Her voice was frightened and jittery. Marissa couldn't understand anything Denise said until the hitching lessened.

"Listen," Marissa said. "I'm just outside of Worcester. I can be on the road in less than an hour. You're not going through this alone."

"Don't come all the way up here. It's too far."

Marissa sighed. Even if she left now, she wouldn't make it to Burlington until the wee hours of the night.

"I want you to call the police and stay with a neighbor or friend tonight. I'll come to you first thing tomorrow morning. You have someone you can stay with, right?"

"It's late, Marissa. I don't want to bother anyone."

"He's stalking you. I bet anything it was the same guy watching you at the hospital. Get to a friend's house, and don't leave until I get there." The line fell silent. "Denise?"

"Okay, I'll start making some calls. It's getting late, you know?"

"Promise me."

"Yeah, I promise."

The line went dead. Marissa's hand trembled as

she stuffed the phone into her pocket. If she left in an hour, she'd have enough energy to make it to Nashua or Manchester.

The need to extract whatever remaining information Jimmy held grew desperate.

"Jimmy."

Jimmy's eyes fluttered in the purgatory between sleep and inebriation.

"Jimmy."

He heard her this time.

"I'm up, I'm up."

"Tell me how to get to your house. I'll drop you off."

After a quick assessment of the surroundings, he told Marissa to take the next right. The sign read *Dead End* as middle-class residences deteriorated to rusty trailers. She wondered if Jimmy was too drunk to navigate.

"Turn here," he said.

She couldn't see the nearly invisible turn until he alerted her. After hanging a hard right that took the back tire over a crumbling curb, she drove them down a pothole-ridden road. Rainfall from recent storms pooled in the holes. The undercarriage scraped mud as the front tires sought and found twin pits cut into the road.

Jimmy directed her to a blue-sided trailer near the back of the lot, the front yard blemished by tire paths. A clothesline hung between a neighboring trailer and a birch tree on Jimmy's property. The clothes had been removed. The line twisted and snapped like a snake.

She pulled up beside the trailer and cut the engine. All the crickets and katydids had gone to ground for the winter, leaving behind a lonesome sound.

"Thanks for the ride," he said and started to get out.

"Wait a second. Finish the story. You were about to tell me about the three girls causing trouble."

"Why should I put myself through all of that again?"

"It's important. It affects the lives of people I care about."

"You told me you aren't from Westland."

She didn't have time to argue. Michael was missing, as was the evidence of Tristan poisoning her, and now Denise was in trouble. Marissa wasn't about to let Jimmy walk away until she had enough clues to piece this puzzle together.

Exasperated, he rubbed at his temples.

"Fine," he said. "I'll tell you what I remember."

"Thank you, Jimmy."

She placed a hand on his. The pain from a long-ago tragedy twisted his face as he turned to stare out the side window.

"You should know that Alisha and Monica both went out with Tristan when we were younger, and there was a rumor about Krista and Tristan getting it on in the backseat of Krista's car right after Jess and Tristan broke up. That's how tightly knit we were. Heck, we'd all known each other since grade school—Westland is a pretty small town as you've noticed."

"Small towns hold some pretty big secrets."

"It was weird the way we passed dates back-and-forth between us. It was like that until Jess and I, and Jamie and Tristan, started going steady. I think the other three felt left out. They all had boyfriends—sometimes they'd bring them up to the barn—but their relationships weren't serious. Not like Jess and me, and not like Tristan thought he had with Jamie. Krista made a play for Tristan around that time. It felt desperate, like all she wanted was to break them up, not because she secretly carried a torch for Tristan. That didn't get very far. Then Monica and Alisha followed Jamie and took pictures of her with the college guy."

"That was a mean thing to do."

"Yeah, it was pretty sordid stuff. But instead of

showing the pictures to Tristan, they broke into Jess's locker and taped them to inside of the door. Left them hanging so we'd all see."

"Why put them in Jess's locker?"

"They wanted to set Jess up for taking the pictures, I guess, make it seem like Jess still had a thing for Tristan. You know how teenagers get, especially the ones with…"

Something stopped him. Jimmy peered into the mirror again, concentrating on the pale ribbon of dirt road running back into darkness.

"…especially the ones who start to feel left out," Jimmy said, worried again. "Tristan and I used to meet Jess at her locker after chemistry lab. Tristan got there first and saw the pictures. I never saw him that angry, not even when he beat the hell out of that guy in the Jeep. He just stood there, didn't even say a word. I tried to get him to talk but he turned and walked away, quiet as death. It scared the living shit out of me because I *knew* he'd get even."

"Didn't you stand up for Jess?"

Jimmy swallowed.

"Of course, but it was too late. Jess convinced Alisha, Jamie, Krista, and Monica to meet her at the barn. It was almost finals time, and everyone was pretty stressed."

Marissa didn't like the story's new path.

"The plan was for them to hash out their differences," Jimmy said, continuing. "And nobody was allowed to leave until they cleared the air. I didn't like the idea. I didn't trust the other girls. You know that creepy feeling you get when someone is standing right behind you in the dark?"

"Yeah, sure I do."

"I had that feeling all day. I tried to talk Jess out of going, but she laughed at me for getting spooked over nothing. Jess made me promise I'd stay away even as I tried one last time to talk her out of it. When Jess left my house I knew it would be the last time I saw her."

Marissa held his hand. A sickle moon emerged from behind the clouds.

"I was sitting on my front porch when I smelled the smoke. I knew where it was coming from, knew something terrible had happened. I could hear the sirens screaming up the hill. I kept praying Jess hadn't gone to the barn, but I knew better. When I reached Holly Hill the barn was nothing but embers. Nobody could have survived the fire."

"I'm so sorry, Jimmy."

She sat quietly with crawling skin. After he finished the story, Jimmy was depleted.

"Did the police determine how the fire started?"

"Sure, but none of their theories made a damn lick of sense. The lantern, they said. Somehow the lantern overturned and caught the hay. But the girls would've seen it happen, right? Even if they wasted time trying to stomp out the fire, they could've escaped out the barn doors. Fire spreads fast on dry hay, but not that fast."

"Why then? Did someone lock them inside?"

Jimmy stared hauntingly up at the moon with the face of a dead man.

"Difficult to say with everything burned to cinders," said Jimmy. "And it was Westland cops running the show, not a Boston CSI unit. They wouldn't let me anywhere near the barn, but it didn't matter. The smoke was so thick I could barely make out the shapes of the emergency workers searching for bodies. I wouldn't have known anything about the findings, except a buddy of mine was a volunteer firefighter. He said they'd found the remains of five bodies. They were all clustered around the center of the barn like they'd never attempted to escape. Some idiot on the police force tried to play the mass suicide angle, but no one else was buying it. No, I think someone else was there with them that night."

"Five girls. That's a lot for one man to overcome. But if he put them to sleep..."

He scarcely nodded, his eyes fixed on the moon-bathed trailer but seeing another time and place.

"Sure. That would be one way."

"It would take someone who knew a thing or two about chemistry."

Jimmy glanced warily at Marissa.

"Like a knockout gas," he said.

"It's not hard to get hold of chloroform, and if you know what you're doing—"

"—you can make it in a lab. Like you said, *if you know a thing or two about chemistry*."

A motor gunned a block behind them. Swiveling around on her seat, Marissa sighed when the car turned into a driveway.

"You think your friend, Tristan, was involved," she said.

He started nodding then shook his head.

"I don't know what I believe."

"Didn't the police ever question him?"

"He had motive, but where was the proof? A big city forensics team might have found evidence. Then again, maybe not. I always thought whoever did it was really intelligent and careful about it. Anyhow, Tristan had an alibi. His prick father claimed he'd been home in bed that night, sick as a dog."

"You believe it?"

Jimmy shrugged his shoulders, defeated.

"It's possible. But I saw Tristan coming out of Mike's Hardware the next day. He didn't look too fucking sick to me."

The warm engine ticked, keeping beat with night's march toward midnight.

"I told you everything I remember," he said. "I don't figure you'll ever tell me why you need to know."

"Maybe I will someday."

"Sure you will."

Marissa felt remorseful. She'd coerced him into digging up the dead. Tapping on the steering wheel, she considered telling Jimmy the truth before he laughed mirthlessly.

"This night couldn't get any stranger. First, you sit down next to me as a dead ringer for Jess and convince me to spill my guts over the worst tragedy Westland ever experienced. And if remembering isn't surreal enough, I think Tristan is back in Westland."

"Tristan is here?" She swung her head around, staring into the secretive night. "Why do you say that?"

"Remember the guy brighting us at the gas station? That's what Tristan used to do. He'd pull into my driveway and flash the headlights through my bedroom window until I came outside. Someone in a sports car did the same thing to me recently. It had to be Tristan. Why he came back after twenty years—"

Marissa threw her door open. The dirt road was silver in the moonlight. Trees bracketed the road and threw shadows across the lawns. The distant purr of a car engine seemed to be coming closer.

"What's wrong?" Jimmy said, looking confused and frightened as Marissa braced herself against the car.

"When was the last time you talked to Tristan?"

"I don't know," Jimmy said, climbing out of the car to join her. "At graduation, I guess. Not since he left for Brown. Why?"

"Would Tristan know your current address?"

"I'm not in the phone book, but it's not like half of Westland doesn't know me. What's this about?"

God, the road was dark.

"It's probably nothing."

"You act like you know Tristan." When she didn't answer, he slammed the car door and stumbled over to her. "My God. You *do* know him."

Marissa didn't say a word. She lifted her hand and touched her wedding ring.

"Jesus," he said. "You could be Jess's twin sister."

"Show me her picture."

"What?"

"A picture of Jess, Jimmy. You still have one, don't you?"

"Yeah…yeah, I do. My old yearbook is somewhere inside. Hold on while I get it."

Darkness stirred at the end of the block. It could have been a neighbor out for a stroll or somebody's pet slinking down the walkway. It could have been anything.

"I'm coming with you," Marissa said.

The screen door to the trailer hung askew as Jimmy led her up the steps. Inside, the smell of alcohol was permanently ingrained in the walls. Flies buzzed around a stack of dirty dishes in the sink as the stink of spoiled meat trickled out of the garbage disposal. Looking embarrassed, he hurriedly tidied the unpaid bills on the kitchen counter.

"Sorry about the mess."

"Don't waste time. Get me that yearbook."

He hurried back into the trailer, flicking on lights along the way.

Could it be her marriage was a lie? Tristan had chosen Marissa because she looked so much like Jess.

As she pictured Annie Wallace, slaughtered on her bed with a single rose laid upon her chest, Jimmy's words hurtled back at her.

I knew he'd get even.

Jimmy cursed and spilled the contents of a cardboard box on the floor. Then he was on his knees, desperately sorting through the mess until he pulled a purple book out of the pile.

"Got it."

He rushed back to her and started paging toward senior pictures. The haircuts and flannel shirts dated the pictures from the 1990's.

"Here she is," Jimmy said, stopping on the second page of yearbook photos.

For Marissa, seeing Jess's picture was akin to finding a forgotten photo of herself. The resemblance to her teen years was striking, down to the pulled back hair and the mischievous smile. But it was the photograph above Jess's that scared her to death.

Jamie Bracket.

The final piece of the puzzle fell into place—a monster out of her darkest nightmare. She knew Denise's stalker.

"That's Jamie," Jimmy said when he noticed Marissa staring at the picture. "Tristan's old girlfriend, the one who cheated on him."

Marissa fell back against the wall, sought the phone in her pocket and fumbled it to the floor. The trailer floor tilted and spun.

"Marissa, what's happening?" Jimmy touched her face and peered nervously into her eyes. "I'll call you an ambulance."

"No...I'll be okay."

He helped her to her feet.

"On second thought," she said. "Call the police. Tell them to alert the Burlington police—"

"Burlington?"

"Do it, Jimmy. Denise Moretti on Maplecrest Drive. My husband is going to kill her."

CHAPTER TWENTY-SIX

Denise in Danger

The yearbook lay open on the table.

Marissa's mind raced back to the love letters. The poor, stilted handwriting, the penmanship more like a man's than a woman's.

Tristan had written the notes to himself. The walls of Jimmy's trailer felt too close.

She couldn't take her eyes off Jamie Bracket's picture. If Marissa strongly resembled Jess, Denise Moretti was Jamie's identical twin. The same flowing blonde curls, ocean-blue eyes, and high cheekbones. Marissa didn't need to see the other girls' pictures to know they looked like Annie Wallace and the women in Syracuse and Medford.

She'd been so stupid not to put the clues together.

Tristan's facial recognition software. That was how he found the lookalikes. Marissa had seen one of Tristan's victim's on the computer the night she caught him in his study.

Jimmy came back from the bedroom. He didn't look happy.

"The cop thought I was full of shit or drunk," he said. "And he's probably right on both accounts."

She had told Jimmy her theory of Tristan repeating the murders from high school, and that her husband poisoned Marissa for several months to keep her bed-ridden. Jimmy's face had been full of doubt. Now he looked furious.

"Are you telling me the police won't protect Denise?"

"Oh, they said they'd send a car to her house and check things out," Jimmy said with a sneer. "But I wouldn't expect more than that. Maybe you haven't noticed, but I'm not exactly convincing when my speech is slurred and I'm trying to tell a flat-foot two hundred miles away that a psycho I haven't seen since high school is stalking a woman I've never met. Come to think of it, the whole goddamn thing sounds crazy to me, too."

"Look me in the eye and tell me you don't think Tristan started the fire and burned those five girls alive."

Jimmy's folded his arms.

"It would have taken someone who knew about chemistry to knock them unconscious. You said that yourself, Jimmy. How much chemistry do you figure it would take to poison a water filter?"

"I wouldn't know anything about that."

Marissa snatched a Jack Daniels bottle off the table and shook it in Jimmy's face.

"*This* is who you are, Jimmy."

"You don't know shit about me."

"You wouldn't have been this person had Jess and the others lived. Tristan did this to you, and now he's murdering your friends all over again. He was here tonight. In Westland. The car with its brights on. What do you think he intended to do? Are you next on his list?"

Jimmy believed her. She saw it in his eyes, even if he stubbornly refused to acknowledge the danger.

"I can't wait any longer," she said. "He's going after my friend."

"You aren't driving to Burlington by yourself. If what you said is true, you're walking into a deathtrap."

Marissa pulled the keys from her pocket. How long had it been since they were at the gas station? An hour or 90 minutes? Rushing to do the math in her head, Marissa estimated Tristan was about two hours away from Burlington if he'd departed from the gas station.

"Unless you're coming," she said. "I'm going alone."

Invisible tethers seemed to pull Jimmy in too many directions. When Marissa stormed out of the trailer, Jimmy cursed and followed her.

As they merged onto the interstate Marissa called Denise's phone again. No answer. After the call went to voice-mail Marissa redialed. She told herself Denise was on route to a friend's house or was already safe and asleep. She couldn't convince herself.

Tristan couldn't be two places at once. If he was after Denise, that meant Jennifer Tompkins was safe. With Worcester's lights fading in the mirrors, Marissa phoned the girl.

"No, I still haven't heard from Dad," Jennifer said.

Marissa could hear the terror in Jennifer's voice.

"Did Mr. Benoit call the police?"

"Yes, but they haven't told us anything yet."

As Jennifer began speaking again, the phone beeped. Another caller.

"Sorry, Jennifer. I have to take another call. Let me know as soon as you hear from your dad."

The caller wasn't Denise. A woman identifying herself as Officer Mantel was on the phone.

"Where are you now, Mrs. Carrington?"

"Coming out of Westland, Massachusetts."

"Do you know the whereabouts of your husband, Tristan?"

"No...no. Is this about the filter—"

"We have reason to believe your husband may be armed and dangerous."

"Oh, my God. Michael Tompkins—is he safe?"

"We've been unable to locate Mr. Tompkins, but a teenager claimed he saw a man who resembled Tompkins getting dragged into the backseat of a Camaro this afternoon. We are aware your husband drives a Camaro. Do you have any idea where your husband might be tonight?"

Thank God someone believed her.

"I think he is heading to Burlington."

"Why Burlington?"

"A friend of mine. Her name is Denise Moretti. Tristan is going to kill her. Please, please call the police in Burlington and let them know—"

"How do you know he is—"

The call went dead.

Her service reconnected after several seconds. Another call to Dense went to voice-mail. This time Marissa left a desperate plea for Denise to call her and mentioned Tristan by name. That would get her attention.

Please let me get there in time.

Night rushed at the windshield.

Jimmy buckled his seatbelt as Marissa pushed the gas pedal to the floor.

CHAPTER TWENTY-SEVEN

House in the Woods

Denise pulled into her ex-husband's driveway on the outskirts of Burlington. Could she fall any lower? Besides her neighbors, she hardly knew anyone in Burlington, having grown up in southern New Hampshire. Most of her neighbors' lights had already turned off when Marissa convinced Denise to get to safety earlier in the evening. She wrestled with herself over banging on doors and waking her friends unnecessarily. In the meantime, she'd wasted another hour weighing hotel options in her head. Staying in a hotel made the most sense, but a convention in Burlington had taken up most of the room availability. Several frustrating phone calls confirmed Montpelier and Plattsburgh were overbooked, as well. It was either she gas up the car and drive to Albany or ask Ben for a big favor.

She didn't want to believe Tristan was stalking her, but the memory of him standing on her porch in the rain, all pallor and vacant eyes, gave her chills. One thing she felt certain of: if Tristan was as dangerous as Marissa believed, if he'd been the man following her at the hospital, she didn't wish to be anywhere near Maplecrest Drive tonight.

The dark Gambrel was gray in the pale moonlight. Tall pines framed the construction and led back to several acres of forestland. Twin quarter-moon windows, eerily reminiscent of the Amityville house, stared with black eyes from the top floor.

Only one light, a living room table lamp, shone in the dark house, and that light was on a timer. Ben and Erin were vacationing in the Keys, stealing a few weeks of summer before winter kicked into high gear in New England. Choosing to stay alone wasn't the best solution, but Tristan didn't know Ben, let alone where he lived.

Besides, she would spare herself the humiliation of explaining why she needed to hide from her new boyfriend. Denise had told Ben an electrical issue knocked out her power, requiring her to find a place to stay for a few days. Ben insisted Denise stay at their house for as long she needed and make herself at home, even though Erin could be heard in the background questioning why Denise couldn't just get a hotel room.

Denise turned on the flashlight and followed the brick paving stones to the porch. Reaching behind the evergreen bushes fronting the house, she squirmed and jerked her hand back as something scurried through the branches. Gingerly, she reached behind the bush again and felt for the dryer vent. When her fingers touched the key on the far side of the vent, exactly where her ex-husband said it would be, she yanked her hand back with a shiver.

Thank you, Ben. I owe you one.

Stale air met her in the entryway. She laid her purse and overnight bag down in the foyer and walked the long hallway, past the living room and den, to the kitchen. Too many phone calls had drained her phone battery, and coverage in the countryside was spotty at best. She plugged in the charger and hoped the phone would be ready to use soon. Turning on the kitchen light made her squeamish. Anyone watching the house would know she was inside. That was her mind playing games with her, as the closest neighbor was a hundred yards down the road and a dense thicket lay between. Still, she found herself sheepishly peering out the window as she ran her hands under the faucet.

Cold. The water heater was off.

The basement stairs led down from the back of the kitchen. Unlike her finished basement, Ben and Erin's was mostly concrete and cobwebs. Except to do laundry, she guessed nobody ever went down there. She stepped down the wooden stairway, paint-chipped but sturdy. The pull-chain light bulb did little to throw back the darkness. Denise swept the flashlight down the steps until she reached the bottom.

Two rooms sat off the stairway—a room in the back full of unpacked boxes, the laundry room to her right. The LED strip lighting pained her eyes after traversing the gloomy staircase. The water heater slept along the back wall. The dial was set to *vacation.* She twisted it to *warm* and a whoosh of blue fire lit the water heater from below.

Denise climbed the stairs to the kitchen. At the sink, she opened the faucet until the water warmed.

As she splashed water on her face a shape lurched past the window.

She jumped.

Something.

Heart thumping, she flipped the wall switch. The outside world began to take shape, first in amorphous grays and then sharp angles. She saw the pines rocking in the wind and nervously laughed to herself. No monsters, no stalkers at the window. Craning her neck, she saw the tops of the trees stabbing into the night sky, where a cloud canopy choked out the stars.

The solitude of the huge house smothered her. It would have been better to drive to Albany for the night, maybe stay in a nice hotel for a few days until this crazy business with Tristan cleared up. *If* it cleared up. Who was to say she'd be rid of him next week, next month, or ever? She wondered how much help the police would be. The officer she'd spoken with earlier promised to send a patrol car to Maplecrest Drive. The sheriff's office lay closer to the countryside. Though the policeman confirmed a sheriff deputy would swing past her ex-husband's house, she hadn't seen a vehicle yet.

Rubbing the chill off her arms, she walked to the living room. Every shadow frightened her.

On the television, the sports channels were debating the baseball playoffs, and that was better than sitting in the dark and wondering where Tristan was.

Her phone buzzed. She hurried back to the kitchen and saw the phone had enough power to retrieve her messages: one from Ben making sure she was able to find the key, the other from Marissa. Denise wrote a quick text message back to Ben and thanked him again for his generosity. For the first time since before they'd married she felt a flutter move through her chest thinking of him. Neither had been prepared for marriage. But if they'd waited a few more years, maybe the timing would have been better and they'd be together now.

Hearing Marissa mention Tristan by name nearly caused her to drop the phone. Denise never told Marissa his name, so how could she know him? Marissa, who'd decided to drive straight to Maplecrest Drive to see Denise, claimed Tristan was on his way to Burlington.

Her hands trembling, Denise checked the time of Marissa's call. Over an hour ago. If Marissa was right, it was possible Tristan was already in Burlington.

But he doesn't know where I am.

Maybe, maybe not.

She rushed to the front door and ensured the deadbolt was thrown. Unfamiliar with the house, it took her a while to locate the back door off a small sitting room across from the kitchen.

The door was all glass. Flimsy. Easy to punch through and unlock the door. Floor-to-ceilings windows created another vulnerability.

Moving quickly through the downstairs, she checked the windows. Most were non-opening Tudors until she found two double-hung windows where the locks weren't engaged.

Satisfied the downstairs was secure, she climbed the stairs. A home office with a desk, bookshelf, and plenty of open floor space sat next to the stairs. The next two rooms were guest bedrooms. She found the master bedroom at the back of the house. A quick check confirmed there wasn't a way to climb into the house. No fire escape, no deck hanging off the second-story.

The bedroom smelled of Erin's perfume, dewy and floral. As she sat on the edge of the bed, she realized this was the first place she'd felt safe in the house. A pair of sturdy, wooden doors guarded the bedroom and locked from the inside. She had a straight sight line to the stairway.

The drone of the television downstairs echoed off the tall ceilings as though it played in a cavern.

Pleated curtains hung open at the bedroom windows, allowing her to look into the backyard. Denise began to relax.

She pulled the curtains shut.

Then someone pounded on the door.

She crouched next to the door and looked out at the long, empty hallway. Did the front door have a peephole?

Holding her breath, she sneaked to the top of the staircase. The pounding started again.

Damn her for turning on the television. Whoever was at the door knew she was in the house.

She started down the stairs. Halfway to the bottom she gained a good enough view of the door to confirm there wasn't a peephole.

A fist pounded on the door again. She heard the hinges of the storm door creak as someone held it open.

Denise crept down the stairs, hugging the wall so no one could see her through the windows. She poked her head around the corner and saw headlights glaring off the front of the house. An emergency vehicle of some type. Exhaling, she yelled she was coming just as the pounding started again.

She pulled back the deadbolt and opened the door. A man with a white handlebar mustache and clothed in a sheriff's uniform stood in the doorway.

"Ms. Moretti?"

"Yes. Denise, please."

He stared around her, surveying the interior of the house.

"Deputy Niles. Just passing through and making sure you're safe tonight. Are you alone in the house?"

"It's just me."

"I understand your boyfriend, a Tristan Carrington, is causing you issues. Has he attempted to contact you tonight?"

Carrington. Marissa's last name.

"Ma'am?"

"Sorry, no," she said, stammering. "Not since this evening."

"Did Mr. Carrington threaten you in any way?"

"No, not exactly."

"Not exactly?"

"He didn't threaten me."

She realized how ridiculous she sounded. If they'd seen Tristan's face, witnessed the way he acted...

Deputy Niles impatiently glanced back at his idling truck. Scratchy banter came out of the radio. Denise knew it was a busy night due to the convention.

He blew out his mustache.

"I'm not sure how soon we can get another vehicle out this way," he said. "We'll do our best to have someone drive by before morning."

"I understand."

Seeing how frightened she was, he sighed.

"Tell you what. I'm gonna take a look around the grounds, make sure everything is all right before I head back into town. You mind?"

"Of course not. Thank you for troubling yourself to check on me."

"Not at all." He started to turn away and stopped. "Make certain to keep the doors locked, and don't answer for anyone you don't recognize. If Mr. Carrington contacts you again, give us a call."

"I will."

Deputy Niles tipped his hat. He walked back to the truck, turned off the engine, and removed the keys. Sweeping a flashlight across the trees, he hobbled on tender knees across the yard as she pushed the door closed and engaged the dead bolt.

She couldn't force her mind to slow. Was Marissa related to Tristan? His wife? Wondering threw into question why Marissa had visited Maplecrest Drive. The likelihood Marissa was trying to catch Denise and Tristan together made her tremble.

The flashlight searched past the den window. Denise followed the deputy's progress to the backyard, then picked up her phone in the kitchen. She accessed Marissa's number.

Denise couldn't bring herself to call.

Tristan's wife.

When they'd first met, hadn't Marissa asked Denise about a woman named Jamie something? She couldn't recall. Her instinct told her the name was important.

She walked back through the house to the living room, sat on the recliner, and placed the phone on the coffee table. She couldn't see the deputy's flashlight anymore. A glance out the window confirmed the truck was still in the driveway. Now she really felt ridiculous.

Not only was she caught in a bizarre love triangle, she'd taken Marissa into her home.

No wonder the deputy was annoyed. Denise was annoyed with herself for getting into this mess.

The phone's ring startled her. She grabbed it and saw Marissa's name on the screen.

Dammit.

It rang a second time. Then a third and fourth.

Denise wasn't ready for this conversation.

On the fifth ring, she still couldn't bring herself to answer.

CHAPTER TWENTY-EIGHT

The Truth

The exit signs for Montpelier materialized like ghosts out of the night. Less than an hour's drive from Burlington, Marissa raced northward on I-89. Tristan was already in Burlington. She felt the cold truth in her bones.

Denise didn't answer her phone.

Marissa had one hand on the wheel and the other clutching the phone to her ear as Jimmy's head bobbed. He'd been in and out of sleep since Boston, snoring sometimes and darting awake as though something dead and gnarled came out of the seat and grabbed him. She wondered what phantoms from Westland's past haunted his dreams.

Finally, Denise answered.

"What do you want, Marissa?"

Denise's caustic demeanor shocked Marissa.

"Did you call me?" asked Marissa.

Marissa heard talking in the background but couldn't tell if it was the television or a group of people. She prayed for the latter.

"About a half-hour ago, yes."

"Are you safe?"

Denise took too long to answer.

"Yes, I'm at my ex-husband's house."

"Thank God. I feel so much better knowing you

aren't alone."

Another pause.

"Well…"

"Please tell me he's there with you," said Marissa.

Marissa's panic bled through the phone when Denise admitted Ben and Erin were vacationing in the Keys.

"But it's all right," Denise said. "Nobody knows where I am except the police."

"Are they keeping an eye on the house?"

"As a matter of fact, the sheriff's deputy is patrolling the yard right now."

"Good. Listen, Denise. I'm about forty-five minutes outside of Burlington. Tell me the address and I'll come to you."

Denise didn't answer.

"Denise?"

"I'm here."

"Don't try to do this alone," Marissa said, pleading. "You don't know what you're up against."

"You called him *Tristan* in your message. How did you know his name?"

"I can explain if you let me help you—"

"Tristan Carrington. That's the name the deputy used."

Marissa couldn't bring herself to answer. Jimmy was muttering in his sleep, something about fire and the devil.

After a moment, Marissa said, "That's right. He's my husband."

"Shit."

"I'm sorry. I didn't know you were the woman Tristan was having an affair with. When I found out my husband was stalking you…"

"You targeted me," said Denise.

"No."

"You came straight to my neighborhood and gave me a bullshit story about looking for deals at yard sales. As if anyone would come all the way from Cape Cod to do such a thing. That bruise on your neck—I bet Tristan did that to you."

"It's not like it seems. You have to believe me. I didn't know about the affair until I found Tristan's letters hidden in the attic."

"But I didn't write Tristan a letter. I didn't even know him until a few weeks ago."

"I know you didn't write the notes. Tristan wrote them."

Silence.

"What are you talking about?" asked Denise, growing exasperated.

"Listen closely, Denise. There isn't much time to explain. Tristan murdered a girl a long time ago, a girl named Jamie Bracket."

Denise stammered, seeming to remember something from her past.

"Tristan called me Jamie."

"My God."

"Oh, Marissa. I don't understand any of this. What does this have to do with me?"

"Jamie was his lover and you look just like her. He thinks you're Jamie. How did you meet Tristan?"

"Marissa, I…"

"Don't worry about hurting my feelings. Tell me the truth."

"The bank. My supervisor has an account with Tristan's firm. He must have…seen me and noticed the resemblance. Marissa, do I really look like that girl? Like Jamie Bracket, I mean?"

"Someone showed me Jamie's picture tonight. I would have sworn it was your senior picture from high school."

Marissa could hear Denise trying to piece herself together.

"Tell me where to find you," Marissa finally said.

After another pause, Denise surrendered the address: a countryside road outside of Burlington.

"Hurry. Okay, Marissa?"

"I'm driving as fast as I can. Stay where you are."

When the call ended Marissa shook Jimmy's shoulder. He awoke with a curse, blinked, and scanned the car, unsure of where he was.

"Thanks a lot," Jimmy said. "I was just getting to the good part."

"Didn't sound like a very good dream from where I'm sitting."

He fixed his eyes on the mile markers whipping past.

Marissa tried to picture Tristan, the man who she'd fallen in love with and vowed to spend the rest of her days beside, setting fire to the barn. Murdering five girls.

Over a failed relationship? It didn't make sense. Jimmy was holding out on her.

"You didn't tell me the whole story," said Marissa.

Jimmy gave her an irritated look, a front which failed to cover how uneasily he shifted in his seat.

"What in the hell gives you the right to keep pestering me? I told you everything that happened."

"Not everything. I know Tristan is violent, but I can't believe he killed those girls over two failed relationships."

"As I told you, they made his life a living hell."

"Enough to burn five of his friends alive? What aren't you telling me, Jimmy."

"Goddamn you!" Jimmy kicked the glove compartment hard enough to knock the door crooked. "I never should have trusted you. Tristan's wife? Oh, did I ever step in shit this time."

The glare she gave him would have melted a

lesser man. He threw up his hands.

"There's more to the story," Jimmy said.

"Tell me."

"After the girls planted the pictures of Jamie and her boyfriend on Jess's locker, Tristan was furious and didn't want anything to do with the rest of us. The next night we decided to go back to the barn to party. This time we didn't invite Tristan, but he found out somehow and followed us. It was Jess and me, Jamie and Chris, that snobby college kid I told you about, and the other three girls. It was after ten, and we were all pretty high by then. The door flew open, and there was Tristan with this look on his face like he wanted to kill us."

The car rounded a bend, and Marissa saw the first lights of Burlington burning in the dark.

"Chris was a good-sized guy, but he was no fighter. He took one wild swing at Tristan that must have missed him by half-a-foot. The guy never threw another punch. Tristan broke his nose. I didn't give two shits about Chris, but I couldn't sit there and let Tristan beat him to death. I didn't want to fight—Tristan was my friend—but when I tried to pull him away, Tristan turned on me and almost threw me through the wall."

Jimmy dropped his face into his hands and yanked his hair.

"I shouldn't have fought back. Tristan would have let it go at that point, but I was out of my head. He never saw me coming. I took him down from behind at the same time Chris got up and jumped into the fight. Chris could barely speak with so much blood pouring out of his nose. That didn't stop him from booting Tristan's ribs while I held him down. Neither one of us would have stood a chance against Tristan in a fair fight, but together we hurt him bad. Chris, mostly. I was just trying to make Tristan stop, get him to calm down, you know? So I didn't even realize Chris had hurt Tristan. Tristan didn't have any fight left when I let him up. Before I knew what he was gonna do, Chris stomped down on the back of Tristan's head. Knocked him unconscious."

"Didn't you help Tristan?"

"Yeah. Of course, I did. I threw Chris against the wall and told him if he ever came back to the barn I'd kill him myself. He whispered something in Jamie's ear before leaving. I don't know what he said, but I shouldn't have left Tristan alone with the girls. Jamie played it up like she was mad at Chris and wanted to help Tristan. I bought it, so Jess and I left together. The last I saw, Jamie was holding Tristan's head in her lap and telling him she loved him and everything was gonna work out, and maybe a stupid part of me thought it might. We were halfway down the hill when we passed Chris, standing along the road in the dark and watching us like he was waiting for something. After we rounded a curve, I couldn't see him anymore because of the trees and brush. I got this sick feeling that Chris might circle back to the barn after we left."

The car felt preternaturally cold as if an ice fog rose out of a shallow grave.

"There was this big oak by the side of the road that had fallen over in a storm. The five of them—Chris and the four girls—carried Tristan down the hill, stripped him naked, and bound him to the tree. Somebody spray-painted *pussy* across Tristan's chest. Tristan was a stone's throw from the county road. Anyone driving by could have seen him, and judging by the way people laughed when he walked into school on Monday, my guess is everyone did see."

Jimmy punched the door.

"It was my fault," he said.

"No, Jimmy. How could you have known what they planned to do to him?"

"Would you have left Tristan alone with them? Wouldn't you have at least waited to make sure Chris wasn't coming back?"

Marissa didn't know how to answer. It didn't matter. Guilt was the demon Jimmy couldn't outrun.

"One mistake in judgment. One goddamn mistake got Jess killed. *I* killed her."

"That's not true, Jimmy. You know it's not true."

"Do I?"

Resigned and emotionally spent, Jimmy had all the animation of a dead man. Marissa wondered what had become of Chris and couldn't convince herself he was alive.

Marissa needed Jimmy. Despite her two decades of marriage to Tristan, she didn't know him as well as Jimmy did.

"He's killing them again," said Marissa. "I know you don't want to believe it, but he already murdered a woman in New York who looked just like Krista Steiner. You know what he did to me, thinking I'm Jess. Now he's after a woman he thinks is Jamie, but we can stop him this time. We can make this right."

"Nothing will ever be right."

Flared by the headlights, every tree that blurred past might have been Jess's ghost glaring in accusation. Marissa felt the chill and knew Jimmy did, too.

CHAPTER TWENTY-NINE

Awakening

When she heard twigs snapping behind the house, Denise jumped awake. For a disorienting moment, she wasn't sure where she was. Then she realized she was on Ben's couch.

The whole house was dark and the television off.

She reached up to turn on the table lamp. It clicked once, twice, and no light flared. The power was out, which didn't make sense because the wind whipping at the house wasn't strong enough to topple trees and wires. Maybe a fuse was blown.

How long had she been asleep? No more than thirty or forty minutes, or Marissa would have arrived by now. It was strange awakening to the powerless dark, like finding herself in a nightmare world where the sun never rose and shadows touched everything.

Remembering the noise that roused her, she jumped up and parted the curtain. The deputy's truck was still in the driveway.

Strange. He'd told her he would make a quick check of the backyard and head into town, yet he was apparently still here, pawing around the trees. He should be dealing with the convention traffic by now.

Unless he'd seen someone behind the house.

Her phone battery nearly drained—unless the

power came back soon, she'd have no communication with the outside world—Denise crept to the den window and peered out. She couldn't see anything except the pine trees, which seemed unsettlingly close to the house, almost near enough for Denise to open the window and place her palms upon the cold, sappy bark.

The darkness, her isolation, and the loss of power were three elements that, when combined, were far more terrifying than their sum. She wished she'd never left Maplecrest Drive, with its well-lit porches and closely bunched homes.

She saw a flash of light and shrank beneath the sill. Something in the dark. Hidden in the trees.

The hallway from the den to the back door was all gloom and silence as she edged through the hallway, her socks swishing across the chilly floors. The cold had found a way into the old, drafty house.

In the sitting room across from the kitchen, Denise touched the door handle, jiggled it. Still locked.

Biting her lip, she threw back the lock and opened the door.

The wind whipped her clothing and dug into her ears, making it difficult to hear.

"Deputy Niles?"

She waited several seconds and listened. Swaying pines threw shifting shadows.

Goosebumps rose over her body as she clutched her arms to her chest.

"Deputy Niles, are you back here?"

No answer.

Three wooden steps led from the door to the grass. She descended them. Dry needles pierced her feet.

"Hello?"

From far off, she thought she heard a voice answer. The wind masked everything.

Cold bit at her, slithered down her shirt and up her

pant legs like water moccasins from the bottom of a frozen pond.

"Deputy Niles, where are you?"

The door slammed behind her. She caught her breath and spun around.

Rushing up the steps, she yanked on the handle. The door wouldn't budge.

Denise pulled harder. The door unjammed and flew open, blasting the side of the house with a bang that echoed off the trees.

Inside, she locked the door and stood wheezing. The cold felt like it was under her skin.

Denise checked the windows. Nobody was outside, not even the missing deputy.

Driven by the furious wind, trees swayed and bled shadows across the windows.

On her way back to the living room, she pocketed her phone and slipped into her sneakers.

The deputy's truck was still in the driveway, blocking her own car. So much for driving back to the lights and perceived safety of Burlington.

Denise stuck her head outside and called to the deputy. The gale swept her voice into the copse.

Before she could talk herself out of going, she lowered her head and ran to the truck. Finding the door unlocked, she slipped inside and pulled the door shut.

Dammit.

Deputy Niles had taken the keys.

She honked the horn and waited. Still no sign of Niles. Several honks in succession failed to rouse help. Not even a neighbor.

As Denise reached for the door handle the radio crackled. The display was a puzzle of white, faintly glowing buttons. A curling cord ran out from the display unit to the microphone, which hung on a clip.

She spoke into the microphone.

"Hello. Can anyone hear me?"

The radio crackled again without reply.

"This is Denise Moretti at 3240 Long Hollow Road outside of Burlington. Is anyone listening?"

From the truck, the front door to the old house seemed a mile away. Dead leaves blew across the walkway.

"Repeating, this is Denise Moretti at 3240 Long Hollow Road. I'm inside Deputy Niles' truck."

A moment of silence, then a man's voice answered her.

"Ms. Moretti?"

"Yes."

"Is Deputy Niles with you?"

"No, sir. I'm at my ex-husband's house. Deputy Niles checked on me about an hour ago and said he was going to take a look around the property. I fell asleep for about a half-hour. When I woke up his truck was still in the driveway, but I can't find him anywhere."

A long moment of quiet followed. Then—

"Ma'am, we're sending another officer out to your position. It might be ten or fifteen minutes before he gets there. Go inside the house and lock the doors. Don't answer the door for anyone until the officer arrives."

"What's happening?"

"No need for concern, ma'am. Do as I say and you'll be safe. Do you have a cell phone?"

"Yes, but the battery is almost dead and I lost power at the house."

She heard him asking another officer to check on power outages.

"No reports of power outages in your sector," he said. "It could be a tree limb fell on a line just down the road. Happens all the time on windy nights. Until the power starts working again, keep your phone powered off unless you need it."

"I will."

"And remember to lock the doors. The officer will be there soon."

"Thank you."

The run from the truck to the door seemed to take forever. The bushes whispered in the wind and scratched at the side of the house. Shapes seemed to dart out of the darkness along the periphery of her vision.

Finally inside, Denise bolted the door. The house was impossibly dark, held too many secrets.

She was still standing in the entryway when a knocking sound came from the back of the house.

It came again.

Feeling for the walls, she edged down the hallway.

There it was again. That noise.

The kitchen was ahead and to the left. She saw where the wall opened up to the kitchen and the shape of the cabinetry. Nothing else.

Three knocks. From the back room. She couldn't see the door from the hallway.

"Help me…"

She froze at the anguished voice.

A fist banged against the door.

"Please…it's Deputy Niles. I'm injured."

Denise rushed into the sitting room, nearly colliding with the jamb as she bolted through the entryway.

She could see the shape of the deputy slumped over outside the door.

He swayed in the wind. Unnaturally stiff. A standing cadaver.

She reached for the handle. Deputy Niles crashed through the glass door.

He lay twitching on the floor with a knife jutting out of his back.

It was then she noticed the dark shape behind him.

"Help me," the voice in the night mocked. "Help

222

me, Jamie."

Stepping through the shattered doorway, Tristan yanked the blade out of Deputy Niles.

Denise screamed.

CHAPTER THIRTY
Where is Denise?

Marissa came around a dark curve, still unsure if she was on the correct road. Some of the streets outside of Burlington proper were recently built, and the GPS had twice taken her down incorrect turns.

The road followed a gurgling creek, pearly under the rare streetlight and black where the light failed to reach.

"There it is."

Jimmy pointed at a dark Gambrel set about fifty yards back from the road. Marissa braked, then backed up and turned into the driveway. The headlights swept across the truck, revealing it as a sheriff cruiser, then across Denise's car.

"The police are already here," Jimmy said.

"Then why are all the lights out?"

"Power must be off."

"It wasn't down the road."

They stepped out of Marissa's car. Jimmy started climbing the driveway and halted, noticing Marissa had stopped beside the truck.

"You coming?"

Something was wrong. All around them, the wind urged the pines to dance, limbs rubbing together and creaking with each gust. A branch snapped and thudded against the earth in the gloom of the copse.

Marissa nodded after a moment of consideration.

They walked side-by-side up the incline. Hadn't it been almost an hour since Denise told her the deputy arrived?

Marissa followed a wire running from the house and back to a power pole growing out of the roadside ditch. Still connected.

Upon the top step, Marissa paused before knocking. Quietly pulling open the storm door, she turned the doorknob carefully until it clicked. Locked.

Marissa looked up at the second-story windows. A blackness deeper than secrets spilled against the glass.

She knocked. When no response came she knocked again and pressed her ear to the door.

"Anyone in there?" Jimmy asked.

"Shh."

It was hard to hear anything over the wind.

After knocking again, she crossed the lawn and tried to peek through a curtained window. A row of bushes kept her away from the house.

"Nobody's home," said Jimmy. "I say we leave."

"You think the deputy left his truck and walked back to Burlington? Follow me."

She rounded the house. The meager pathway between the wall and closely-knit pines felt claustrophobic. Jimmy jogged to keep up.

"Enough of this shit," Jimmy said, his arms wrapped around his body. "It's cold, goddammit."

"So go back to the car. I won't be long."

"And let you trounce around in the dark by yourself? Not a chance."

From the road, she'd been able to see the lights of Burlington on the horizon, glistering like a great moon folding into the earth. Not here. The backyard was nothing but shades of black. The wall of trees boxed her in, trapped them.

It was then Marissa felt something in the night and knew they weren't alone. She froze in place, eyes searching. Jimmy noticed, too. He shifted nervously, turning in a circle at the corner of the house.

"There," he said, pointing.

Her eyes followed. The back door was smashed. Glass sparkled on the ground.

He started forward and she yanked him back. Her eyes warned him not to move.

She waited and listened. No sound came from inside.

At her nod, they edged closer to the broken door. Just past the glass shards, a bulk lay on the floor, too dark to see.

Please, don't let it be Denise.

While Marissa did her best to avoid the broken glass, Jimmy stepped down and crushed a piece in the entryway.

The darkness moved inside the room.

Marissa shouted at Jimmy as a knife swept at her face. She ducked and felt the blade rip through her hair.

Her right hand seemed to move on its own, thrusting upward with an open palm like a chainsaw kickback. It clipped Tristan under the chin and sent him stumbling backward. Screaming Tristan's name, Jimmy threw himself at the dark form. They crashed over a table, crushing a lamp and picture frame.

Their bodies twisted and rolled as one. Tristan's knife was somewhere on the floor, along with the shape Marissa now recognized as the deputy, a pool of blood spreading out from his body.

Marissa blindly swept her hand across the floor and couldn't find the knife. She heard them struggling in the corner. Jimmy's pained grunts told her Tristan was killing him, beating him to death with his bare hands. On the return sweep, her hand closed over the hilt. As she picked it up, Tristan rushed out of the dark and threw her against the wall. Her face smacked hard against the jamb. Tristan ripped the knife from her grip.

The blade cut across her chest. She cried out and struck Tristan's face, knocking him back a step. He came at her with the knife. The tip bit into her ribs.

Kneeing him in the groin, she forced him to drop the knife. She felt her shirt sticking to her chest with spreading blood.

His hands gripped her neck, crushed and strangled. She couldn't breathe. Beating fists against his face had no effect. She was too close to use her leverage. As Tristan pressed her against the jamb she twisted herself into the doorway and backed away through the grass, his hands clutched around her windpipe.

Stay on your feet. Don't go down.

Tristan was at arm's length. Her vision already began to cloud. She punched her arms up and under Tristan's and knocked his hands off her throat. A look of astonishment crossed his face. Then disdain. He lurched after her, screaming *Jess* with spittle flying from his mouth.

She struck him hard in the mouth, then twice in the chest. Blood trickled down his lip. Each strike fired pain across her chest.

"Stop calling me Jess. Think, Tristan. It's me—Marissa."

He cocked his head slightly, animal-like in his primitive simplicity. If she'd held any hope of reasoning with him, it was gone now.

"What did you do with Denise?" He stalked forward without a hint of recognition. "With Jamie…what did you do with Jamie?"

His lips curled into a grin.

"She will be reborn, as you will be."

He lashed out. A fist clipped her forehead and sent Marissa reeling. She lost her footing and fell backward onto a bed of dead pine needles and shriveled branches.

Tristan landed on top of her. One hand bludgeoned her face while the other curled long, bony fingers around her throat. Thrusting her hips, she tried to throw him off. He was too strong.

She couldn't breathe. He squeezed tighter, hands shaking as though tremors ran under his skin.

Tears left a blurry sheen across her eyes. All was indistinct—the maniacally swaying trees, the dark clouds racing across the moon, Tristan's wide and crazy eyes—everything bleeding together into one nightmare vision.

Marissa pressed her heels into the dirt and tried to bridge him off, but the ground was too soft and debris-ridden. She lost leverage, her sneakers scouring soil before her legs collapsed.

Tristan smiled as she began to lose consciousness. To her eyes, there were two of him, their bodies separating and merging as the life ran out of her.

Her eyelids fluttered and drooped shut. Wavering on the border of consciousness, she heard a loud slapping noise like two boards smacking together. Tristan groaned and released her throat.

Marissa gagged and felt Tristan fall aside. She desperately gulped oxygen.

The world was swirling blacks and reds.

"Let's go!"

A hand gripped hers and pulled. She gained her footing and immediately toppled forward. A pair of arms circled and supported her.

"Move, Marissa!"

Her mind struggled to process what was happening as she recognized Denise's voice.

Before Marissa had full control of her legs, Denise tugged at her. They ran toward a wall of black—trees,

Marissa realized. Her legs kept giving out.

Behind them, she heard Tristan stirring.

The scent of tree sap and pine exploded when they entered the copse. Denise weaved between trees and bramble scrub, taking them deeper into hiding. Rough, sticky bark clipped Marissa's shoulders. Limbs like devil claws scraped her hair.

Tristan was somewhere behind them, screaming incoherently.

At once, Denise stopped and dropped to one knee. Marissa's heart thundered as she touched her neck. She could still feel his fingers around her throat.

"Why are we stopping?" Marissa asked.

"I heard voices." Denise crouched beside Marissa and put an arm around her shoulders. "The second patrol car—I think it's here."

Marissa looked down at her chest and discerned a darker shade where blood pooled.

When she moaned, Denise noticed the blood.

"Oh no," said Denise. "It isn't deep, is it?"

When Marissa didn't answer, Denise tugged at her own shirt, trying to tear a strip of cloth.

"It's okay, I'll be fine."

"But you're bleeding."

"There isn't anything we can do about it now."

Marissa listened. She couldn't hear Tristan anymore. From beyond the trees, a light flashed momentarily and was gone.

"Flashlight," Denise said.

There were two voices…men's voices…coming from near the house. They called out for someone. Niles, Marissa heard them say.

Marissa and Denise yelled out to them, but the wind was too loud.

Flashlight beams swept along the trees and disappeared as the officers circled around the other side of the house.

"I didn't know where you were," said Marissa. "Did he hurt you?"

"He would have killed me if it wasn't for you. You pulled into the driveway right after he broke through the back door."

"You should have fled while you had the chance."

"And left you alone with that maniac? What kind of person would that make me?"

A branch snapped behind them.

Denise and Marissa huddled together, shielded by a pine bough.

Denise's eyes faintly glowed in the dark, wide and terrified. They crouched in silence but the sound didn't come again.

"What do we do?" Denise asked.

"Get to those officers and get the hell out of here."

"And if we run into Tristan instead?"

It was a good question. One Marissa couldn't answer.

Rushing out of the copse across the open lot was a Russian roulette gamble.

"I say we make a run for it," Marissa said.

Denise struggled with indecision before nodding.

Staying low to the ground, they ducked under branches and stepped carefully upon the forest floor. Something tore through the leaves behind them. Marissa pulled Denise behind a tree and waited until the sound faded.

A gunshot exploded nearby. Denise fell to the ground with Marissa across her back, shielding her. Someone cried out, then another shout, followed by return fire. It was impossible to tell how far away the officers were. Their cries echoed off the trees and came at Marissa from all angles.

A third shot boomed from near Ben and Erin's

house. The blast resonated to the far horizon as a series of echoes strung together, like a low-flying jet passing overhead.

Then dead silence.

"Please tell me they got him," Denise said.

They crawled forward to a tight grouping of trees.

The quiet disturbed Marissa.

"Marissa…" Denise's voice quavered. Marissa pulled her in and hugged her. "He killed the officers, didn't he?"

"Don't say that. We're almost back to the yard. If we can get to the driveway—"

"Yes, and someone must have heard the gunshots. There'll be an army of cops out here soon."

The edge of the trees stood just ahead. The dark bulk of the Gambrel climbed into the sky. The yard was empty.

Parting the branches, Marissa reexamined the backyard. It was at least another 50 steps to the next grouping of trees along the house. They'd be exposed until then.

Denise trailed a step behind, her head swiveling each time a branch creaked. The driveway lay hidden behind the house, the windows black.

They were almost to the back corner of the house when the crackle of twigs stopped them. Her back pressed against the wall, Marissa peered around the corner. She could see the shattered back door and the shape of the dead deputy inside.

When the noise didn't come again, Marissa led them along the side of the house.

The driveway appeared. The second sheriff's truck was parked behind and just off to the side of Marissa's. She thought she might be able to squeeze around the truck and avoid the deep ditch at the bottom of the property.

"We're going to make it," Marissa said before something thudded behind her and dropped Denise to the ground.

Then the sound of a gun cocking.

"Where do you think you're going, Jess?"

She turned just as he brought the handle down on her head.

CHAPTER THIRTY-ONE

Phoenix Rising

Marissa's head throbbed.

Bindings prevented her from moving her legs, and her hands were tied behind her back.

She remembered the rough walls of the Gambrel and a deep pool of darkness between her and the car and then…

What…what…?

And then…

Someone dragging her through brush…away from the house…away from Denise…and…

Rocks had pinged the undercarriage of the car as she drifted in and out of consciousness, while someone lay next to her in the backseat.

A burning pain traveled from her shoulder to across her breasts. Moving made her flesh tear. Her head felt light, her shirt wet. She wondered how much blood she'd lost.

Long, dead grass whipped at her legs like the fingers of dead children. Her eyes flickered open to darkness and she thought, *My God, I'm blind*, but she wasn't blind. A piece of cloth was tied around her forehead, covering her eyes.

Someone groaned. Wherever she was, she wasn't alone.

"Gang's all here."

She jumped at Tristan's voice. Behind her.

"It's not a perfect recreation of Westland. I think it will do."

He touched her neck and slid his fingers down the back of her shirt. All around her was a grassy, fecund scent, the earth frigid beneath her legs.

A harsh slap and a sob brought Marissa's head up as Tristan struck someone beside her, several yards away judging by the sound.

"Please, stop," the voice said.

Denise.

"You will be punished for what you did to me," said Tristan.

"I never hurt you."

Another slap left Denise sobbing.

"Stop saying that. What we had was special. Were it not for Jess, you might have been the one for me, Jamie."

"I'm not Jamie. You killed her, remember?"

"No. I saved you. Do you remember the fire?"

"It wasn't me."

"You screamed and screamed, and you believed the agony would never end. Yet it did end, and you were reborn to this world. Tonight, you will be reborn again."

Something dropped beside Marissa's feet. She smelled gasoline, heard it splashing inside a container. He meant to burn her alive. She struggled wildly against the zip ties as the fumes flew up her nose and made her retch.

She heard a scuffing sound, maybe his shoe sliding over stone. Or a match being struck.

Then he ripped the blindfold from her eyes.

She was on a hill somewhere, exposed to a wind screaming down from the clouds like the fury of a deranged beast. A small community church stood about fifty yards away at the end of a gravel road.

She turned her head and saw Denise seated in the grass, bound as Marissa was. Another shape lay on the ground behind Denise. Jimmy. He wasn't moving.

Tristan glared down at Marissa, eyes unfocused and skittish.

"Do you recall your rebirth, Jess?"

"Damn you, Tristan. Look at me. I'm Marissa, not Jess."

When he touched her cheek she squirmed and turned away.

"Scream if you want to," Tristan said. "No one will hear."

Marissa searched for Burlington and saw only undulating, forested hills. Here and there was a distant light, evidence someone lived this far out in the countryside.

They couldn't be too far from Ben's home.

Tristan killing three officers gave Marissa a sliver of hope. The house was swarming with police by now. If Tristan had left a single breadcrumb for them to follow, they'd track him down.

Tristan knelt before Denise, caressing her chin as she turned her head away.

"I forgive you for your sins, for what you and Chris did to me."

"I don't know who Chris is!" Denise shouted.

The wind yanked her words away and shredded them across distant hilltops.

"Chris had no redeeming value, unlike you. He didn't deserve to rise again."

From his coat pocket, Tristan withdrew a blood-stained knife.

"You're insane," Denise said.

Tristan didn't seem to hear. He walked past Denise to where Jimmy's body lay slumped on the ground.

Marissa turned away as Tristan kicked the body, a wet noise like a sledgehammer striking cattle. Tristan kicked him again and elicited a groan.

"Wake up, Jimmy."

Grabbing a fistful of hair, Tristan dragged Jimmy out of his slumber and onto his knees. Like Marissa and Denise, Jimmy's wrists and ankles were locked together.

"Why are you doing this to me?" Jimmy's voice sounded wrong, nasally and hoarse.

In the faint light, Marissa saw Jimmy's face and felt her stomach quiver. Blood caked his mouth and neck, running down from where the nose had been flattened against the side of his face. A piece of scalp hung from his forehead, a bloody chunk of flesh with hair growing out of one side. A gash from earlobe to cheek marked where Tristan had swept the blade across Jimmy's head.

"You missed the fire the first time. Tonight, you will burn with Jamie and Jess as you should have in Westland."

Jimmy started to argue and caught Marissa's eye. There was no reasoning with Tristan. He dropped his head to his chest, resigned.

Tristan kicked Jimmy in the stomach. Blood sprayed from his mouth. When Jimmy dropped to his side, curled and defenseless in a fetal position, Tristan kicked him again.

"Remember this, Jimmy? Remember Chris kicking me while you held me down?"

Tristan kicked him again. Blood trickled from Jimmy's mouth and puddled on the ground.

"You're killing him!"

Hearing Denise, Tristan smiled ironically. There was sadness in his eyes.

"And you watched," Tristan said. "You watched and laughed while they hurt me."

"No...no she didn't," Marissa said. "It was only

Chris. Jimmy tried to help you."

Tristan's face changed. He appeared confused, then he rushed over and bent down in front of Marissa.

"You *do* remember, don't you?"

"Yes. Yes, I think I remember now."

"I knew you would, Jess."

"It wasn't Jimmy's fault, Tristan. He was your friend, remember? Why don't you let him go?"

Tristan's eyes glistened. Marissa had broken something fragile inside of him. He caressed her face, and this time Marissa forced herself not to turn away despite his dirty, blood-crusted hands.

"Let us go," Marissa said. "Let us go, and things can be the way they used to be. We were more than lovers, Tristan. We were friends. You remember how close we were, don't you? It can be different this time. This time…you can have the both of us."

His mouth hung open. He glanced back to Denise, her eyes encased in black circles, mascara running in streaks like warpaint. Jimmy lay prone, spraying red with each cough.

As if someone snapped a finger and brought him out of hypnosis, Tristan's stare turned dark.

"Lying bitch!" He backhand slapped Marissa. Her ears rung, face numb with shock. "You were no friend to me. None of you were. You demeaned me and left me to suffer in view of the whole town. Did you think you wouldn't pay?"

"But it wasn't us," Marissa said, pleading. "It was Chris."

"Jamie was there."

Tristan stared at Denise, whose expression was twisted in fear and confusion.

"You will remember the truth of what you did to me," Tristan said. "If it takes fire to make you see the truth, you will remember how you hurt me."

Tristan loomed over the three of them. It was quiet now, Jimmy a dark clump on the ground.

"My name is Denise Moretti," Denise suddenly said, giving up the charade. "I manage loans at First Burlington Bank. I've only known you for a few weeks, Tristan."

"You feared the fire," Tristan said, continuing as if he hadn't heard a word. "I promised that you'd be reborn, that the pain would be only temporary."

Struggling against the bindings, Marissa thought she felt them loosen.

"You were reborn and I found you," Tristan said, standing over Marissa. "You used a different name and didn't remember your past, but your love for me proved your true identity. You knew before the fire that I would attend Brown. There you awaited my arrival, evidence that you were Jess reborn."

Jimmy coughed hard, a wet, injured sound.

Marissa slid her wrists inside the ties. She'd worked up a sweat. If her skin became slick enough, she might be able to wiggle her hands free.

Tristan's fingers twitched as he approached Denise. Sweat dotted his upper lip.

"Can't you see he's dying?" Denise asked, choking on each word.

Under the cloudy night sky, Marissa saw the pallor of Jimmy's face. His eyes appeared to be sinking into his skull.

"He may yet live again," Tristan said. "If he is worthy."

Tristan grabbed Jimmy by the ankle and dragged him across the field. Jimmy flopped onto his back, limp as Tristan pulled him to where the hill steepened and fell away toward the road.

"What do you think, Jimmy? Are you worthy?"

Jimmy's arms trembled. Another horrible cough,

more blood. He tried to raise his arms. They fell uselessly to the earth.

"Stop it!" Marissa pleaded. "You can't murder your friend."

"Murder or save?"

"Will you listen to yourself? What you're saying is impossible."

"You came back, Jess."

"God damn you, I'm not Jess! My name is Marissa. I was born in Providence and was in high school when you killed Jess. For Christ's sake, Tristan. You know my parents."

Ignoring her, Tristan lugged the sloshing can of fuel back to Jimmy. When he passed by with kindling cradled in his arms like a newborn child, Denise began screaming.

He tossed the kindling at Jimmy's feet. Jimmy twitched as if sensing what was about to happen. Tristan laid the wood in a tepee pattern, the tops forming a crude point above Jimmy's belly.

Picking up the gas can, Tristan doused the kindling as the wind carried the scent of benzene back to Marissa. Jimmy didn't stir.

Make it quick, Marissa whispered in prayer for Jimmy.

After he was done, Tristan stood back with his arms folded, admiring his work as if appreciating art.

"You don't have to do this," Marissa said. "Leave him be. He's your friend."

"He must pay for his betrayal. Rejoice, Jess. We may see him again."

Tristan brought out the knife. He stood examining the blood stains, which appeared black beneath the night sky.

Running his finger along the blade, he glared down at Jimmy and plunged the knife into his shoulder. Denise turned her head away as Tristan dug into the soft flesh, cutting and sawing as Jimmy squealed like a pig brought to slaughter. Blood geysered. Tristan tore something out of Jimmy's shoulder. When he rose to his feet, Marissa saw the slab of flesh dripping in Tristan's hand. Jimmy continued to shriek as Tristan squeezed the excavated tissue and wrung out crimson.

"You never should have crossed me, Jimmy. Do you know how long I've waited for this night?"

Kneeling beside Jimmy, Tristan ran his eyes over the fuel-drenched clothes. The gas continued to drip down from the peak of the tepee, splattering Jimmy's exposed skin.

"It's a shame," Tristan said. "Perhaps Jimmy isn't meant to rise again, and if that is the case, may he rot in hell with the other girls."

He dug into his coat pocket and his hand emerged holding a pack of matches. The fuel smell was cloying, a part of the wind that stung Marissa's eyes.

Tristan struck the match.

The light left a white-hot imprint on her eyes and caused the night to disappear.

"Don't. Please don't—"

Whoosh.

The tepee ignited in flame. First blueish-green, then hellfire orange.

When Jimmy started shrieking, Marissa screamed, as well, hoping her own anguished cries would drown out Jimmy's. Between the wood slats, now glowing and exploding sparks into the darkness, she watched Jimmy's body convulse and jerk across the ground as if electrocuted.

"Time to burn, Jimmy. We're just making up for lost time, dear friend."

The smell of burning flesh blew back at Marissa. A sizzling pop mingled with the breeze as blisters sprouted and ruptured across Jimmy's body. He stopped convulsing. The fire grew until she couldn't see Jimmy at all, only the white-hot funeral pyre belching torrents of smoke.

Shoulders slumped, head hanging to his chest, Tristan swayed just beyond the inferno's periphery.

"Why did you do this to me?" Tristan asked.

He was crying.

"I loved you, Jess. I cherished you. When you left me…when you left me for Jimmy, you might as well have plunged this knife through my heart."

Tristan lifted the knife and turned the point on himself. He gripped the hilt, knuckles white and straining.

Do it.

"You could have stopped them. You knew what they were capable of, and you still left me alone with them."

Tristan's eyes glazed over, his mouth pulled back in a death mask's rictus.

As the blaze washed Tristan's skin in fiery reds and shadows danced out from the surging fire, his demeanor shifted again.

He shook with rage now.

"I never wanted to hurt you, but you left me no choice."

He strode at Denise with the gasoline can swinging at arm's length.

Defenseless, unable to crawl away, Denise drew her knees toward her chest as he threateningly swished the fuel. Her eyes were full moons reflecting the inferno.

"Your turn now, Jamie. Tell me—do I look like a pussy now?"

Turning over the container, Tristan dumped gasoline on Denise's pant legs. As she cried and attempted to squirm away, he stomped down on her ankle, bringing forth a scream. Denise curled up as Tristan stalked back for more kindling.

Tristan returned with the firewood and threw it next to Denise. His back was to Marissa as he surrounded Denise with kindling.

Marissa averted her eyes from the fire engulfing Jimmy, raised her legs and slammed them hard against the ground, trying to smash the zip tie around her ankles. The bindings held firm.

They would all burn at his hands tonight.

Marissa yanked on the ties, couldn't break them. The slack around her ankles absorbed the energy from her escape attempts. Frantic, Marissa bit down on the zip tie. Straining, she pulled back with her head and neck. The ties tightened, squeezing her bloody wrists together.

Smoke flew at her face.

Eyes watering. Nostrils choked on fumes.

Pull it, dammit. Harder.

She bit harder, felt the sharp plastic gouge into her gums, clasped the tie between her front teeth and pulled until she was sure her neck would snap.

Marissa clenched her hands into fists, extended her arms in front of her and ripped them back into her belly. The tie refused to snap, biting into her bones. Trembling from the pain, she brought her arms out and pulled them back again. Her wrists collided with her stomach and drove the air from her lungs.

The binding snapped apart.

She fought up to her knees and blindly felt her way through the layers of smoke. She heard Denise's cries. She grabbed hold of the zip tie around her ankles and pulled. The plastic slipped through her bloody fingers. Grabbing hold again, she held the tie in place and doubled herself over until her teeth closed over the plastic. She felt the chest wound open wider. Her shirt dripped with blood.

The gas smell grew. She heard the fuel splash as Denise begged Tristan to stop.

Simultaneously pulling back with her head and extending her legs, Marissa felt the tie tighten against her ankles. She swung her legs up and smashed them against the cold earth.

The plastic broke.

Marissa ran sightlessly into the billowing smoke.

The smoke pulsed orange where Jimmy lay burning, a part of her fearing the fire had reached Denise and *no…please, no, just let me get there in time and*—

Denise screamed when Tristan struck the match.

Jimmy's bonfire exploded and almost made her lose her footing. The flare of the match led her to Denise. Still time.

The wind shifted, parting the choking veil between Tristan and Marissa. His head shot around in surprise as Marissa burst out of the dark.

Shoulder lowered, she drove the wind from his ribs. Something inside him broke.

Marissa prayed the match wouldn't tumble from his fingers and ignite the kindling.

Tristan shouted and stumbled. Marissa drove with her legs, steering him away from Denise and toward the dragon fire behind him. Tristan caught hold of Marissa and turned her momentum against her. He was so much stronger. Her feet left the ground. She whipped through the air and smashed shoulder-first against a bed of rock and hardened clay.

Pain turned her vision black and red. She gulped air, but it refused to return to her lungs.

Somewhere, Denise screamed for Marissa to get up…Tristan stomped through the grass, closing in on Marissa.

His knee struck her head and knocked her neck sideways.

Her ears rang, nose pouring blood.

Tristan yanked her up by the belt loop and

slammed her to the earth. She landed on one arm and felt the shoulder dislocate.

Roaring, he turned from her and pulled the matches from his pocket. As he started after Denise, Marissa, still unable to breathe, swung her leg out of the dark and swept his out from under him. Caught off guard, Tristan pitched forward. His head glanced off a jagged rock.

His head was bleeding as he lay stunned. Marissa wriggled onto all fours. The ground undulated, the field whirled around her.

Crying out, she slammed her shoulder into the ground. Once, twice. A third time popped the dislocation back into place.

She started crawling past him. His hand shot out and grabbed her ankle, pulling her backward as she splayed flat on her chest. She could feel her lifeblood spreading out from the gash as she screamed and kicked free of his grip.

Groggy, he came at her again. She was quick to her feet this time, ignoring the pain and swimming head and fighting on instinct. He staggered into range. She drove the heel of her foot into his chest and knocked him back. One hand reaching behind him for the knife, he climbed back to his knees, but she was faster again, smashing her knee against his face and splitting his nose open.

Tristan fell onto his hands and knees, crawling lost and confused. The knife had fallen from his pocket and was somewhere in the weeds.

Marissa staggered, gained her balance, then ran on buckling legs.

Tristan struggled to his feet behind her, insane and screaming. The charred scent of Jimmy's remains brushed her nostrils as the flames burst higher. Sparks rained down.

"I'm coming for you, Jess," she heard him say.

She had fifty yards on him, then thirty yards as her wounds became an undercurrent dragging her down.

Scrambling back to her feet, Marissa reached Denise and pulled the kindling off of her, breathing the fuel vapors through her mouth.

"Let me get it," Marissa said, tugging at the zip tie as Denise yelled in warning.

Tristan clubbed Marissa across the back of the neck. She pitched forward onto Denise as the firewood lay collapsed around her.

Rolling onto her back, she watched Tristan pull a glinting object into the firelight. He'd found the knife.

Tristan sliced the blade at her face. She ducked and felt the tip rake a shallow wound across her forehead. Then her legs shot up, kicked the blade away, and locked around his neck, dragging him down until she could clamp her thighs around his belly. She guillotined his neck under her arm and pinned it to the grass, squeezing and choking as he struggled to pull her arms away. Marissa knew about leverage, knew how difficult it was to escape the choke once it was applied. His legs scrambled, shoes gouging up clumps of dirt as she squeezed.

The knife lay on the ground, reflecting the fire. Denise crawled to the knife and pressed the zip tie against the blade edge.

Tristan powered up to his knees and started to stand. Marissa clamped harder and pulled him down, but he was so much larger, so strong. He got back to his knees and wedged his arms under her back, lifting her.

He stood up—her legs still wrapped around his chest, Tristan's neck locked under her arm—and struck her in the ribs. Marissa couldn't maintain control as he hoisted her higher and tossed her into the night air. Her head struck the kindling.

Marissa's legs shook and refused to obey as he thundered after her. Tristan howled in pain and landed on his stomach beside her, one hand clutched behind his knee. Marissa turned and saw Denise holding the knife, wet with fresh blood, in her hand. Marissa urged the feeling back into her legs and crept to her feet.

Tristan rolled over. When his hand came away from the back of his knee it was dripping blood. Clumps of grass and dirt caked one side of his face. Groaning, he fought up to a kneeling position as Marissa staggered away. Free of her bindings, Denise threateningly held the knife. There was something in her other hand, an object Marissa couldn't discern.

From the corner of her eye, Marissa saw the blackened remains of Jimmy's body. He was curled into a ball, a ghost sleeping. The fire had collapsed to embers, with a few belligerent flames receding into the weedy overgrowth.

Tristan's lips curled into a knowing smile, eyes shooting between Marissa and Denise.

"So this is what it's come to—the two of you aligning against me one more time."

"Get on your knees, Tristan," Marissa said.

"Why should I?"

"Because we have the knife."

He laughed and mockingly lunged at her. Marissa flinched but refused to back down. She was finished cowering before him. One hand clenched across her breasts to keep her chest from splitting open, Marissa breathed deeply, then again. The agony dulled.

The dying fire's glow framed Tristan from behind, made him appear ethereal. It helped her focus.

A siren wailed in the distance, soon joined by another.

Tristan's grin faltered. Over his shoulder, a line of flashing red and blue lights swept down the valley. The fire was their homing beacon.

Tristan gazed back at the Camaro parked halfway up the hill. Back to Marissa and Denise. Indecision in his eyes, teased by the sirens.

He leaped at Marissa's throat. She swatted his arm away with her left hand and thrust the palm of her right under his chin. His teeth clicked together and his eyes rolled back.

Seeing he was stunned, Marissa kicked down on his kneecap. Tristan's leg snapped, the point of his foot angled backward. As he screamed and grasped his ruined leg, she leaned back and rammed her knee into his groin. Before he could recover, she recoiled her hips back to center, ready to strike again. He bent over and staggered into her. She snagged him by the hair and slammed a forearm on the back of his neck.

Tristan collapsed onto the firewood and Denise plunged the knife into his back.

Reaching into her pocket, Denise pulled out the object Marissa had seen her snatch off the ground.

The matches.

"No!" Marissa screamed, diving at Denise and shoving her out of the way as the wind rained sparks upon the kindling.

The fire caught immediately and fanned out with the wind. It greedily sought Tristan, starting at the cuffs of his pants and racing with yellow fury past his knees. Screaming, he swatted at the spreading flames.

Tristan rose to stand on one leg, the broken leg hanging uselessly. The fire exploded and seized him. By frantically swinging his arms, Tristan urged the flames to spread faster. He was a whirling fireball stumbling across the field, still coming after the women as they backed away.

Then he collapsed and lay convulsing.

Pain and blood loss slammed into Marissa. Her knees buckled, and suddenly she was on the ground with no memory of how she'd gotten there, Denise supporting her head and neck as a throng of sirens and twirling lights surrounded them.

An officer ordered her to put her hands up where he could see them. She fell unconscious.

CHAPTER THIRTY-TWO

Epilogue

Marissa floated through the darkness amid a sea of concerned voices. Forcing herself awake, she knew she lay on a stretcher. A male and female EMT slid her into an ambulance, where Denise was seated inside with another EMT shining a flashlight into her eyes.

At the hospital, an endless procession of doctors and police officers vied to see her. The physicians prevailed. The police officers' lines of questioning over her involvement in the deaths of the two burned figures in the field softened after they discovered the cop killing revolver in the trunk of Tristan's Camaro. Yet they still had questions to ask, and Marissa was too groggy to understand much of what they said.

Next to the bed stood a monitor with green, blue, and red letters which she couldn't read due to sleep deprivation and an assault of medications. When she was finally able to keep her eyes open, she saw the empty room and knew she'd lost a lot of time. She'd been through at least one surgery. The picket fence of stitches across her chest tugged angrily when she tried to sit up.

Better to lay there and watch the monitor slowly come into focus, because the numbers and sawtooth lines kept refreshing, and as long as they did she knew she was alive.

Raised voices from the hallway sent her heart rate higher. She had a vision of Tristan, blackened and oozing, staggering down the corridor and searching for his Jess. A gurney pushed by two orderlies in green scrubs shot past. The shouting ended and her eyes fell shut.

The light was different when she opened her eyes again. It was tawny and amber and cut into parallel rectangles by Venetian blinds.

Someone was in the room with her. She painfully turned her stiff neck and blinked the sleep from her eyes. Denise was seated in a chair next to the bed, gazing at the end of day and wholly unaware that Marissa had come awake. When Denise saw, she gave a start. Marissa started to laugh at her surprise but stopped when the stitches protested.

Denise held a coffee cup between her knees as she cautiously placed her hand on Marissa's arm, searching for open real estate between the mess of probes and IV lines. Marissa knew Denise, whose eyes were bloodshot, hadn't slept much.

Marissa tried to ask Denise what happened, but only a dry whisper came forth. Denise leaned closer and Marissa asked again.

"You lost a lot of blood," Denise said. "You were in surgery for a few hours yesterday morning."

"Yesterday?"

Hearing she'd lost two full days without noticing gave her an anxious feeling, as though the entire universe had been drawn into a black hole with Marissa left behind.

"How do you feel?"

"Like a train hit me."

Her throat felt sandpapered. She motioned for the water cup. Denise held it for Marissa and maneuvered the straw to her lips.

"The doctors have been standoffish with me

because I'm not family or anything," Denise said. "But I convinced one to talk. He assured me you're doing great and won't be in here much longer."

The water tasted stunningly cold and seemed to coat the inside of Marissa's chest with ice. Parts of her voice broke through the whispers when she spoke again.

"I want a mirror."

"Marissa, you're fine—"

"Please, I just want to see."

Foraging through her bag, Denise came out with an oval case that snapped open to a mirror. She held it in front of Marissa's face.

A purple mound grew from the side of Marissa's head. A small brick of hair was shaved away next to the swelling, with more stitches sewn in. It was her eyes she most interrogated. They were tired, swollen, but lucid. Tristan's drugs were out of her body.

The tangled mop of hair appeared darker. That might have been the dappled window light playing games with her, yet the new roots were as dark as they'd been before the illness.

Six months of her manufactured disease, finally over.

Marissa waved her away when Denise tried to gloss over the injuries and reassure Marissa she'd look fine after healing. Marissa didn't care. She was free of Tristan.

"I don't know whose blood is swimming around inside of you, but it's in for a rude awakening if it gets on your wrong side," Denise said, shaking her head in wonder.

A nurse knocked on the window.

"The whole time Tristan courted me he thought I was a dead girl," Denise said. "Why did I fall for him?"

She caught herself, realizing Marissa's entire marriage had been a lie, and immediately became apologetic.

"Don't worry about me," Marissa said. "Worry about the people he killed. What I don't understand is *why* he believed those things."

The nurse knocked more insistently. It was time to go.

Denise leaned close and lowered her voice.

"I have a friend inside the police department. She said they found anti-hallucinogens in his car. The bottle was full. I wonder how long he was off his medication."

"Anti-hallucinogens?"

"Yes…you didn't know he took them?"

The sun burned a hole into a distant hill and disappeared. The room grew dark.

When the nurse poked her head around the corner and cleared her throat, Marissa said, "Just another ten minutes. She's family."

"My supervisor will have my head. Ten minutes." The nurse said to Denise, "If anyone asks why you're still here, leave my name out of it."

Marissa listened as the nurse walked down the hall. When she couldn't hear the footsteps anymore, she motioned Denise to slide her chair closer. Denise switched on a small lamp affixed above the bed. It cast a tired, yellow light that only made the rest of the room appear darker.

"I'm so sorry, Denise."

"Don't you dare apologize. None of this was your fault, and nobody suffered longer than you did."

"Tell that to Jimmy."

Nightfall slid down the window like oil. Perhaps sensing Marissa's discomfort, Denise pulled the window shade down.

"That better?" Denise asked.

Marissa nodded.

"Is Tristan really…"

"Dead?"

"Yes."

"Gone forever," said Denise. "I watched them wheel him out in a body bag, myself."

"Then it's finally over."

October turned to November on the day the hospital released Marissa. The stitches made her chest feel tight and forced her to hunch when she walked. Marissa insisted on driving herself back to the Cape. Denise only agreed if she could follow Marissa home and stay a few days.

Marissa's house appeared alien. The exterior white seemed darker than she remembered. Inside, the walls felt too close, and the light couldn't push back the shadows as if all the lights had dulled in her absence. Marissa had a queer feeling that something was hidden behind every corner. She kept expecting to hear Tristan calling to her from somewhere in the house.

Denise sat at the kitchen table with a mug of coffee while Marissa sifted through the stack of mail. Halfway through the stack, Marissa's heart froze.

A letter. From Tristan.

She used a butter knife to break the seal and carefully removed the letter.

It was handwritten. The print was easily recognizable—it was the same for all of the forged love letters she'd handed over to the police. Holding it under the light, she bit her thumb and started reading.

Dear Marissa,

That you are reading this letter means I am dead. I appreciate you are upset with me, but please understand that my actions were for your own good. In time, I believe you would have come to remember who you really are— my beloved Jess. The fates were not on our side for this turning of the wheel. Know, however, that the wheel spins eternally. We shall meet again.

I love you, my dear.
Forever.
Tristan

"Is it from him?" Denise asked.

Marissa began to weep.

The next day, Marissa phoned the realtor and listed the house for sale.

A week after Marissa's release from the hospital, she followed Denise back to Burlington under a late-autumn sky that seemed a reflection of the ocean.

"I have to go back to work tomorrow," Denise said, sipping on a soda at the final rest stop before they crossed the state line into Vermont. "You okay with that?"

"Sure. I don't mind staying alone."

The Halloween decorations were gone from the Maplecrest Drive houses and replaced with Thanksgiving-themed turkeys and pilgrims. Youngsters in light coats played in the yards, most of the bicycles stored away for the long winter to come.

Another body had been found—a woman buried in the woods not far from the apartment in Medford. A woman who looked a lot like Alisha Morgan. Her picture had been in the newspaper, but Marissa avoided looking. Staring too long might awaken sleeping ghosts.

Hours turned to days, and days to weeks. The time Marissa spent with Denise waiting for the Cape Cod house to sell comforted her. She enjoyed the companionship and sensed Denise needed her, as well. It was when Denise left for work that the big Colonial seemed to hold too many unexplored corridors. That was when the nightmares were particularly bad. She dreamed of waking and hearing Tristan climbing the stairs, of Annie Wallace lying in pool of her own blood with a single rose placed upon her chest. In time, her physical wounds mended. The mental wounds would take longer.

On a cold December afternoon, one of Denise's volunteer days at the children's hospital, Marissa drove into Burlington. Snow sparkled in the street lamps and dusted the sidewalks. Everywhere was Christmas, from the garish lights and garland strung between poles, to the harried rush of shoppers searching for last-second Christmas gifts.

To them, she was another holiday shopper or tourist. They didn't see the horror hiding behind her eyes, and no one paid much attention to the way she turned sideways and made herself thin in the crowd as if their touch would scald like a hot oven door.

Sometimes she saw Tristan's face in the crowd, only to blink and see a man who didn't look the least bit like him. Other times, the phantoms of the dead Westland girls weaved through the rush.

But the Christmas shoppers didn't care, for they didn't understand murder and betrayal and two decades of hidden insanity.

She caught her reflection in plate glass and touched her forehead. A scar, too faint to see from more than a few feet away, ran from ear to scalp. Minor cosmetic surgery had made the scar nearly invisible, but Marissa would always know it was there.

For years people had told her how pretty she was, how she defied the passing years until Tristan poisoned her. What difference did beauty make?

In a Westland grave slept a girl named Jess who looked strikingly like Marissa. Jess should be 45 now, the same as Marissa.

Examining her face in the glass, as the phantom images of holiday shoppers merged with hers and passed on, Marissa understood beauty was a fallacy. We manufacture beauty, pass judgment on the desirability of our friends and neighbors. The animals are the only ones who have it right—survive and procreate. They don't see beauty. Only we do.

She touched her face and wished she looked nothing like Jess.

Her phone hummed with a received message. She opened Denise's text and slumped against the storefront.

Marissa, someone was inside the house. Is it happening again?

Marissa sank to her knees.

The snowflakes fell harder. From where she knelt, she could only see the hazy colors of traffic lights and cars slipping uncertainly along the icy macadam. The garland had blown off the power poles, which stabbed bloody shadows into the skin of the sidewalk.

Winter was here again.

Connect With Me

Mailing list members get to download my latest novels on Kindle for **only 99 cents** on release day. You will always be the first to know when my latest story is released and where I will be appearing. Please join in on the fun by signing up at
http://www.danpadavona.com/new-release-mailing-list/

You will only be contacted once or twice a month, or whenever a new book is about to be released. Your address will never be shared, and you can unsubscribe at any time.

Sign Up

Her Shallow Grave

Keep Reading!

Correspond directly with me. Each month I answer questions about my stories, give readers the scoop on my latest projects, review great books and movies, and run giveaways. Please join in on the fun by signing up at http://www.danpadavona.com/new-release-mailing-list/. You will only be contacted once or twice a month, and whenever a new book is about to be released. Your address will never be shared, and you can unsubscribe at any time.

If you liked The Face of Midnight, you'll LOVE my full-length, vampire horror novel, Storberry. Visit http://www.amazon.com/Storberry-Dan-Padavona-ebook/dp/B00N0D2LUG to start reading Storberry right now.

Storberry is an old-school thriller that returns the vampire mythos to its horrific roots. See what others are saying about Storberry:

"A Genuine Gem of the Horror Genre"

"A Classic Horror Novel"

"[Padavona's] descriptions paint vivid portraits in the mind and help with the visual 'Drive-In movie feel'."

"Finally a vampire story where the monsters are actually scary."

"Foreboding and moody. I love it!!!"

"[Padavona's] descriptive imagery is outstanding. I truly 'see' this town and the characters."

Ready to be scared? DOWNLOAD STORBERRY at http://www.amazon.com/Storberry-Dan-Padavona-ebook/dp/B00N0D2LUG and turn the lights to low.

Read on for an excerpt
From
Crawlspace

"Just as Jack Ketchum, Richard Laymon, and the splatterpunks did a generation ago, Dan Padavona's CRAWLSPACE represents a seismic shift in the horror genre. An instant -- and important -- classic." - Bram Stoker Award–winning author, Brian Keene

I flew over the crest of Court Hill without a bike helmet. My headphones were on, which is why I never heard the pickup truck creep up on my back wheel.

When the driver laid heavy on the horn, I nearly jumped out of my skin. You can't appreciate how loud a big truck's horn is until the grille is two feet from your ass. You don't just hear the horn, you feel it blasting hot air against the back of your neck while the wail rattles through your bones. The horn made me lose control and nearly careen over the curb, but I straightened the front wheel and managed to stay upright. I twisted my head around and saw the hardened, beady eyes of a man laughing at me over the steering wheel.

Doing what any sane person outweighed by 6000 pounds would do, I edged toward the curb to give the driver room to pass.

He didn't pass.

He swerved the grille directly behind me again and blared the horn. I inched closer to the curb, afraid the bike pedal would clip the concrete and I'd tumble over the handlebars. He flicked on his high beams.

The smartest choice would've been to hop the curb and get onto the sidewalk, but it was too dangerous to attempt at high speed. The sun was almost down, and downtown, at the bottom of the hill, was still a mile away. I realized we were the only two people barreling down the incline. If the driver was crazy enough to run me over, there would be no witnesses.

When I looked over my shoulder, the driver stuck his middle finger up at me and rode the horn for several seconds. I swerved into the oncoming lane, hoping he'd finally pass. As I angled across the road at over twenty mph, the headlight beams swept across the pavement and followed. I veered back, the driver right on my tail.

We zigzagged again; I couldn't shake him.

The horn brayed in triumph, and I did another stupid thing: I flipped my middle finger back at him.

The pickup lurched angrily forward and grazed my back wheel. The touch was so subtle that I wouldn't have noticed if every nerve in my body hadn't been on high alert, red-hot and standing at attention. The bike trembled dangerously. I white-knuckle-gripped the handlebars, knowing that if I so much as touched the brakes, the bike would fly out from under me, and three tons of steel would drag me under.

The faster I pedaled, the more the driver pressed down on the accelerator. We were one entity, the truck and I, accelerating in lockstep toward downtown. A quarter-mile below, a train of vehicles crossed the intersection, growing closer by the second. I felt the trap closing around me. The motor growled down the back of my neck.

Then the truck whipped around me and passed. He shot downhill doing highway speeds in a residential zone, the red eyes of the taillights glaring back at me. Watching the truck instead of the road, I lost control. The bike tires flew out from under me, and for one awful, frozen moment, I saw the cruel macadam rush underneath and imagined the amount of skin it would tear off my body when I landed.

In that precious split second, I had enough

presence of mind to clutch my arms protectively around my head. The bike careened over the curb. I smashed shoulder-first against blacktop.

The air rushed from my lungs, and the pavement peeled away skin from shoulder to hip. It seemed as though I slid forever across that cheese grater of roadway before I finally stopped. Ringing trailed through my eardrums, and when I tried to make a fist, my hands refused to respond.

Shaking, I rolled gingerly onto my stomach. I didn't want to see how much skin I'd lost. Strips of shirt were torn away and in pieces up the incline. What I saw of my arm I didn't recognize: the layer of skin the macadam had excavated was as white as January snow, dotted by pinpricks of blood. I think my body was too shocked to bleed.

As I lay at the base of the hill, a car pulled up beside me. A middle-aged man in glasses leaned out the window.

"Good Lord. Are you okay?"

His wife stared from the passenger seat, both hands over her mouth. A young girl in the backseat held a stuffed dog in front of the window, making it dance for me. She seemed quite amused.

Putting his phone to his ear, he waved reassuringly and said, "I'm calling 911."

"No, don't," I said to his amazement. My school health insurance had lapsed because I took the spring semester off, and my family's health plan wasn't worth the paper it was printed on.

"Look, you could have broken bones and a concussion—"

"I'm fine," I said, cutting him off. He shook his head, muttering something about idiot college kids, and squealed off toward downtown.

Then *she* was there.

A thousand wasp stings stabbed my skin when I moved my shoulder, but when she knelt down and offered me her arm, I took it and crawled up to my knees, vaguely aware of her car, a pearl blue Mazda RX-8, purring curbside. The first thing I noticed was her legs—tan, fit, and sexy beneath a jean miniskirt that barely caressed her mid-thigh. I must have stared for too long, because she said, "My eyes are up here, Don Juan."

I rushed my eyes to her face, thinking she wouldn't take kindly to them lingering elsewhere. My legs were gelatin, and if she hadn't grabbed hold of my arm, I would have collapsed.

"You okay now?"

"I don't have a clue."

I looked into her eyes and gasped. I know how corny this sounds, and believe me, I'm no romantic, but I wanted to melt in the endless depth of those blues. My knees buckled again, and this time she ducked under my arm and let me lean against her. I caught scent of her perfume, subtle yet alluring, redolent of distant wildflowers after a warm rain. The sun flooded orange and red into her blonde curls, which draped down to her shoulders and tickled my nose.

Her eyes considered the bike—twisted, bent carbon, the brand name nearly scraped away by blacktop.

"Hmm. No saving the bike, I fear. But if you want me to throw it in the trunk—"

"Just leave it," I said.

I turned away. The scrapes across the bike's body reminded me of what had become of my skin. I found no sign of my headphones or MP3 player. They were probably halfway up the hill, in worse shape than the bike.

"All right. Can you walk to the car if I help?"

I told her I could, though each step made my head swim and my stomach turn. She watched me closely as we took it one step at a time, concern etched into her face.

"We should really get you to the hospital."

"No doctors."

I expected her to protest, but she just shrugged her shoulders.

"Good. I don't trust doctors."

I pulled the passenger door open, and she eased me into the car. New car smell and pungent black leather met me as I slumped into the seat. I should have told her to drive me to the hospital, insurance or not. My head seemed to float off my shoulders, and the yellow stripe of dividing line snaked and slithered out the window as though alive. Maybe I had brain trauma. Maybe I was minutes away from an aneurysm.

Screw it.

I rolled the dice and put my life in her hands. There were worse fates than dying in the front seat of a sports car with the sexiest girl in Kane Grove beside me.

"What do they call you, Don Juan?" she asked, slipping into the driver's seat. I would've stolen another glimpse of her legs, but I felt sure I would vomit if I didn't keep my eyes fixed on the undulating road.

"Jerry."

"Jerry like Seinfeld, or Jerry like Cantrell?"

I smiled to myself. *An Alice in Chains fan.* Could she be more perfect?

The last thing I remember was trying to form an answer.

"Jerry…Laymon."

Everything went black.

My eyes squinted open to a blur of traffic lights whipping overhead, the windows rolled down, letting in a cold splash of upstate New York air. Where was she taking me? What if the short skirt and pretty face were meant to lure me into her car before she slashed a razor across my throat, stole my wallet, and left me in a countryside ditch?

I still hadn't asked for her name. Or had I? My mind was a needle on a skipping record.

After losing consciousness for several minutes, I awakened to the grumble and jounce of tires along a gravel road. The high beams were on, painting field grass in monotonic whites and grays. A creek sluiced beyond a line of barren trees, reflecting the twilight, mirroring her eyes.

She swung the Mazda up a rocky incline of a driveway. Just up the hill, a long apartment complex seemed to grow out of the earth, like the dead rising.

"Where are we?"

She jumped, the dashboard lights cast back against her face.

"Jesus, you scared me. I thought you were asleep…or dead."

"I feel like I am," I said, trying to rub away the sensation that a layer of putty lay beneath my face.

The beams swept across an apartment on the lot's right end and shut off. She killed the engine, and a chorus of cricket songs rang through the open windows.

"Home, sweet home."

Home, sweet home?

The L-shaped complex, with its chipping paint and dingy windows, made me think of the Bates Motel. One of the apartment's shutters hung askew like the broken wing of an injured bird, and there was a smell—a stale, musty odor that blotted out the scent of spring rising off the dewy grass. I wondered why she chose to live here, why she of all people scraped my carcass off the blacktop and drove me to her house without knowing the first thing about me. That got me thinking again about who she was and whether or not I should trust her.

As she helped me up the steps, I took in the string of connected apartments, a queer familiarity tickling recollection down the less-traveled corridors of my memory. I'd seen this place before. But where? A faded wooden sign welcomed all to Gardenia Apartments. At the base of a pitched roof, five dark letters spelled *MOTEL*, each letter flickering and dying like moths to a flame. I should have known this place, but the memory hid lost and unrecognized, like a ring in the dark, smutty murk of a catch pipe.

She unlocked the door, and I limped with her assistance from the entryway to the couch. The downstairs barely looked lived in—little in the way of furniture, a small television, an absurdly small dining room table. While I slouched against the cushions, she disappeared around the corner to the kitchen. I heard cabinets opening and closing and the sound of running water, and a few minutes later she returned with a first aid kit, a box of gauze bandages, and a glass of water.

"You look prepared for the worst," I joked, as she dunked cotton into a bowl of iodine. She didn't answer.

"This is gonna hurt," she said, holding my gaze until I nodded that I was ready.

She dabbed the cotton, soaked with purple savagery, against the newly-exposed layers of my excavated skin. It felt as if she'd run a blowtorch across my arm. I bit down on my tongue to keep from screaming. Even after she took the cotton away, the burning went on incessantly.

"The hurt means it's working," she said, giving me a wink. "At least that's what Mom always told me."

"My mother said the same," I said through gritted teeth. "I thought she was full of shit back then, and that iodine is payback for all the hell kids give their parents. Iodine and Bactine—the suburban parent's favored choices for torture devices. Nothing since has changed my opinion."

Now she held a pair of scissors. A needle and thread rested on the end table, and I hoped to hell she didn't intend to stitch any wounds.

Ready to find out what happens next? Download Crawlspace at:

https://www.amazon.com/dp/B01CM3HVUY

Please join my VIP community list at http://www.danpadavona.com/new-release-mailing-list/ to be notified as soon as new novels are released.

Author's Note

After completing **The Face of Midnight,** I felt a little "slashed out" and knew my next story needed a different direction. I spent a few months sputtering along, starting projects and killing them off, searching for what I wanted to write next. **Severity** began with an opening line. "She found the love letters stuffed inside a cardboard box in the attic." When I added the second sentence, "Like finding a scorpion under the pillow," I knew I had something.

Over a period of days, Marissa's story began to surface. Then the writing took off, the storyline beginning to feel like something between **Sleeping With The Enemy** and a Jack Ketchum novel.

Since **Dark Vanishings**, I've gravitated toward strong female characters, and in many cases they've become lead characters and leaders. The choice isn't conscious but innate. Marissa is one of my favorite created characters, a bad-ass if there ever was one. I couldn't wait for her to break the chains of her sickness and seek revenge.

A fellow writer questioned my decision to include Tristan's past. His psychosis is the result of severe abuse, not only from the friends who betrayed him but also from his father. Was it wise to allow readers to sympathize with a monster?

I struggle with this puzzle often. My favorite killers are cyphers—Michael Myers in **Halloween**, Billy in the 1974 version of **Black Christmas**. The mystery behind their characters makes them more frightening and allows our minds to fill in the details with our most repressed nightmares.

As counterpoint I give you Francis Dolarhyde, the devilish creation from Thomas Harris' **Red Dragon**. Does sympathizing with Dolarhyde's history (he was abused as a child) make him less frightening? I think not.

In fact, I believe any murderer, cypher or sympathetic, can be utterly terrifying. The key is creating characters who we care about so when the monster is unleashed, we fear for our protagonists.

Here's one nugget for you. Perhaps the most frightening scene from **Severity**, and one of the scariest scenes I've ever written, was cut from the novel.

"What in the hell is wrong with you, Padavona?" you are probably asking right now. I've taken liberties to delete your most colorful expletives.

Unfortunately, the scene didn't fit with the storyline. It felt contrived and so it had to go.

Fear not. The offending subplot was rescued from the waste bucket and is currently being reinvented as a standalone story. You will see it soon, and you will thank me. Or not.

Horror author and friend, Chad Lutzke, provided impeccable editing for **Severity**. Chad brought the storyline into focus and reigned me in when I wandered, as I tend to do. After Chad's editing, the manuscript was a well-oiled machine. Thank you, Chad, for bringing out the best in me.

Jack Musci, Lydia Capuano, and Terri Padavona were invaluable, catching mistakes during the beta reading process and offering suggestions which made for a better reading experience. Thank you to my A-team.

Special thanks to my wife, Terri, and our children, Joe and Julia. You are my reasons for being, my motivation. Without you, I would not be the man I am today.

Although many of the locations in **Severity** are actual places, Westland and the novel's characters are wholly of the author's imagination. Any resemblance between the people in this book and people in the real world is purely coincidental and unintended.

About the Author

Dan Padavona is the author of Severity, The Face of Midnight, Crawlspace, The Dark Vanishings series, Storberry, Shadow Witch, and the horror anthology, The Island. He lives in upstate New York with his beautiful wife, Terri, and their children, Joe, and Julia. Dan is a meteorologist with NOAA's National Weather Service. Besides writing, he enjoys visiting amusement parks, beach vacations, Renaissance fairs, gardening, playing with the family dogs, and eating ice cream.

Visit Dan at: www.danpadavona.com

Her Shallow Grave

Made in the USA
San Bernardino, CA
25 July 2020